THE FRAGILE TRUTH

by
E.J. Ivory

"Write the tale that scares you, that makes you feel uncertain, that isn't comfortable. I dare you. In a world that entices us to browse through the lives of others to help us better determine how we feel about ourselves, and to in turn feel the need to be constantly visible, for visibility these days seems to somehow equate to success – do not be afraid to disappear. From it. From us. For a while. And see what comes to you in the silence."
She concluded, "I dedicate this story to every single survivor of sexual assault. Thank you."

-Michaela Coel
Emmy Acceptance Speech

I heard these words at a time when I was struggling with the choice to publish this novel or not... at the time I was so scared because the story was too personal and uncomfortable. But that's the very reason why I went ahead and published this. Because the truth is often scary and uncomfortable. And nevertheless it still needs to be told.

Disclaimer:

First, thank you for getting this book. But also warn you, this book paints a very vivid and detailed depiction of grooming and rape. I didn't do this for shock value; I wrote the details to accurately portray what an actual victim goes through. Many survivors live with the vivid details replaying in the memory every day. There is nowhere a survivor can hide from these disturbing images. Nevertheless, these victims and survivors suffer in the dark, or quiet moments of their lives for the rest of their lives. So, warning this novel may trigger and disturb you, but I'm not apologizing for that sexual assault and rape *IS DISTURBING*.

I dedicate this to all of those who see the cracks in the mirror, but still have the courage to find themselves in the reflection.

TABLE OF CONTENTS

Preface

Not again...

THREE MORNING, I awake in a complete panic attack; my chest hurts, and I struggle to catch my breath. It's the first time in a while that I've woken up from a nightmare feeling a sense of dread and hopefulness. I can never escape him. I can never escape it...

It's still dark outside; the city is calmer than usual, and I wonder if anyone besides me is up this early on a weekday. I have so much on my mind. It's a miracle I slept at all, but I'm up now, with no desire to go back to sleep again.

Don't think about him, Lisa...

I have so much to do today. I needed a good night's sleep, but I can't focus on work. Ever since these allegations sprang up on the internet, I haven't been able to concentrate on anything for the last couple of days.

Don't think about it...

Since I can't sleep, I have to find another distraction and decide to go to Central Park East. It's my favorite place, and it's not too early to head out. The place I go running and clear my head.

First, I head downtown, through the nearly empty streets of the city; only the insomniacs and early birds are up this early.

On mornings like this, my body is wired, and I can appreciate everything that's beautiful about living in Manhattan.

I run along the Reservoir running trail: The soft surface of crushed gravel and the 1.58-mile loop offers the best views of Central Park's and the Midtown skylines. I run the counterclockwise direction around the track with one thing repeating in my mind.

Keep running… Don't stop…

I jog harder, picking up the pace. My muscles ache and joints strain, but I push harder.

Don't stop… don't think about him…

My lungs are on fire now as I run into a full sprint. I run until my body nearly collapses, but no matter how hard I try, the thoughts linger in my mind. He stays in my mind.

It was 5:45 when I finally stopped, sweat dripping from every pore and my clothes completely soaked. I gasp for air, almost wanting to throw up.

You push too hard, Lisa. My mind screams at me.

I thought a run would help me, but it never does. It's just another temporary distraction, and the runner's high never lasts long.

I huff and walk down the path for another thirty minutes, watching the sun slowly rise over the city's skylines. I can't think about him or what he's done.

No one knows what he and I did in the past. Or who I was. And I don't know these women either. These accusations have nothing to do with me, and I'm going to keep it that way.

Oh, Monty…

I think, stretching my sore muscles on a nearby bench. *What have you done?*

I pull out my phone and read the Twitter thread:

"NFL athlete Lamont Johnson is being sued by several women for sexual misconduct and assault. After the first woman came forward last week, three other women have come forward with similar accusations."

I've read the words so many times; it's engraved in my mind. I try not to process how I'm feeling, but I know one thing... this isn't going to go away.

I head out of the park and feel no better than when I woke up.

Don't think about it.... My mind sighs. *You have enough on your plate right now... Focus, Lisa...*

Focus.

I'm relieved that I have so much work to do at the office. I won't have time to think about anything else once I walk through the office doors.

"None of this has anything to do with me," I tell myself repeatedly.

I get home just before seven, shower, and grab a cup of coffee in my hands as I leave out the door. I figure I'd hear from Monty soon; he always calls me when his life is going to shit. But I can't let him get to me, not this time.

It is 8:45 when the phone chimes; it's Katie, and I ignore it. I can't think about her right now either, even

11

if she's my sister. She's a part of the problem, and frankly, I don't know what to say to her either.

"Are you up?" her message reads.

I don't answer, catching a cab to head downtown to my offices.

Another chime.

"Are you busy?"

"Christ," I sigh. "It's too early for this."

I know by now, Katie's heard the news about Monty too, and that's why she's blowing up my phone, but I don't... can't deal with this right now.

I have to keep moving... and outrun the past... the darkness.

"I can't think about him." I shake my head, "Or it will ruin me."

ONE

Monday... March 10th, 2016

"I love my business, and business is good. There's no doubt about that."

I've worked my ass off for the last five years, and it's finally paying off for me: my black double-breasted blazer, flare pantsuit that matched with stiletto heels that murdered my feet, screams success. But I look damn good, like a fierce businesswoman; it's a good disguise.

"Your eleven o'clock is here, Ms. Rose." Russell, my assistant, declares, peeking his head through the door. "Shall I show her in?"

"Yes, please."

The woman walks in, looking like a young supermodel. She's dressed in a red business blazer and a skirt that rests just above her knees. The look announces her professionalism and catches my attention immediately. She has that effortless beauty like she doesn't have to do much in the morning to look this flawless. Nothing is out of place, from her crop-cut hair to her fresh manicure nails. It's impressive.

She comes across as intelligent but high maintenance. I examine her as she confidently strides in, taking a seat in the chair in front of my desk. From her attire to her demeanor, as she lowers into the seat, I realize she is sizing me up as well.

"Do you have a resume for me?" I ask.

She smiles, and her cheeks flush. "Although I am very impressed with your invention and how far your company has come along in the last five years... I'm not here for an interview."

Curious.

"Then why are you here?" I hiss. "I don't have time for games."

The woman pulls out a large portfolio case stuffed with papers. Every page-aligned perfectly and organized. A part of me is impressed, but that quickly dissipates.

"My name is Chloe Roberts; I'm a reporter for HotFire News, it's a news website. I was wondering if I could interview you?"

"I'm confused. Why would you want to interview me? Obviously, I know that there have been rumors about a business deal with a certain company. But I can't comment on that at this time, and I wasn't aware that this was common knowledge. So, I'm afraid that I can't—"

Chloe clears her throat.

"I'm not interested in your business dealings, but with your relationship to pro football player Lamont Johnson. I'm sure that you might have heard that there have been over a dozen women who have recently accused him of sexual misconduct and assault. And two other women who have recently accused Mr. Johnson of rape came forward publicly on social media."

Lamont Johnson? It was a name that I hadn't heard in a while but was always on my mind. I hadn't heard about any of this, but maybe because I'm not on social media too often.

"No," I hide the pain in my voice, hiding behind my walls. "I had heard nothing about that. Furthermore, I don't know why you're asking me about Mr. Johnson. Or why you even assume that I know him at all."

I watch the young woman rummage through her papers and pull a stack of documents from a folder. Then neatly placed them in front of me on the glass surface of my desk.

No… it can't be. That is the only thought that pops into my mind.

"What are these?" I ask, already knowing the answer.

The reporter smirks, knowing that I'm full of shit. "I've recently come across these copies of text messages and emails between Mr. Johnson and a young girl that I assume is you. The time and date stamps reveal you exchanged these messages when you were in your early teens, and some of these messages are very sexually explicit."

I sink back in my chair and weigh the gravity of her words. I don't know how she got her hands on these messages. It was so long ago… another lifetime ago. And no one knew about them, and I had all but forgotten that they existed at all.

Lamont was my first crush, but he was dating my sister, Katie. We hung out from time to time. What we shared was intimate and personal, something special between him and me, and it was a secret. And now all I can think about is, what did this woman want with me? Who hired her? And more importantly, what did she plan to do with these copies?

Chloe takes a deep breath, sensing the tension shifting in the surrounding air. "Listen, I'm not here to exploit or expose you or what happened to you, Ms. Rose. You seem like you have a good life and a prospering business, but what he did to those other women has ruined their lives in one way or another. Some are trying to press charges, and soon it will come out that Lamont has been doing this for years, whether or not you want it to come out... It's clear that he has been doing this long before he was a famous wide receiver and Super Bowl champion."

Her eyes pierce through me, gauging my response, my body language, and the tone of my demeanor.

"What do you want from me?"

"I just want to talk to you and find out the truth." She says.

My heart sinks deep into my stomach, stalling for a moment, knowing that I already have an answer for her. "I'm sorry, I can't help you. I haven't spoken to Mr. Johnson in years, and I'm afraid I can't help these girls. And have nothing to say about these accusations or the past."

"Fine," Chloe says.

"I'm sorry," I say again.

The reporter shoves the papers back into her portfolio. "Ms. Rose," she adds. "I'm not a great investigative reporter, and somehow, I stumbled across these messages. It's only a matter of time before someone else does. You should talk to me before some other person uses these emails and text messages and plasters them all over the internet."

I stand, frustrated and annoyed. I'm done with this meeting, or ambush, or whatever the hell this is.

"Look, Ms. Roberts, I don't know if any of these accusations are true. What happened to innocent until proven guilty?"

"There's no such thing as innocent on the internet, Ms. Rose. I will leave you my card, and I have yours — think about what I said. What has happened, and what these women have gone through, is a tragedy. You can help them and make sure that Lamont gets punished."

She stands, placing her business card on my desk. Then makes her way to the door and out of the office without speaking another word.

I'm lost in my thoughts — my memories — my nightmares. Lamont was instrumental in my success. He gave me the first startup money to start this company. He believed in me when I didn't believe in myself and molded me into the woman I am, in one way or another. I owe him so much.

Right on cue, my iPhone vibrates against the glass of my desk. Quickly, I flip it over and gaze at the screen.

It's a text from my sister, Katie, like I need this right now.

"Meet me for dinner tonight." She says with a sense of urgency in her tone.

"Fine," I reply.

I know there is no use in arguing with her. If I don't come to dinner, she will show up at my apartment. Or keep calling and texting until I meet with her. I don't want to be bothered, but I know I don't want to be alone with these thoughts right now, either.

I'm stuck between a rock and a hard place. I think to myself. And could use a drink...

****

The Beginning....
September 18th, 1999

Katie introduced Lamont to me when I was twelve. He was twenty-one and a star athlete for UCLA. I remember that day; I was in the living room reading, and he'd been dating Katie for three months. She finally brought Lamont home to meet our dad and me. At first, I thought very little of him. Everyone seemed so impressed with who he was and what he could do on the field, but to me — he was just 'Monty.'

We lived near Westwood, Los Angeles, so Katie could stay home while attending the university. And my dad, Joe, had a 24-hour babysitter for me. Lamont always seemed to be over at our house after that day, spending all his free time with us when he wasn't practicing football or studying. He would hog the remote and eat all of our food, which annoyed me so much. It was like he didn't have his own home to go to of his own.

I noticed almost immediately how Monty treated me differently than nearly everyone else around me at the time. He never treated me like the annoying younger sister and spoke to me like I had a brain and an opinion. It felt nice in an unexpected way. Above all, he and I seemed to click very well, liking the same movies and T.V. shows. He would often say I had an old soul and many talents that he admired. I never knew exactly what he meant by that, but it made me feel good.

"Are you sure that you're only twelve," he would often say to me in private moments, "I've never met any twelve-year-old who is as cool and as talented as you."

"There's nothing special about me," I'd blush, "you're the star athlete that everyone loves... you're the popular one."

For my thirteenth birthday, Lamont gifted me a red Nokia 8210 cell phone — it was my first phone, and the first number programmed in it was his. I'd been asking for a phone for a while, and most people at my school had one. I wanted to seem cooler than I was at school, but dad would always respond, "No to a cell phone."

"Here you go, Lisa," Monty said, handing me the phone. "Happy birthday... We can keep this between us so that no one can take it away from you."

"Okay," I beamed. "Thank you so much, Monty."

"My number is number 1, so we can talk anytime you want." He continued. "But no one should be around when you call me because—"

"They will take it away."

"Exactly." He leaned closer. "It's our secret for now."

It was the first of many secrets we'd keep from everyone else...

The way he would say things made me feel unique and meaningful — like an adult. It didn't sound like we were doing anything wrong but sharing a private moment together. I never questioned the things he did or said to me at first because I liked it.

The boys at my school seemed stupid and immature compared to Lamont. They were childish, grabbing my breast in the hallways between classes, writing notes to me, telling me what sexual things they wanted to do to me — or constantly trying to make me touch or look at their private parts. I had developed my breast over a year ago, which brought me more attention than I wanted. I just wanted to be left alone and draw on my sketchpad.

The privacy and Monty's insistence on taking precautions and being discreet was something I grew to appreciate. His glances towards me were so subtle that no one noticed but me. It was intimate when he touched me, yet he did it in a way that didn't draw attention to him or me. He'd give a compliment here or a wink there. It felt like a secret dance that only he and I knew about. And I liked it...I grew to like him more and more.

Now and again, he slipped notes into my sketch pad, knowing that I took it everywhere with me:

"Thinking of you all day, have a good day."

"You looked so cute today in that outfit."

"I'm winning my game tonight… for you."

When things started, I didn't feel bad about keeping it a secret; it felt good. I looked forward to finding notes in my room or between the pages of my books from Monty. I felt like he loved me as much as he loved Katie. He told me he wished I was older all the time so that we could be together. He did all of this, making me feel important and unique for months before he even kissed me or before we spent any time alone.

The first time I can remember him kissing me was on November 21st, during the Thanksgiving break. He, Katie, and I were sitting in the living room. I walked to the kitchen to get a Coke, and Lamont walked up behind me, startling me. I assumed he wanted to tell me to grab him a drink too, but he leaned down and pressed his lips against mine, sliding his hand underneath my T-shirt and cupping my breast. It stunned me how different it felt from what I'd experienced at school. It didn't feel intrusive or offensive… it just felt right.

"You're my favorite girl, beautiful." He murmured in my ear.

And with that, I was tethered to him from that moment on…

TWO

Present Day

After the reporter leaves, I can hardly focus on my work, still feeling her presence. Around four in the evening, Katie and I meet at Masa restaurant. Somehow, Katie can get reservations for the two of us. I'd been trying to get into this place for months now, but I guess when you are an agent for A-list celebrities, they can pull strings, even at a moment's notice. The warm, intimate setting is breathtaking.

We settled down with our menus and ordered dinner and drinks. The only downside is the moment I finished the most exquisite sushi I ever had and secretly wanted more. Also, Masa is located inside a shopping mall, so now and again, people will walk by and casually wander into the restaurant, which is very distracting. Chef Masayoshi Takayama serves us his fantastic, delicious food that is meticulously prepared.

The food, service, and décor are incredible. And for nearly six hundred dollars a person, I am glad that Katie is picking up the check.

I trace lines into the sweat on my glass, wondering what's the sudden urgency to meet up for dinner. Usually, we only meet up for holidays and special occasions. And the last holiday we spent together was Christmas.

"As much as I appreciate the free dinner, why did you call me and want to meet up? What was so urgent?" My voice says low.

"I just had a bad day." Katie lowers her gaze to her drink. I've been thinking about a lot of things lately. I wish Mom could have been here."

Katie takes my hand in hers from across the table. "I know in my heart that mom would have been so proud of us both and how far we've come. We've both become successful and are living our lives. We graduated from school, and I know she'd be proud beyond words."

I avoid her eyes, unwilling to succumb to the emotions after my conversation with that reporter Chloe. I want to cry, but not right now. Not in front of my sister. I keep my thoughts and emotions in check; the alcohol is helping.

Katie looks up at me, her eyes glistening from the tears that are swelling in them. "Have you heard about Lamont? Have you heard what these women are saying about him?"

I raise my glass to my lips, nodding through the sadness, feeling my heart fall to my stomach once again. I never thought Katie would be so emotional or affected by the news. After all, she broke up with him years ago, turning down his marriage proposal, and breaking his heart.

"I heard that there were accusations," I say, taking a healthy swallow, savoring the burn of my rough liquor as it stings all the way down.

"Lisa?" She looks down, tears falling onto the table. "Lamont and I dated throughout college – four years. He practically lived with us; he was over the house so often. There was never a hint that he was capable of any of this."

What makes you think he did this? Those women could be lying. The thought enters my head before I can catch it.

I let my thoughts drift back to what the reporter said. But with all the current pressures of this pending business deal with Apple and my company. With my lack of sleep for the last several nights, I can't afford to dwell on this.

"You never really know anyone, do you?" I say. "They could seem so perfect on the surface level, but it's just a mask."

She wipes the tears from her eyes with the napkin, being mindful not to mess up her well-applied mascara as she dabs and pats.

"Lisa," Katie's voice drops into a serious tone. "I need to know… I mean, I have to ask."

I know what her following words will be, and it takes everything within me to keep this very expensive sushi down that I just ate as my stomach twists.

"Okay?"

"Did Lamont ever? I mean—was there ever a time when?" Katie struggles to get the words out.

"Did Lamont ever try anything with you? Was he ever inappropriate with you?"

I gulp the rest of my drink quickly. Time feels like it's standing still; suddenly, the room feels like it's spinning…warping… and pulsating all at the same time. It's disorientating. And I hate going through this every time I think about my past. Everything fades into the background, including Katie, and I'm lost in my memories…of him.

"Lisa?" A voice echoes in the darkness. "Lisa?"

"No, Katie, I'm just as shocked at these recent accusations as you are. It's all just hard to accept or believe." The lie comes out so quickly; I'm taken aback by how natural it feels.

I moved to New York about three years ago. And I decided that when I left California, I'd leave all the secrets of the past there and not let the darkness consume me in this new city. I've managed to do that for three years, until today, until some reporter comes into my office and throws my dirty secrets on my desk.

"So, Lamont never touched you?" She asks more directly.

"No." I signal the waiter for another glass of whiskey. "Famous people are always targets, while in the public eye. Some distraught fan or stalker gets mad and starts accusing a famous person of some misconduct. Most of the time, they want something."

Ever since our mother died, Katie took it upon herself to be more like my mother and not so much my sister. Our relationship with our father became strained because he was always on the road as a truck driver. As a child, I used to follow Katie like a shadow; I wanted to be her. Strong, determined, and beautiful. She's everything that I wanted to be...even now.

The sadness in Katie's eyes reflects my internal regret. I know she loved Lamont deeply and probably still does; he was her first genuine love. I don't know the details of why they broke up; she doesn't talk about it. And I never pressed the issue because I always feared that I was the real reason in one way or

25

another. The guilt of that thought is sometimes too much to bear.

"Did you ever hear from him after you two broke up?"

"No." She sighs.

"You miss him?" I ask softly, mirroring my guilty thoughts.

"Sometimes," She confesses. "We never got proper closure."

I remember that night. There was a lot of shouting coming from Katie's room as she and Lamont had a shouting match. I don't know the specific details of that night, just that after everything was said and done, he stormed out of the room, then the house. And I only saw him again a few months later.

"This is bringing up so many emotions for me, Lisa."

"I know."

"Do you think the accusations are true? Do you think he could've done this, that he has that in him?"

I sigh.

"I don't know."

"I don't want to think about this anymore. How are things going with your Assist App? How is your love life?" Katie smirks, changing the subject to another intrusive topic.

Flashing a smile, I know she's fishing for information on the enigma that is my life. I'm such a private person with few people ever knowing what's really going on with me. I'm not particularly eager to keep anyone close because I'm so afraid of hurting someone I care about.

"I have a meeting with Apple at the end of the month. They are interested in buying my app, and they're offering somewhere around three-hundred million. As for my love life, there's nothing to report."

"What about Dante Kingston?" Katie smiles. "Have you heard from him lately? Whatever happened between the two of you?"

I fucked it up like I always do.

"No," I roll my eyes. "I haven't spoken to Dante in a while."

My busy life has provided me with my share of short-term flings, and I prefer things that way because relationships are so complicated. And they are also emotionally draining. I'm not looking for love or any more complications right now. Running my own business eats up most of my time; I don't have a social life, nor do I want one.

We finished, and Katie agreed to share a taxi with me. I know it's just her way of ensuring that I don't go to a club or bar for more drinks.

She knows me too well... and sometimes I hate that.

THREE

I enter my three-bedroom apartment at Wall Street in the financial district, in downtown Manhattan, around eight at night, and behind closed doors, finally, I'm alone. I rush to the refrigerator and grab a bottle of Crown Royal from the freezer. Downing two glasses immediately, I work up the courage to pick up my iPhone and search for the articles and posts that have anything to do with Lamont. While gulping my third glass of Whiskey, I read the words carefully on the link on Yahoo. Below the article, I see over 30k shares are trending. I hate the internet sometimes. People play judge, jury, and executioner, ruining many people's lives while sitting behind the safety of their computers.

This is a fucking nightmare...

I place my phone on my coffee table and leave my apartment, deciding to go to the bar that's a few blocks away from my loft, the Dead Rabbit. I love their hours since the bar stays open from 11:00 a.m. to 4 a.m. the next day, and those hours are perfect for an insomniac like me. And I'm addicted to their lobster devil eggs, which are a permanent staple in my diet.

I sit at the end of the bar on the second floor, staring at the Irish Whiskey on the shelves against the wall. And I eat my fifteen-dollar devil eggs. I am trying not to think about Chloe Roberts or those text messages. And not think about how I might be ruined if these text messages get out somehow. I can't stop my thoughts from racing through the memories and interactions Lamont and I used to have. He made me feel fearless—and deep down, I love him, even now.

I'm about to down my refill when I feel the presence of someone sitting next to me. The subtle scent of Marc Jacobs's cologne fills my nostrils. And the smell only grows stronger.

"What are you drinking?"

For a moment, there's only dead air, and I freeze, my eyes fixed on my drink.

"Crown Royal," I reply coldly.

The handsome stranger exhales and smiles with his perfect white teeth. "Can I buy the next round?"

"Sure," I reply. "Thank you."

I'm not in the mood to be hit on by some random stranger, even with his sexy southern accent and fitness model physique. But this guy doesn't take the hint and is determined to strike up a conversation with the woman sitting alone at the bar. He talks about what he does for a living, assuming that I'm mildly interested at all, which I'm not.

He confidently assumes that he's more charming than he is.

"My name is Jason." He finally says. "I'm a real estate agent."

I don't care... and I feel like my 'fuck off' vibe is abundantly clear, but he persists.

"Jasmine." I lie and never give my real name to people I randomly meet; it's better that way, just in case things get out of hand... it protects me.

I was not focusing on the man in front of me at all. My mind is stuck in the past, thinking about the last time Lamont and I spoke. I told him I was moving to

New York. And he told me we couldn't see each other anymore. I struggle to remember the specifics of what he said, but he told me he'd met someone and wanted to marry her. The only thing I thought about at the time was that he didn't want me anymore, and I wasn't good enough to be with him publicly. I was so mad and wanted to profess my love for him, and I tried to remind him that we had something special. The one thing he always used to tell me, but I didn't do or say anything.

"So, what do you do?" Jason asks, tearing me back into the moment.

"I'm bored with this mundane attempt of flirting. I'm only in town for one night and staying at the DoubleTree downtown." I lie, feeling the effects of the liquor kicking in. "Do you want to get out of here?"

This is crazy... my mind screams. You need to stop Lisa...now.

"Yes, we can get out of here if you're okay with it."

"I'm okay with it." Another lie, but this time, I'm only lying to myself.

We walk to the nearest hotel conveniently on Stone Street, in the Historic District of Manhattan, which is a few blocks away from the bar. It's late, but I'm not tired at all. My mind is racing with thoughts I don't want to think about and emotions I don't want to feel. I want to feel better and forget this day and what happened. I want to feel good, and liquor just won't do it tonight.

Arriving at the hotel, Jason gets an important call and stops short of entering the building. Allowing me to go inside and rent a suite for the night quickly.

"Is everything okay," I ask. "Do you need to leave?"

Jason shoves his phone into the breast pocket of his blazer and smiles. "No, it's just work stuff."

He's lying, but I don't care...

The hotel room is cold and empty, mirroring my own feelings as we settle in. I stare out the window as Jason takes a shower, and I raid the mini-bar. Outside, the night is frigid for it to be Spring. The news says that a storm is coming.

Jason steps out of the shower with a white cotton towel wrapped around his waist and water dripping to the floor... glistening on his almond skin.

I say nothing but subtly admire the stranger's thick muscle and fitness model physique, looking like he does CrossFit or something.

"That pricey suit doesn't do you justice," I say.

"Oh, really?" he smiles. "I could say the same thing about you, and your beauty struck me from the moment I laid eyes on you at the bar."

Deep down, I know it's a line, but I couldn't care less at the moment. And with that, Jason walks towards the bed, lowers down, and plants his lips on mine. "I've wanted to do that all night," he says.

His words are unoriginal, but I'll give him credit because he's a pretty good kisser and too fucking fine. Embolden by all the liquor I consumed, I lean closer to him and kiss him back, long and passionately.

I just want to fill this hole I'm feeling, and Jason will provide the perfect distraction. I don't care that I just met him, or that he's a stranger... I never do. At least for the moment.

"Come here." He says, allowing his towel to drop to his feet.

And I do... shifting my legs towards the edge of the bed. He towers over me like a statue in all of his impressive glory.

I need this. I convince myself. *I need to feel good, even if it's a lie.*

FOUR

"What do you want?" Jason asks quietly, his gaze traveling over my naked body.

I feel his eyes studying every freckle and crease of my body; my cheeks flush, my skin heats up under his intense gaze. This is what I need. After the day I've had, it only fits that the night ends in bed with a stranger, but it wasn't planned; I'm winging it from here on.

After my thing with Monty, I'd been with other men and had them as frequently as I needed. Most of them meant nothing; their only purpose was to scratch the sexual itch that porn and toys couldn't fulfill. It felt like putting a Band-Aid on something that can't be fixed, but it made me feel good — at least for the moment. I am always detached and lose focus when getting physical or intimate with anyone, but I crave this.

"I want to taste you," Jason says, pulling my legs towards the edge of the bed. "It's all I could think about since I first saw you."

How original. I roll my eyes.

He doesn't hesitate, allowing his fingertips to graze over my skin and play with my breasts. "You're sure that you want this?"

"Yes," I say, against my better judgment.

I close my eyes for a moment, silently accepting the ill course of action that I've taken. Sometimes, I get a little reckless, and this is one of those careless moments, which has the potential to be incredibly dangerous, but none of that concerns me, nor does it cause me to change my mind.

"Lay back, beautiful." Jason says, "I want to make you feel good tonight."

"You think you're that good?" I smile, scooting towards the headboard.

He raises his eyebrows. "I'm pretty confident in my skills."

I laugh playfully. "We'll see."

His emerald eyes darken, traveling down my body, focusing on the most sensitive areas between my legs for a moment.

"Challenge accepted."

I breathe in sharply as he gently kisses me between my legs, licking and sucking, pleasuring and feeding my cardinal desires. I want him to keep going and never stop. I can care less about the repercussions or anything else in this brief moment because I just want to stay in the moment and hold on to it.

I let out the breath that I was not aware I'd been holding in. And let go of every thought that has been lingering in my head all day. I lose myself entirely to this one-night stand.

Fuck it.

"Don't stop." I moan softly, feeling the sensation building in my body.

Unable to take it anymore, I pull Jason up towards my face, firmly kissing him hard and aggressively. He touches my breasts, again, which now are a lot more sensitive than before. His fingertips trail down my body, setting me on fire with every second.

It feels deliciously good.

My head rolls back onto the pillow, and I moan again, feeling my body react to his touch. His lips kiss, suck and tease me, tasting and nibbling my overly-sensitive areas tormenting me. He overwhelms me as he tickles and tugs on my nipples with his warm tongue.

"Do you like it, Jasmine?" his lips brush against my hard nipple.

My mind unravels, losing all sense of reason and speech. Arching my hips into him is all the answer Jason needs. Our bodies touch; I run a hand down his sculpted chest, down towards the complex curves of his abdomen. Then to his waist and still further down. He feels so incredibly impressive, firm, and hot.

"I want you now," he whispers against my skin.

"Then what are you waiting for?" I exhale. "I want this too."

"Jasmine, come here."

I feel his hard erection pressing against me. After a few deep strokes with my hand, he grows even harder in my grip.

I suck in a sharp breath as he climbs on top of me, kissing me again.

"You taste so good."

I ache for him, to have him inside me; I don't want to wait a moment longer.

His erection throbs, gently grazing my inner thigh, feeling long and as hard as a rock, and then Jason pauses, rolling a condom over himself.

"You ready?"

"More than ever," I answer quickly.

It's the point of no return. I couldn't stop if I wanted to at this point. My body is screaming for more.

He positions himself and postures as his thick thigh muscles push my legs apart. Then he skillfully wraps them around his waist.

Slowly, I feel him ease inside of me, filling me. After a brief pause, he thrust hard and deep within me.

"Jason," I say, sucking in the air as he settles himself.

I struggle to take him all in at first, feeling my insides shift to accommodate his girth and size. Jason eases out of me a little, then pushes inside again. A small cry escapes me as he fills and stretches me. The sensation is a relief beyond words or description, and nothing matters or feels righter than this moment. My legs try to accommodate him, feeling him find his stride and rhythm.

"Oh God, you feel so good." his breath is ragged as he thrusts again and again.

It's slow at first, but he soon picks up his pace. Suddenly, as I close my eyes and relent to his punishing pace, I feel myself slipping out of the moment.

No. My thoughts struggle. Not now.

Trying to stay here, I think about him and how good he feels, but I can't stay in it. My mind feels like it's leaving my body after a few minutes, and my feelings slowly fade to nothing. I'm numb.

Fuck...

He moves with deliberate and calculated strokes, not holding back or relenting. My body feels him there inside me, but my mind sinks further and further away. Each movement of his thrust feels more distant and foreign to me.

No... not again.

I moan, breathing harder and faster as he keeps thrusting deeper and slamming harder against me. His rhythm is crazy, but I've disconnected. No matter how hard I concentrate on him and the pleasure of his touch... I can't get there, and I can't climax.

"I'm almost there." His voice cracks as he keeps his punishing pace.

He doesn't slow it, as all that time in the gym pays off. "Are you almost there?" he whispers against the nape of my neck.

"Yes." I lie, moaning in response.

I've become an expert at faking it. I've mastered imitating all the motions and sounds to make it seem that I'm on the edge and being pushed to my climax. But in reality, I just can't get there... it's only genuinely happened a handful of times.

"I'm cumming." Another lie. "Jason, I'm cumming."

The words encourage and excite him, and without warning, his hands grip my ass and thrust hard into me, picking up speed. His breath is shallow, and with every second of punishing thrust, I feel his muscles tighten, and his grunts get louder. He's determined to give me all that I can take... the best fuck of my life and everything that comes with it.

But I feel nothing. There's no earth-shattering explosion that radiates and vibrates through my body.

I'm just numb. There's only a sense of hollowness that deepens in the pit of my soul with every thrust. An emptiness that lingers and will grow long after tonight.

"Fuck!" He stiffens, quivers, and his muscles tighten. Still, inside of me, his body feels hot, and sweat glistens over his skin. I gripped his hair, moaned loudly, and trembled.

"Just relax, baby, and let go," he breathes. "You're okay."

It's all routine at that moment; I clench my legs around him and shudder. I'm out of breath and sweating myself. My body feels sore and tired, but mostly, I'm ready to go home.

Jason rolls onto his elbows, groans, and smiles. "Damn, I can honestly say that's one of the best times I've ever had. I'm so glad that our paths cross tonight."

Soon his eyes get heavy, and he collapses on the pillow next to me. He's exhausted and satisfied that much is clear.

Fucking is the one thing I know I'm good at…

I sigh. "It's my turn to take a shower now… again."

He smiles and kisses me. "Okay, hurry back, though. We have all night to have some more fun."

"I'll be quick." I smile, "in and out—only five or ten minutes."

Jason gives me a soft kiss and pulls away, smiling and settling his head on the pillow, pulling the sheets up over himself.

"I'm so happy we met." He says again. "You're so beautiful."

I shake my head and walk into the bathroom. "I'm glad we met too."

As he disappears from my sight and I close the door behind me, I avoid the mirror at all costs, turning on the shower and sitting on the toilet for a moment.

Why do you do this to yourself? My mind protests.

I don't dare to search myself for a genuine answer and just wait for the bathroom to fill up with steam.

Stepping into the shower, the scolding water cascades over me. The water is so hot that my skin turns red as it hits my flesh. I take an extra-long time in the bathroom, knowing that Jason will probably be tired or gone by the time I'm finished.

After thirty minutes, I slowly open the door, and just as I predicted, Jason is well asleep and even snoring comfortably on the bed.

Thank God for small favors...

FIVE

I quickly collect my clothes and sneak out of the hotel room before Jason even wakes up. This is the way I prefer things to be; it's less complicated and messy this way. It's around 2 a.m., and I'm still not tired. As my taxi moves through the empty downtown streets, I'm somewhere else, staring out the window of the back seat. I try to hold it together just long enough to reach my apartment.

In the safety of my apartment, I undress in the living room, take another long shower, take off my makeup, and pour myself another drink. I've lost count of how many drinks I've had tonight, but somehow, I am still conscious. My body aches, and my limbs feel heavy, but not as heavy as my heart.

Monty is still on my mind...

I slowly lower myself on the soft cushions of my sofa, and something shifts within me as I reach for my phone that I'd left on the coffee table. Initially, I was only going to head to The Dead Rabbit and return home after a few drinks, but stupidly, I've been out all night without my phone. Feeling the comforter on my feet, I pull the fabric, sliding it up to my waist, and exhale the stress away for the first time all night.

Suddenly, I notice it—a new alert appears from Facebook messenger, and I lift the screen to eye view.

"Hey, it's me.
Monty."

No... my mind screams in disbelief.

Immediately, I sit up against the cushions. Am I dreaming? Drunk? Have I finally lost my mind? Is it Lamont? After all these years, he messages me.

It's like I thought him into existence, but I stay strong and don't reply. Pacing, I wait several minutes before replying. But I stare at the message, thinking about everything, feeling overwhelmed and unable to process anything.

"I've been thinking of you." He types. "Can I call you?"

My mind protests, but my fingers still type—yes.

A moment later, my phone vibrates, an *UNKNOWN* number, but I know who it is. I pick up. But he says nothing at first… and there's an awkward pause between us.

"Lisa." His voice sounds like I remembered, and my heart skips a beat…just like it used to. Every memory rushes to the forethought of my mind, ambushing me in a split second. "Lisa, are you there? I'm sorry. I don't mean to call you like this and intrude on your life. I know it's late, and I have no right calling you like this."

My mind draws a blank. I can't think. I just stare out the window and look down at the quiet streets below. My eyes travel along the block from one end to another. Monty is only calling because he has no one else that he can talk to—no one else is as loyal, loving, and understanding as I've been to him.

"Monty," I say. "It's late. Why are you calling me?"

"I'm sorry." He whispers into the phone. "I'm sure you've heard about—"

"I've heard rumors—yes."

I pause.

"And a reporter came to my office today. She was talking about the messages that we used to exchange back when—you know."

"What?" He gasps, "you mean the messages that we used to send back and forth."

"Yes, this woman found them. I don't know-how, since you had my phone."

I can't sit still. My body is in a frenzy and full panic mode. And it's hard to think. At that moment, I just wanted Lamont to keep talking to me. I don't want to hang up the phone because I might lose him again if I do.

I sit back down on the couch and listen carefully to the phone. To hear his voice again makes every memory, every sensation and feeling swell and stir inside me. Nothing makes sense, and I'm that thirteen-year-old girl all over again. The room feels like it's spinning out of control. I can't breathe.

"I want you to know," he finally says. "I think about you all the time and track your success and check in on you from time to time. You have never left my thoughts. Now and again, I find myself thinking about our special time together. I miss you so much."

Listening to him, I close my eyes, and I'm back in that place. The first time we ever did anything intimate. The first time that Monty confessed, he saw me as more than Katie's little sister. The way he pulled me into the kitchen while Katie was getting dressed, and he kissed me while playing with my breast and tugged on my underwear.

"The first time we kissed." Monty breathes hard into the phone. "My soul felt complete. You made me so hard that I wanted you right then and there in the kitchen. You were beautiful and so mature. And we had so much fun playing Tomb Raider on PlayStation. I remember when you told me you wanted to be Lara Croft, and you were such a badass."

It's a memory that I can hardly remember at all. And I stopped playing video games years ago. Listening harder on the phone, I hear raspy breathing.

He's jerking off... Unfucking believable.

"I miss the way you taste," he says. "The way you came for me."

I grip the edge of the comforter, trying to push out the thoughts as he describes them. My body tingles with confusion and excitement, but I try to collect myself long enough not to get stuck in the flashbacks.

But I do...

The thoughts consume me, and I'm there again, thinking about the way Monty smelled. The way he tasted. The way my body would unravel when his hands would slip in my pants, rubbing me, and the way his fingers felt inside me.

Fuck...

I shake off the memory.

"Did you do it?" I ask, steadying my breathing, not sure if I want to know the answer. "Some of these women are claiming that you raped them."

He goes quiet for what seems like forever. "Lisa — you know me, and you know that I'm not like that. Several of these women tried to blackmail me, and when I didn't pay, they threatened to ruin me. I even have text messages from one of them saying they would do this, and then I'd be sorry. And two of the other women work as strippers at a club in Las Vegas that I visited once or twice."

After a moment, there is an alert that chimes on my phone and a snapshot of a text message from a girl named Brittney Baby. It's from Monty as proof, confirming what he is saying.

"I need for you to believe me." He adds. "I need you to be here for me, and I could lose everything over some fucking accusations."

He pauses.

"But none of this means anything if I don't have you in my corner."

I feel an overwhelming sick feeling in the pit of my stomach. I'm not a fool; a part of me knows there is some truth to what these women are saying. But I am a fool—for him.

"I'm here, Monty." I exhale, feeling the gravity of the earth pulling me down. "I'm always here for you. But it's late, and I need to get up in a few hours for work."

"Okay," I hear him smiling in relief through the phone. "I will let you go. And don't worry about those messages, I'll take care of it. Goodnight, beautiful."

"Goodnight."

I want to feel better about this whole situation, and deep down, I thought hearing from Lamont would make me feel better, but it doesn't.

Looking at the lock screen, the white numbers beam in the darkness.

4:07 a.m.

I make one last call...

"Nichole? It's Lisa; I need to speak with you as soon as possible, please. Call me back. Thank you."

SIX

Tuesday, March 16th, 2016

"I did it again," I confess. "I didn't plan for it to happen, but it did."

Ever since I tried to kill myself six months ago, I've been seeing Dr. Nichole Owens. At first, it was for regular therapy, but it's evolved into trauma therapy. I told her how I can't sleep at night, how I am a control freak regarding my work, and how I feel about everything. It's a necessary evil, even with Nichole's helpful insight on what's going on with me — I am still not used to talking about myself and having someone listen.

Her office is located at 34 West. 25th Ave, a ten minutes drive from my office. Once I get there, a weight of guilt presses on my shoulders. Sitting in the soft leather chair in her office I fidget, while Nichole sits across from me on a sofa. I take a sip from the water bottle and place it on the glass end table next to me. The cream-colored curtains are drawn together, and the room is dimly lit.

I can appreciate the warm and inviting atmosphere, and it fills me with a sense of calmness, which I'm sure is intentional. Nichole is around the same age as me but seems wise beyond her years. I've seen several therapists in the past, but they never last over six or seven sessions at the most. I can appreciate her fierce sense of style, wearing a black Italian blazer and a red satin shirt with stiletto four-inch 'fuck me heels.

"You did what again, Lisa?"

The doctor leans back against the leather of her sofa. I know she has already deduced what I am referring to, but still, she waits for me to open up willingly, which I love.

"I went to a bar, picked up a guy, and—" I hesitate, fidgeting with the buttons on my blouse like the act is too shameful to say out loud.

"You slept with him?" She asks.

"Yes." I clear my throat.

"Okay." She says, without a hint of judgment in her voice.

I don't have many friends, but even my close ones scoff and joke when I have these minor slip-ups, and that is reason number fifty-two of why I don't tell anyone anything anymore and why I love coming here and talking to Nichole.

"Let's examine this," she continues. "Why did you do it in the first place? You have been doing so well. So, that is the real question. What's been going on? Have there been any additional stresses manifested in your life other than the demands of your job?"

Additional stresses, that's the understatement of the year.

"No," I lie, trying to save face. "It's been business as usual."

Nichole's eyebrow raises slightly as if she has a bullshit-meter that's beeping rapidly. "What about these recent allegations about Lamont Johnson? It's been all over CNN, Facebook, and ESPN... I've heard. Wasn't it four different women that have come forward and stated that he sexually assaulted them?

Didn't your sister date him? He was a family friend, right?"

Damn… she's good. I think to myself.

Although, she doesn't strike me as someone who would watch ESPN or have a Facebook account.

"Yes, I knew him a long time ago. And yes, he dated my sister, and that's all. I heard something about accusations, But none of that has anything to do with me," I choose my following words carefully. "An investigative reporter or blogger or someone in that field did contact me, and to dig up any information about Mr. Johnson's past…but I told her that I couldn't help her."

"Why did she contact you?" Nichole leans forward. "Is it because your sister dated him, or was it because he helped you start your business? Or was it something else?"

"It seems like it's all the above." I sip more water. "Although the woman wasn't very specific."

"Lisa, I know we spoke about you being abused and raped in the past. And now this reporter is contacting you about Lamont. Does one have to do with the other? Are you one of his victims too?"

Damn, she's excellent.

There are certain words I hate to be associated with when describing my past:

Abuse…

Rape…

Victim…

I don't see what happened as any of these words, even though people have told me that's exactly what it was. And I have a hard time accepting that because I don't see myself as a victim. I mean, who does. But to me, those words sound tainted and horrible. When I think of rape or abuse, I think about that movie, I Spit on Your Grave, the 2010 remake. The girl in that movie went through something horrible and traumatizing—those men raped her. She was a victim. And that's not what I went through at all. I loved Monty with all my heart for a long time... I still do.

My experience was nowhere near that horrible.

"I have nothing to do with Lamont or what's happening to him. He was my sister's boyfriend, and that's it," I lower my gaze, fearing that if Dr. Owens saw me, she would know the truth. "And I won't help these women ruin his life either."

"I understand your loyalty, but what if the accusations are true?" Nichole asks. "Is this somehow bringing up what happened with Derek Page? Is that what is triggering you?"

I shrug my shoulders, saying nothing.

"And now, in response to those triggers and stressors, you went and had sex with some random guy you met at a bar...just like you used to do in the past."

She removes her glasses and sits back again. "Lisa, it's normal to feel overwhelmed and conflicted about these recent accusations. You knew Lamont Johnson before he was an MVP wide receiver for a Superbowl-winning NFL team. You knew him when he was just some hotshot college football player for UCLA and your older sister's boyfriend. You saw him as a friend, and I'm sure that even though they aren't together anymore, you still care about him deeply."

Nichole pauses, taking a deep breath before continuing.

"Did anything ever happen between you and him?" She asks again.

"No," I lie. "I had a crush on him, but that's it."

We shelve the topic for a moment only because Nichole senses how antsy and uncomfortable I am feeling and doesn't want to push me. We discuss work and how I've been sleeping since our last session. And if I'm still using Crown Royal and Diet-Coke to self-medicate.

Which I am...admittedly.

We go through exercises that will help me relax when it's time for me to sleep. And discuss healthy ways to deal with the potential shit storm that might come if these accusations turn out to be true.

"Okay, Lisa, I know you didn't come here just because you slipped up and had a one-night stand," Nichole finally says, "Why did you really call for this emergency session with me today? Is it just because of the reporter or something else?"

"Katie asked me if Lamont had ever tried anything with me before when we had dinner last week."

"And it disturbed me that she could turn on him like that."

"Why?"

"Because she knows him," I finish my water.

"Did you think she asked because she wants to know or — some other reason?" Nichole asks.

I don't know how to answer the question.

"I'm afraid," I reply. "I'm afraid this will ruin everything for me. I've worked so hard to build my business, and Lamont was vital in helping with that. I'm afraid this will ruin me, especially if the information gets out about him helping me."

I'm close to Katie, but I keep many things from her, especially when it comes to Monty. What he and I had was our thing, and she doesn't need to know the details. Like I don't need to know the details of what she did with him either.

"You're afraid that you will try to harm yourself again. Or spiral out of control again with the drugs, the alcohol, and sex."

"Yes," I whisper, lowering my head. "I find myself being pulled in that direction."

"Okay," Nichole smiles, reassuring me in her own way. "Now we are getting somewhere. Let's talk through this; clearly, recent news about Lamont is triggering you in some way. Tell me what you can about your abuse. What do you remember? I'm here to listen for as long as you need. Just take it slow."

I remember everything. My mind sighs.

"Okay," I say. "You mean the first time I ever had sex?"

She shifts her body on the sofa, nodding her head — yes.

I begin to tell her, but I omit the fact that it was with Monty... I know lying is counterproductive, but I just don't want to tell her all of the truth at the moment.

****

December 19th, 1999

"I know I shouldn't be saying this, but you are so beautiful." Monty leaned in and whispered to me.

He said this out of nowhere one night when we were sitting in the living room. My dad, Joe, was out working a shift at the trucking company, and Katie was babysitting me for the weekend during Christmas break from UCLA. She had invited Monty home for the holidays.

Beautiful? My mind questioned. Me?

I'd been called beautiful before, but only by relatives and strangers. It felt so different coming from Monty, like it meant something different... or something more. That night, Katie was in the shower for what seemed like forever while Monty and I watched a scary movie... The Mummy Returns with Brendan Fraser in the living room.

We'd been exchanging text messages for weeks now, nothing but innocent banter back and forth. Monty even kissed me the last time he stayed the night on Thanksgiving break, but I brushed it off at first. But now, it felt like he wanted more, though he never said it directly, only hinted at it now and again.

Monty listened for the shower, then snuck a kiss on my lips, causing my cheeks to flush, but he didn't say or do anything else, just winked at me. When Katie returned to the living room, he ignored me and focused on the movie. I must admit I was a little confused and upset that Monty wasn't his usual playful self. He looked like he had something on his mind but said nothing.

I tried to focus on the movie for the rest of the night, but Lamont was firmly on my mind. Why did he kiss me? What did he mean in his text messages when he said he wished he could lay with me all night? Was he just pretending to still like Katie, to be near me? Or was I just reading too much into it when he was just trying to be nice to me.

Too many confusing questions...

"Okay, kiddo," Katie chimed in after the credits of the movie roll. "It's time for bed."

It was nearly 11:30 p.m. and way past my bedtime.

"I'm not tired."

"But I am," she snapped. "Time for everyone to go to bed."

"Fine." I hissed, storming to my room.

I lay in my room for what seemed like forever but couldn't sleep. Deep into the night, I heard what sounded like a door opening down the hall, but when I listened harder, I heard nothing else. I settled back in the sheets, not wanting to admit that the movie scared me more than I wanted to admit. Then my room doorknob moved, and it took everything within me not to scream, especially after that horror movie. But I didn't.

"Hey, it's me," Monty whispered through the opening. "You awake?"

"Yeah," I replied.

The door opened and closed, but it was so dark I could hardly see anything but his dark silhouette coming close to the edge of my bed.

"I can't see anything." He laughed, keeping his voice just above a whisper. "Do you have a nightlight or something?"

I did, a plug-in light that I sometimes used to stay up and read long after I was supposed to be asleep.

"I think so," I said, reaching for the switch that was next to the bed. "Wait, a sec."

The switch flipped, and the low dim light illuminated his face.

"Ah," he smiled, flashing his perfect teeth. "There you are. Sitting there looking so beautiful and sexy."

Sexy? First beautiful and now sexy...

It's the first time someone ever said that I was sexy. I always felt like an awkward thirteen-year-old with stringy hair and boobs that didn't fit the rest of my body. I hardly saw myself as sexy, and I didn't see myself as anything, to be honest.

"I want to kiss your lips again." He added. "I know it's wrong to say that, but I enjoyed it. Probably more than I should. I feel so close to you."

He paused and lowered his head.

"Can I lay here with you, only for a few minutes?"

"It's okay." I blushed, suddenly feeling self-conscious. "I liked it when you kissed me too tonight. Probably more than I should."

Monty smiled, then slowly leaned in and pressed his lips against mine. At first, his lips were closed, but then his tongue slowly opened my mouth and played with my tongue. It's not my first kiss, but it's my first grown-up kiss like the way I'd seen people do it on T.V.

After that, everything happened in a blur. I felt Monty's hand slip under my T-shirt, which was something he only did briefly before – he grabbed my breasts while continuing to kiss me.

"Is this okay?" He asked, massaging me.

I stayed silent; it felt like my body was frozen, and no words could come out at that moment.

I thought back to all the messages that we'd exchanged. When he told me all the things, he thought about doing to me. He'd been drinking that night; I could smell the beer on his breath. I knew I didn't want to do all of the things that he wanted to do...at least right at that moment. I wasn't ready, but there he was, trying to convince me that I was. I blinked, and Monty lifted my shirt over my head before I knew it, and the upper half of my body was exposed. He slipped his hand underneath the fabric of my pajama pants and gently rubbed in between my legs around my special area.

"Are you okay?" He continually asked in the beginning. "We can stop if you want to."

I didn't know what I wanted...

He didn't wait for an answer either; although it appeared that he was concerned, it didn't feel genuine.

A part of me wanted to stop, but somehow the words, 'we can stop if you want to' felt hollow. And I didn't feel in control at all, and I just felt weird... and confused.

"It's okay." Monty said, "I promise this will feel good. I've wanted to do this with you for so long. Don't be afraid."

"I'm not."

But I was… I didn't feel right. None of it felt right. Nothing felt real.

"You trust me, right?" He asked.

I nod — yes.

My pajama bottoms came off, and a split second later, my underwear followed them onto the floor. Then I felt Monty's fingers slip inside me, but before I could react, my body went limp. My brain couldn't think properly or send any commands. There was pain. And I felt outside of myself. After a few more minutes, he stopped checking to see if I was okay less and less and just kept saying.

"You're okay." He said. "Just relax. I know you want this just as much as I do."

His body weight shifted to the foot of the bed, and he positioned his head between my legs.

"You're okay. Just relax." He repeated.

The words faded further and further away.

I'm not okay… I wanted to stop… but I couldn't speak.

I was afraid and caught off guard as he kissed and licked me down there. I'd seen porno movies before at my friend Amber's house, so I knew what Monty was doing, but I'd never had it done to me before.

I didn't like it…it just felt weird to me.

I wanted to go back to just kissing, but my mouth felt dry, and I hesitated to say anything at all, fearing that Monty would see me as a baby and not want to talk to me again.

He pulled me close towards the edge of the bed and licked me in my sensitive area — it felt good, in a way I couldn't register. My muscles tightened, and my body felt weird. A moan escaped my mouth before I could even catch it. Monty stopped abruptly and handed me a pillow, and said, "Here, bite down on this...you have to be quiet. Okay?"

I did as he instructed, biting into the dry cotton fabric while he went back down, licking and sucking me. I felt one of his rough callus hands reach up as he played with my breast and hard nipple, causing even more confusion in my head. I bit harder, and more moans vibrated in the pillow until I couldn't hold it in anymore, and my body reacted.

"You're so wet," he said, embarrassing me to the core as my body quivered uncontrollably.

Then he stopped and sat next to me on the bed, looking very pleased with himself.

"You're okay," he said. "You just came for me, and that means that you liked it. And that's normal, and that's what happens when you love someone."

He smiled, looking as smug and arrogant as ever.

My legs were shaking; I couldn't keep them still. My mouth couldn't talk because my throat felt dry. My mind couldn't think; nothing made sense. And the room felt like it was spinning.

"You're okay. Just relax." He said.

But I couldn't.

My breathing returned to normal after several minutes went by. I assumed Monty was now satisfied and would go back to Katie's room. But he stood up, slipped his penis out of a hole in the front of his shorts.

Then he pulled me by my wrist closer to him, forcing me to sit on the edge of the bed in front of him.

"I don't know how — ," I said.

It's the only words I managed to form.

"It's okay." He said, placing my hand on his soft penis, then he put his hand firmly over mine. "I'll show you what to do. Don't be afraid. Trust me."

But I was sort of afraid... not of him, but my inexperience. I was scared to continue. Afraid to stop. Afraid to disappoint him.

Afraid...

I know what he wanted me to do. I remembered it from one of the scenes in the porno, and I just didn't think I could.

"I just made you feel good." He said, guiding my head closer to him. "Don't you want to make me feel good too? Just open your mouth. And relax, you'll like it too."

I opened my mouth and felt it stretch as he slowly eased himself inside it. He placed his hands on the back of my head and moved his hips back and forth as he steadied me.

It felt like I was going to choke. It's hard to breathe, but I didn't stop... neither did he.

"You're so good at this," he reassured me. "I knew that you would be. You're driving me crazy. I want you so fucking badly."

I was happy that I could make him feel good, hoping that it would be enough. I just wished the sides of my mouth weren't hurting so badly. I'm grateful; the dim light masked the tears that formed in my eyes as I tried to keep up with his relentless pace. I wanted to stop and take his thing out of my mouth and go to bed, but I feared doing that would make him mad.

He said he'd been thinking about me for days now. I did not want to disappoint him. It didn't matter that my jaw hurt or that I couldn't breathe thoroughly. Making him happy was all that mattered. As he said, I just needed to relax more, and everything would be fine.

Minutes seemed like hours until he grunted and stiffened in my mouth.

"Can I make love to you?" Monty breathed in sharply, towering over me with his intimidating build.

I understood the words, but not the meaning. We'd already done more tonight than we've ever done in the months before. It started with a little flirting and touching, but now — I was ready to stop it there.

And I wanted to stop it there.

I assumed that Lamont knew that he was very special to me. That I had a crush on him. I haven't done any of this stuff or spoken to anyone the way I talked to him. Sure, the boys at school sometimes grabbed my breast or pulled their penis out and showed me, but this was all new to me. I loved him because he treated me like an adult and took me seriously.

Can I make love to you? That was something so different; it meant going all the way, like in the movies. Like in those sex education classes I went to last year. Am I ready for that?

Again he didn't wait for the answer.

He laid me down in the middle of the bed, climbed on top of me, and positioned himself between my legs. The muscles in them strained to stretch to accommodate his massive athletic frame.

I didn't want this, maybe some other night, but not that night.

"What if we wake up Katie?" I whispered, hoping that would deter him from going any further.

"We won't," he sucked on my nipple, then looked up at me. "She took her sleeping pills, and nothing short of a house fire will wake her up right now. It's just you and me. Don't you like me? You said you did."

"I do," I replied.

I did like him... I really liked him. I had wanted to say those words for almost a year now, but now it just made my soul feel empty.

"You're okay. Just relax." He said again, stroking his erection. "Trust me. If you like me, then you'll want me to do this."

I did, but I was having a hard time feeling anything.

He pushed himself inside me, using his upper body weight to keep me in place.

It felt tight. It hurt, and that was all I could remember.

"Just relax, baby," he said. "It won't hurt as much if you relax."

But it did hurt.

I gasped, but Monty didn't seem to notice. He just repeated, 'relax' over and over in my ear. I dug my nails into my sheets as he eased deeper inside. Wet streams of tears rolled down my cheek, but I did not cry, not entirely; I just closed my eyes as hard as my eyelid muscles would allow.

"Almost there," he grunted. "It will only hurt for a little bit, and then it will start to feel good again. Just relax. I'm almost there. You feel so tight and so good, baby."

When it felt like I couldn't take any more of him, Monty stopped. "There you go; I'm all the way inside you now."

As much as I didn't want him to move, he did.

The details became blurry, but the pain was all I remembered. Feeling like I was watching a movie that I was starring in... was how I saw it. Nothing was real to me at that moment.

After what felt like forever, he stiffened, collapsed, and nearly squished me into the mattress with his body weight. He gently swept his lips against my ear and said, "I love you so much. Even though I know I shouldn't. I knew I wanted to be the first to make love to you... ever since I first laid eyes on you."

That was making love? I asked myself.

That December night was the first time we had sex, but we had sex a lot more at the beginning of the year, and it did get easier....and even enjoyable. I didn't feel anything after a while, but it made Monty happy. I even learned the way his body reacted when he came and how to make him finish quicker.

We snuck away every time we got a chance. I got used to it. I began to like it and even craved his touch. I did feel guilty about one thing. Katie, she's my sister, and I love her, but I couldn't help that Monty loved me more.

Present Day...

The room is quiet, and I'm back in Dr. Owens's office again... Nichole doesn't say a word at first. It's a typical response. Most normal people don't know what to say after hearing about my past, and I'm used to it. And I don't say anything either. This has left me feeling some kind of way. I've just told her the story of my first time with an older guy, but leave out the fact that it was Monty, implying that it was another person that Katie dated.

"I'm sorry that happened to you." She finally says. "It should've never happened to anyone. But you were so young."

There it is the most gut-punching sentence that can be uttered to me.

"I'm not a victim," I mutter, looking down at my phone. "We could've stopped at any time, and I wanted it."

"If that were true," she sighs. "Then why do you feel so ashamed and guilty about it? Why does it seem to hurt you to talk about what happened? Why don't you get any pleasure out of consensual sexual intercourse? And why won't you just tell Katie the truth?"

All valid questions, but I don't have any answers. I'm lost--adrift without a compass or any other guidance to help me navigate my way through anything.

Suddenly, it feels like all of the air has been sucked out of the room, and I can't get my bearings. I can't seem to focus on anything. I've ignored the office's several missed calls, the reporter, and mister random guy from last night. And I've held off listening to any voicemails… even though there are so many that it fills my lock screen.

The session has come to an end; Nichole walks around her desk at the far end of her enormous office and takes a look at her MacBook Pro to see what space she has available for me next week. She glances up over the top of the laptop; she catches me fidgeting again.

"Lisa, can I give you my personal number," she asks, "I want you to feel free to call me any time you need me – day or night. And if you feel yourself slipping into self-destructive habits, call me before you do anything."

"Okay."

"I mean it, and you should think about visiting a close friend or someone you trust," Nichole adds, typing feverishly on the keyboard with her polished acrylic nails. "You shouldn't be alone."

"I have a feeling that things will get a lot worse before they get any better," my voice response in a low tone. "No one wants to sweep these accusations under the rug. But he is also my friend."

Nichole nods. "In my opinion, no one should ever sweep abuse, sexual assault, or rape under the rug. Keeping quiet is what allows these monsters to get away with it for so long."

But Monty wasn't a monster—not to me.

I keep quiet.

"Lisa, you were thirteen years old when an older man first groomed you," Nichole's voice drips with genuine concern for me. "You weren't physically, emotionally, or mentally ready to consent to all of the things that he manipulated you to do. This person raped you—repeatedly, and that's not okay, nor is any of it your fault. Even if you liked him too, the sooner you accept that the sooner you can start to heal and accept help."

I know she's right deep down, but my brain is wired to disagree. "Thank you, Nichole, for everything... I'm truly grateful."

I smile—through the shame and guilt and the pain. Put on my 'I'm fine' disguise and quietly exit the office after making another appointment for the following Monday.

I need a drink...

SEVEN

Friday, March 19th, 2016

A few days have gone by since I met with Katie. And the accusations against Lamont are spreading all over the internet like wildfire. The news says they have suspended Monty from his team, pending an investigation, and I hear even the police are getting involved. I want to believe that life will return to normal, but nothing feels normal about my life right now. But then again, I've never felt that way in my life.

I need to focus; I'm on the verge of closing this significant deal, and starting down the road of being a millionaire. And possibly changing the App world forever; still, I can't get him out of my head. Every day, I've been having panic attacks more frequently; the images of my past are consuming my every thought.

For all my wishing that all of this would just go away... or that I could forget the last few days, a minor part of me feels sorry for Monty, wanting to be there for him. Secretly, I hate myself for caring about what people are saying about him — the comments — the breaking news — the articles. I try not to become obsessed with every detail, knowing that it will simply consume me even more if I go down that rabbit hole. I'd broken free from Monty a long time ago, and now, I've convinced myself that none of this had anything to do with me, and that's how it should stay.

Walking into my apartment after another long day at work, I shuffle through the stack of mail that had been crammed in my mailbox and notice a letter from an anonymous person. I don't open it, deciding to head back downstairs again to grab a drink from the bar. When I step out onto the street, I hear my name ring out in the air. The sound is coming from a woman that I don't recognize with long brown hair tucked into the hood of her jacket. And I watch her cautiously as she quickly approaches me from the opposite end of the street. Her voice sounds familiar to me, although I can't seem to place it.

"Lisa," I hear my name again, but a little louder this time. "Is that you?"

The woman smiles, running up to me and throwing her arms around me in an embrace. "Lisa, It's me... Sara!"

Fuck... this is all I need, more ghosts from my past.

I feel like I'm being Punked, looking around for a camera crew or something. New York is supposed to be a city that you can get lost in, but at the moment, it's where everyone appears to be able to find me easily these days.

"Sara." I smile. "How are you doing?"

Like I care...

I met Sara in high school; we both went to Penn Foster together. She was a grade higher than I was, and I even considered her a friend for a while at least, but we grew apart.

"Wow, look at you." She smiles, catching her breath. "It's been ages."

"Yeah," I put all my internal walls up. "It feels like a lifetime ago."

"Where are you headed?" Sara looks around. "Am I keeping you from something?"

"The Dead Rabbit." I hesitate, knowing immediately where this awkward exchange is heading.

"Do you want to get a drink with me? We've got to catch up."

The idea sounds innocent enough, but I'm in no mood for a trip down memory lane or to be socially polite.

"Sure." I force a smile. "Sounds great!"

I try to block out all the reasons our friendship came to an abrupt halt, and I stopped speaking to Sara entirely. I remember there was a time when she'd betrayed my trust, and it wasn't something I could forgive. She tried to friend request me on Facebook once, but I never responded.

God, I hope she doesn't bring that up... I thought.

"Let's go then."

We walk a short distance to the bar; it's only a few blocks away. Once there, we make our way to an intimate corner of the room. We sit at a table for two patrons, secluded from the rest of the bar. We haven't talked since high school, and we knew nothing about each other's lives in the years since Penn Foster. I can only imagine what she wants to talk about with me now.

When our drinks arrive, I take a sip of my Whiskey while Sara stares at her Stella beer. "So, what have you been up to?" I ask, just trying to navigate through the awkward silence between us.

"Oh, you know, just trying to make it through this funny thing called life," Sara smiles and shrugs her shoulders. I'm a teacher now… fourth grade. I love it—I'm married and a mom. You know the usual boring life."

She pauses.

"What about you?"

"I own my own company." I take another sip of the bitter liquid of Whiskey, before continuing. "And I'm trying to expand and throw my hat in with the big boys?"

I smile, still carefully reading her expressions and movements.

"I have an invention, and a big tech company seems to be interested."

"That's so awesome. You were always so talented like that in high school, and I remember you were always reading and sketching in your notepad."

I raise my glass to my lips, finish my drink, then signal for another one.

"How are Katie and your dad?" Sara continues her awkward interogation.

"Everyone is doing well." I pause as the server brings me another glass of that amber liquor. "Katie and I just had dinner the other night, and dad died last year."

"Oh, I'm sorry to hear that," she says softly. Her tone even has a hint of remorse and care in it.

Lowering her gaze, Sara exhales deeply before speaking again. "Lisa, I'm really sorry about the way things went down back in high school. I didn't know things were going to go down the way they did for you, and I was just trying to help. And ever since then, I've felt so guilty."

Here we go…

"It's okay." I shrug dismissively. "It's ancient history."

"I realize how bad I hurt you." She adds. "And I wish I would've gone about doing things differently."

"It's water under the bridge now, Sara," My tone is dismissive, but she doesn't pick up on it. "I understand why you felt like you had to do it. It was my fault; I shouldn't have burdened you with everything that happened."

She shakes her head — *no.*

I gulp down the rest of my Whiskey like it was a shot, knowing that we have arrived at the topic I wanted to avoid this entire time.

"I'm sure you've heard about Lamont Johnson." She doesn't look at me as she speaks. "I mean, he was your sister's boyfriend. So I assumed you know about his 'situation.'"

"Yes."

I take a deep breath, feeling my stomach sink. There is a strong feeling within me like my Whiskey is fighting to come back up again. I don't want to have this conversation… not now… not ever. It seems like, lately, everyone is forcing me to speak about shit that I've spent years trying to forget.

"Lisa, when I saw you and Derek that night after the party. I felt sick." She blurts out. "I had so many emotions surging through me; I couldn't think straight. All I wanted to do was find a way to make him stop — you were only fourteen — a sophomore, a baby. None of those things should've happened to you at all... and deep down, I felt responsible, so I told Ms. Mayo."

"I know why you did it, Sara." I lower my gaze. "You couldn't have foreseen what would happen next. You were just trying to help, and I understood that."

"Then why did you stop talking to me?" Sara asks. "You cut me out of your life as if I had hurt you worse than he did."

As I think about that time in my life, Sara's voice fades into the distance. It was a dark time for me, after the party. Nothing made sense at all anymore, and everything seemed to spiral out of control. It was the first time in my life that people looked at me like there was something damaged or broken within me. And at that moment, all I wanted to do was die or disappear and never be found again.

"Sara," I sigh. "You said it yourself. I was fourteen. Confused. And being labeled as some kind of slut. I didn't want to hurt anyone. And I didn't want to expose anyone either. I just wanted to go back to being invisible. But after you told Ms. Mayo, my life imploded."

I pause.

"After that day, suddenly, I was asked all these difficult and embarrassing questions. I was forced to have doctors examine me to see if I was still a virgin. My dad wouldn't look me in the eye anymore and left the room every time I entered it. Then came the whispers and gossip while I was at school. I was the girl who went to a birthday party and slept with her friend's older brother—then wanted to play the victim. At least, that was what people thought of me. It was a stigma that I couldn't shake."

"And it was all because of me." She adds.

Yes...

"No." My voice trembles as I play with the condensation on the rim of my glass to hide my emotions. "It was because a teacher reported me to the principal."

Every day, I struggle to forget that part of my life when my world crumbled and crashed all around me. Derek had done something to me...he was older than me, but that didn't seem to matter to anyone. Everyone had their own opinion about me, and Lamont was furious with me for letting another person touch me in his favorite places. For a year, it felt like I was on a runaway train, and all I wanted it to do was crash. It's a lot for a teenager to go through. I became so depressed I stopped eating, which developed into an eating disorder. It felt like I was in Hell.

I look up into Sara's eyes; sympathy and pity are swirling deep within her gaze.

"It's okay." I force a smile. "It's in the past, and I'm over it."

"Lisa, no one ever really gets over going through something like that," her voice falls flat, as if she's speaking from her own experience. "You could've come to me, talked to me — we were best friends. I was at that party too; I saw you and believed you, and I knew what Derek did to you."

Suddenly, I feel even more sick to my stomach as a realization slowly pushes its way to the front of my thoughts. I sit back in my chair, drawing in a sharp breath. It's like a sixth sense among damaged people. Darkness always attracts darkness, and it hits me like a punch in the face. "Derek Page hurt you too, didn't he?"

Sara slowly nods; her gaze is fixed on the table, not daring to look up at me.

"Not that night at the party, but a few months before it," she confesses, pain dripping from every word. "I was so sure that Derek wouldn't do anything with so many girls there that night. But when I realized that you'd been in the room with him, I felt so guilty for not stopping him earlier... or at the very least warning you about him."

"Oh, Sara," I say. "I understand completely."

I grab her trembling hands across the table.

"What happened to me that night wasn't your fault."

Talking to Sara only makes me think about my ex-boyfriend, Dante, even more because she reminds me of him. In truth, he'd been on my mind lately, almost as much as Lamont has been. He was another person who cared about me deeply and was just trying to help, but I pushed him away and hurt him like I always do.

After we say our goodbyes and promise to stay in touch, I'm left standing there alone on the crowded street. I dig my phone out of my pocket and frantically dial a number.

"Hey, Dante," I exhale into the phone. "Are you busy?"

******

72

Friday, March 21st, 2016

I have to admit; I'm fucking nervous as hell right now. And can't believe it's been six months since Dante and I ended our three-year fling. He'd asked me to marry him, and I said, "I couldn't." The relationship really couldn't go anywhere after that. But when I called him and said I needed him, he promised to stop by, without question... even after all these months.

It surprises me when he asks me to text him in a few hours.

After another two hours go by, I respond, "Are you free?"

"I've been thinking about you..." He texts back. "Wanna get a drink?"

Thank God for small favors...

"Absolutely." My thumbs frantically pound the keys on the screen as I type.

Sitting at home, I go over a few things for work. And around six in the evening, Dante texts me, saying he's already outside.

Immediately, once I walk out the front door, I notice how good he looks. It's clear that he's been hitting the gym, and it shows. His broad shoulders strain the fabric of his shirt as he stands there playing on his Samsung phone.

"Hey, Dante," I say, shortening the distance between us, giving him a soft hug. "Sorry if you've been waiting long."

Damn, he smells so good. My mind screams as he squeezes me back. I've missed the way he smells.

"No, I just got here a minute ago. Damn, you look beautiful as always, Lisa; you still take my breath away — even after everything."

"Thank you," I blush, swiping a stray hair from my face.

"You haven't been sleeping, though, have you?" He hugs me again, pulling me into the comforts of his embrace.

"No," My voice is low, resting my chin on his rock-hard chest.

"Nightmares again?"

"Sometimes." I reply. "Other times, I can't sleep at all."

The first thing I notice is that being with him feels like we haven't been apart at all. I immediately feel safe and like a human being again. And I didn't realize how much I missed the way Dante made me feel.

"How is work?" I tiptoe around the purpose of this abrupt meet up.

"Work is work…" He smiles. "But that's not why I'm here."

We skip the rest of the small talk, heading to Jacob's Italian restaurant for dinner. And I'm right back to where I was six months ago — feeling confused but somewhat comforted by his presence. Minutes after we enter the restaurant and the host gives us a booth, Dante sits opposite me and smiles warmly. A part of me is disappointed that he doesn't want to share a booth with me like we used to. There used to be a time when we couldn't keep our hands off each other. And lately, I've missed those days.

"Lisa, what's wrong?" He asks, just as his Guinness beer arrives. "You look — upset."

"I'm just stressed," I downplay things. "That's all."

The server comes around, and we order; I'm eager just to get rid of her and be alone with him again.

"You could've called me when everything went down, you know," Dante finally says to me. "Truthfully, I wanted to call you, but I was afraid of how you would react."

Of course, he knows... The words echo in my mind, and it's been all over the news.

"I'm fine."

"Bullshit, Lisa."

"No, really." I smile.

The server brings our appetizers to the table a few moments later—Spinach Artichoke and chips.

"Has he contacted you?" Dante leans in, whispering.

I subtly nod my head... *yes.*

"Jesus Christ, Lisa."

I told Dante about Lamont in our second year of dating. I had a nightmare, and when he pressed the issue, I confessed all that I could bear to tell. Naturally, he was pissed and wanted me to see a professional to talk about my feelings,' but at the time, I refused. And it caused a lot of friction between us.

"I'm okay." I smile, putting up my armor. "But last week, a reporter came to my office, asking about him."

Dante gives me a long look, not blinking for a while. "A reporter? Are you serious? Are you doing okay? Tell me what's going on—the truth, Lisa."

I sink into the cushions of the booth, taking a drink. "There are old emails and text messages between Lamont and me. This reporter somehow got her hands on them and is threatening to make them public. My therapist thinks — "

"You're seeing a therapist now?"

I frown, angry at my slip up. My entire life, I've managed to lie to everyone, but not Dante. Thirty minutes in his presence, and I'm confessing like a defendant in an interrogation.

"Lisa, when did you start seeing a therapist? I begged you to go when we were together, and you were adamant that you wouldn't ever go."

"Six months ago," I sigh. "After I tried to kill myself."

"Wait, after we broke up?" A look of shock and horror beams in his eyes. "Lisa."

"It's okay. I'm fine now."

Dante lowers his gaze before speaking again in a soft tone. "I've been so worried about you. I wanted to call you so many times, but my pride wouldn't let me because of how we ended things, but the thought of losing you..."

He shuffles out of the booth, then scoots next to me, throwing his arm around my shoulders. The warmth of his body immediately fills me with a sense of safety that I didn't know I'd been longing for.

"I don't know what I would do if I lost you."

Dante squeezes me and exhales.

"I'm okay." I fight the tears.

"No... you're not."

No... I'm not.

Dante asks me about my business and my family, mercifully changing the subject. By the end of dinner, it's clear how much he still cares about me and loves me… and how much I'd never stopped caring for him either like we'd never been a part at all.

"Lisa," he says, "I'm crazy about you, and I'm addicted to you. Tell me, why did you leave me."

I force myself to breathe, not expecting to have this conversation right now. I finish my beer, then lean back against the seat, trying to steady myself.

Lie damn you… my brain screams… *Lie!*

But I can't; I just don't have the strength to.

"Dante, I'm poison." I feel the tears swelling in my eyes. "Every second of every day, I feel ruined and tainted by my past. I have no delusions about that… I didn't want to end up hurting you. And I didn't want you to wake up one day, look at me and see damaged goods… or see me broken and vulnerable."

"Oh, Lisa," he pulls my trembling body closer to him. "I've never seen you like any of those things. You were molested, raped—and abused."

He exhales deeply, so hard it can be heard through his chest.

"I just wanted you to let me in," he says. "Trust me and not have any fear that I will hurt you. Because I won't, I swear I won't."

"But I'll hurt you," I cry softly into the fabric of his shirt. "I'm not right—not normal."

"Normal is overrated."

We leave the topic right there and finish the excellent meal. I have steak and potatoes. Dante has salmon and rice. We close the place down, talking and catching up before we are forced to leave.

Reluctantly, we walk out of the restaurant and into the brisk night air. Each of us wants to prolong every second of this moment together. He places his arm around me, and I don't object... I don't want to.

"I'm so glad you're seeing a professional, Lisa," Dante says. "I just wish that you'd let me be here for you."

I smile, but it's only to mask the fear.

Memories of Lamont push their way in the moments of silence. I don't want him there, but he's always here — within me.

"I won't keep asking you if you're okay," Dante adds, slowly walking by my side. "Because I know that, you'll put your armor on and say yes."

He knows me too well.

"Did you have a good time tonight?"

"Yes — you are a pleasant distraction from the chaos that is my life." I smile, watching the vapor of his breath float in the air.

"Good."

It's late... too late. There are no cars on the street; it's just us. Dante pulls me closer to him, comforting me, and I wish I could know what he is thinking.

"I wish I could kill him," Dante finally says, "he manipulated you. Hurt you. And tried to ruin you."

I know he's hurt and angry, but it's still very awkward to hear that kind of hate coming from him.

We stop at a streetlight, and wait for the signal to tell us to proceed, then turn the corner towards my apartment.

"He wasn't the only one who hurt me, Dante," I confess... I don't know if it's the beer or the shots we took afterward, but I'm too drunk to care anymore.

"What?"

"There were other times. Lamont was just the most consistent and longest one, but it seems like I attract men who want to do these perverted things to me, and I'm used to it."

"Have you discussed this with your therapist? Does Katie know about what he did to you? How many others were there?"

"Not tonight, Dante."

He tilts his head back, looking up towards the sky, cursing under his breath, "Those fucking bastards. Okay, I won't press the issue, that is how I lost you the first time, and I won't make that mistake again."

We reach the steps of my apartment. I wait, but Dante doesn't leave, doesn't move, or even unlock his car. His emerald eyes seem to almost stare right through me, unraveling me with his intense gaze.

"Do you want me to go?"

I shake my head—no.

He smirks and exhales as I reach out for his hand. I don't want to be alone, not tonight—not ever.

EIGHT

We walk together through the entryway of my loft into my enormous living room.

"I like your new place," Dante says, surveying the area. "How many rooms."

"Three."

"Nice island," he adds, running his finger over my stainless-steel fridge in the kitchen. "It's very spacious. You must pay a fortune, and why do you need so much space if it's just you?"

"I like my space." I pull the refrigerator handle. "Beer?"

"Please." He smiles.

This past week has been so stressful. With Lamont, the reporter—work, and my demons, I can barely breathe. But I can't think of anyone that I'd want to be with more, at this moment, than Dante. I'm grateful he didn't turn me down when I called him. And that he's standing in my kitchen with me right now. Still, I'm cautious about taking any of this further, and it seems foolish to add another complication to my life right now.

Dante and I met at Club Nightlife a few months after I moved to New York. At first I thought of him as another one-night stand, but the attraction was instant and intense. For the first few days—weeks, we did nothing but fuck, blowing off any other responsibilities. After that first week, we were inseparable. Dante was dominating and controlling, which, I must confess, was part of the attraction I had to him. The way he took control and owned my body drove me wild. It was thrilling, but not in a stalker or serial killer type of way.

"I like this place." His baratone voice rumbles, "It fits you."

"Thank you. But I know you didn't just come up to see the decor." I hand him a bottle of Guinness, which is both his and my beer of choice.

He pulls his phone out of his pocket, checking the final numbers of his stock options, then silences his cellphone. "I haven't been able to get you out of my mind." He moves the bottle to his lips, emptying half the liquid with one gulp.

He's nervous, which is a welcoming change.

"Why?" I ask. "I left you… hurt you. And I figured that you wouldn't want to bother with me after everything."

"I know, Lisa. But I know I didn't handle things well when you told me about some of your past either." He sighs. "I was so mad…at you—at what happened to you in general. Lamont hurt you…abused and raped you, and you were dismissing it like you didn't care. And worse, you tried to convince me that somehow you were okay with everything because you loved him like any of that was okay or normal."

"It was normal for me." Shame drips from my voice. "My life revolved around Monty when I was younger and even when I realized what he was doing to me was wrong. It was all routine to me, and I simply didn't know how to stop it. And at the time, a part of me didn't want to stop. I wanted to please Lamont and make him happy. He had convinced me I made him happy, and that I was happy too."

Routine, my mind scoffs.

"I don't want to talk about this anymore tonight."

"I understand," Dante flashes a warm smile. "But eventually, I'm going to need you to tell me everything."

"Yes, but not tonight." I take his beer and finish it off.

"No." Dante kisses me passionately, forcing all my old feelings and desires for him to bubble to the surface. "Not tonight."

Looking down, I see the evidence of his desire for me; his sex is pushing against the hem of his jeans.

"Come here," I say, tugging on his Henley shirt.

"What are you doing, Lisa?"

"You're going to help me feel better." I smile.

Dark desire burns in his eyes, but he protests. "This doesn't feel right; I don't want to take advantage of you. I want you, but not like this. You're hurting, and you're upset."

Dante pulls away, putting a little distance between us.

My eyelashes flutter as I process what he just said. "I don't want to take advantage of you..." Those words sound so foreign to me.

"L," He sighs, looking down at the floor. "All the men in your life have hurt you in one way or another. That's not a list that I want to be a part of."

Dante lowers his head, almost appearing ashamed of the thoughts that he's thinking.

"When I'm with you," He begins to confess. "It's hard for me to control myself—you feel so fucking good, and I want you so damn bad that I almost lose control. And after you told me about you and Lamont.

I knew I would rather let you go than lose complete control and have you one day look at me the way you look when you are thinking about him... in pain."

This is why he let me go? I think to myself. Dante's just as afraid of himself as I am of myself.

"Dante, has it ever occurred to you? I'm addicted to you too, and it scares me sometimes as well. I like when you lose control. Don't compare yourself to Lamont or the others, because I don't see it that way at all. And I've never seen you that way. You scare me, yes, but it's because I feel like I could really be happy with you, and I've never been happy before. Happiness could feel like Heaven when you have it, and Hell when you lose it."

My fingertips run over his stiff erection.

"Sex with you never felt dirty or wrong to me," I add. "It felt right... it felt like nothing I've ever felt before in my life."

"Well, if that's true?" He inhales sharply. "Why did you turn down my proposal?"

It's a valid question, and after all Dante has done for me, he deserves the truth.

"Before you," I explain, not expecting to have this conversation right now. "Lamont was the only man who made me orgasm and who made me feel special. And after him, sex and relationships meant nothing to me, and I felt nothing... but then YOU entered my life. When you lose control—I lose control, and my body orgasms and unravels for you. I don't have to fake it. It brought up a lot of confusing and conflicting emotions for me... and I got scared."

I kiss his neck gently, feeling the heat radiating from him.

"Lisa… with everything you're going through, things could get complicated. I don't want to lose you again by moving too fast. These last six months have been Hell for me, and I want to represent something positive in your life." Dante exhales carefully. "You deserve to be happy. And I want to be the one who makes you happy."

I frown at the thought of this man—my friend. My lover, ever thinking that he didn't make me happy.

"You want to make me happy." My eyes narrow. "Take me into the bedroom and fuck me until my legs feel like jelly… don't hold back. Lose yourself in me."

"I don't want to scare you away again or, worse." Dante holds me close to him, looking into my eyes.

"I trust you." I pause, realizing the gravity of the words that just escape from my lips. "Now, trust me to let you do those dark things you want to do to me. Knowing that, I will let you know if it's too much for me."

Darkness attracts darkness… I thought to myself.

"Lose control, Dante, please."

It's the one thing I love about him the most, how he pushes me to the edge of the abyss without making me feel less than. It drives me crazy sometimes. And I don't understand it, but I love it.

"Lisa." His voice was low, vibrating against my lips.

"Don't pull away, Dante."

He breathes deeply.

"This isn't right. This is fucked up."

"I'm fucked up, remember?" I smile.

Suddenly, he grabs me, pinning my body against the wall. I tremble slightly, but it's from excitement and not fear.

"This isn't what I wanted to do tonight."

I graze my lips against his. Then kiss his lips hard and passionately, pulling him so hard that I'm afraid I'll break him. "This is exactly what you want to do, and I want to do. Don't be afraid... I won't break."

"It is what I've wanted to do for months now, but yes, I'm still afraid."

"Shut the fuck up, Dante," I release him. "Let me tell you when it's too much."

He lifts me up; my butt rests on his massive forearms as he guides me to the bedroom.

"I want to toss you on the bed and fuck you senseless... hard." He lowers me down slowly until my feet touch the floor again.

That's what I want — my mind screams. The words pierce through me like lightning.

"I'm not stopping you."

His lips kiss me hard, and his touch sets me on fire from the inside out. A kindle is lit deep down in my belly and quickly sets every cell within me aflame.

My lips press against his, matching his force and intensity. I crave him, wanting him to consume me completely, coaxing the pure animal desire that I felt when we first met. And at that moment, I'm not afraid, just needing.

"Don't hold back," I moaned into him. "Not tonight."

"Fuck, Lisa."

I lick his lips, feeling his erection against my body. He wants this as much as I want him, and when nothing else in my world makes sense, I'm relieved that this somehow makes perfect sense to me.

Slowly, I lower myself to my knees, with Dante standing in front of me. My fingers massage his erection through the fabric of his jeans. Tugging on the button, sliding the zipper down, my fingers tremble from the surge of adrenaline at the thought of what's coming. Freeing his cock, I slide my mouth over the tip and suck gently. He moans, loving the motion of my tongue dancing around him.

He grabs my head, pushing me to suck deeper… tickling the back of my throat with his tip as I move in and out slowly.

"Fuck, Lisa." Dante grunts, grabbing a fistful of my hair. "I missed this. I missed you."

I look up at him; my mouth mercifully releases him for a moment.

"You're still holding back, Dante. Fuck my mouth. You say you missed me? Show me."

He smirks, gripping my hair tighter, thrusting his sex further into my mouth as I take all of him in.

In… Out… In… Out. Faster. Harder. More.

He fucks my mouth, losing himself in the pleasure of it all as he sucks the air sharply into his lungs until his body stiffens.

"Oh, fuck." He grunts.

His touch and being near him are so addictive. I want him all the time. Six months ago, that was part of the problem; I always wanted another fix.

"I can't wait any longer." Dante breathes, toying and tugging at my nipples.

He kisses me hard again with a sense of yearning.

"I want to fuck you now," Dante breathes in.

I feel him grab my thighs and pull them up to his waist. He skillfully spreads my legs around his waist as he thrusts into me in a hard, singular motion, digging his fingers into my hips while easing deeper inside of me.

I close my eyes, allowing myself to absorb all of him inside of me. I don't go away. And stay here in the moment with him. And I'm relieved. I don't hide and don't retreat in the back of my mind.

"Lisa—" He pauses, huffing.

"No, don't hold back. I want all of you, Dante." I arch my hips into him, holding him closer to me. "I want you to ravage me."

He stares into my eyes. Then he drives into me, deeper—harder.

I cry out, feeling my body tense up around him immediately and unravel under him almost just as quickly.

Dante's thrusts are rapid—intense and deliberate, as I tighten around him like a snake coils around its prey. Every nerve in me quakes, forcing my body to tremble uncontrollably as I climax hard. He doesn't waver, thrusting deeper... harder... faster, punishing that particular spot inside me that forces me to explode repeatedly for him.

Yes...

The entire bed is moving. The headboard bangs rhythmically against the wall. Dante grips the edge, leveraging himself, and continues crashing into me, pushing me to the point of madness. Then his hands slip underneath my ass, lifting my hips, allowing him to maneuver even deeper.

"Dante!" The pleasure and pressure ripple through me as everything goes white.

His breath quakes, "I know, I'm there too."

He doesn't relent.

"Lisa, fuck." He threw his head back, his fingers marking my skin.

A split second later, he stills—and stays deep inside me while I tremble underneath him, desperately clawing at the surrounding sheets.

Dante is the only man that drives me this crazy.

"Did I hurt you?" He exhales, trying to catch his breath. "Are you okay?"

When my vision comes into focus again, I look up into his eyes and steady my breathing... I try to collect myself.

"I'm fine." My breath is shallow and my throat is dry. "I'm more than fine. I'm perfect."

Then, when I can't imagine him doing another perfect act. He simply pulls me closer, wraps his muscular arms around me, and just holds me. Before I know it, the warmth of wet tears streams down my cheek and pool on the bed. At this moment, I'm at peace.

"I'm sorry. I don't know what's wrong with me." I bury my face deep into the pillow.

"It's okay," Dante says, squeezing me tighter. "You're allowed to cry, and you don't have to apologize. You put of this vale of perfection with everyone around you. Pretending to be okay, don't pretend with me."

"Please stay with me tonight," My voice quakes, surprised the words are coming from me.

"I'll stay all night if you want me to."

Being with him is intoxicating. And I want more.

Suddenly, the phone rings and BLOCKED flashes on the screen, and I know who it is. It's him... Monty, calling to ruin my otherwise perfect moment as if somehow he knows I'm with someone else.

"It's him," I say, not knowing if I said the words out loud or in my head, as my mind drifts into a flashback of images.

NINE

January 5th, 2001…
The memory is as clear as water…

I'd just turned fifteen back in December; Monty and I were sitting on the couch alone, my legs on top of his, and we were watching Gladiator with Russell Crowe. Katie was in the bedroom, taking a nap before her shift. That night, Monty offered to babysit me for a few hours while my sister rested; although I was feeling grown-up enough to take care of myself, dad didn't seem to agree. But I knew Monty was just hanging around to be around me.

"I should go to my room. And have an English test on Monday." I spoke, stretching, slowly lifting my legs off of his lap.

My phone alerted next to me, and I checked the message, smiling at the stupid text a friend from school had sent.

"Who the fuck is that?" he inquired.

"Just a friend."

I felt Monty move as he sunk into the cushion of the couch and yanked my legs back onto his lap, staring at me.

He was jealous…

"It's no one," I jerked, quickly putting the phone away. "Just a friend from school. We have a project together, and we're collaborating."

Monty didn't blink, just glared at me, staring at me. "A boy?"

I exhaled in, rolling my eyes.

"Maybe we should start setting a few boundaries between you and me." His voice was cold and flat.

I eyed him, not sure of what he was getting at.

"I know you're in high school now and have new friends and all that shit."

"I don't have too many friends." I huffed. "It's just a stupid school project. If I could do it alone... I would."

Under the thickness and cover of the blanket, draped over the two of us, concealing us. Monty slowly slipped his hand under my nightgown and into my underwear, rubbing me at first, before thrusting two of his fingers inside of me—forcefully. His other hand tightly gripped my thigh, keeping me in place.

"So, you're saying that I can trust you, right? And that you know how important it is that we must keep our special time together a secret?"

"Monty." I snapped, "I'm not stupid."

"No, but I need to know that I can still trust you and that you still want to be with me."

Be with him?

I'd been with him, and I didn't seem to have much choice in the matter... It felt like I had even less of a choice now. He's all I knew—and it tethered me to him. I loved him, and we have had this secret affair for a long time now. And this secret had gotten way too deep and complicated that I couldn't tell anyone without the risk of losing everything myself.

"I have said nothing to anyone," I whispered, feeling him forcibly shove the third finger deeper into me. It hurt, but he didn't stop. Nor did he seem to care as I tried to pull away.

But I couldn't move.

"I need for you to know what will happen if someone finds out about us. Katie would be crushed and probably hate you forever. Your dad would find out and definitely be pissed at you and probably think that you were some kind of slut or something. And everyone would look at us differently. They would question why we let this go on for so long. Or why you told no one."

I couldn't speak. The pain was becoming unbearable.

"I would lose my scholarship... and not get drafted. No one would believe that you didn't want this too, and the stigma would follow you forever like an awful stink."

My eyes rolled to the back of my head. "I promise, I wouldn't tell on you. I won't say a word. You can trust me... please. I've done nothing that would make you think otherwise... Monty."

The worse part of what he said was that Katie would hate me. I didn't want that at all. I'd never meant to hurt her. She's my sister and has always been there for me.

"Do you love me?" he asked. "Say you love me as much as I love you."

He kept going, fingering me harder and harder.

"I love you, Monty," I responded in anguish.

"Repeat it." He directed.

"I love you."

"I don't believe you," he scoffed. "And I won't stop until I do."

It hurt... that's all I remembered — the pain.

"I love you, Monty." "I love you," I repeated.

Please stop...

When he did things like this, punishing me for whatever reason, I couldn't think through the pain; my body couldn't respond to the commands that my brain was giving. It felt like he was purposely hurting me because he knew he could. He did it because he was everything, and I was nothing, and he wanted to remind me of that. He knew that even after this, I would still love him.

He could be ruthless when he wanted to be.

"I love you," I repeated one last time. "Please... just stop."

After I begged, Monty seemed satisfied, blinking at me rapidly. He loosened his grip on my thigh and retracted his fingers from inside of me. Through the warm blue light emanating from the television, I could see the shade of red liquid on his fingers and the scent of copper in the air.

"Fuck," he added, realizing what he'd done, "I'm sorry... Lisa, I'm so sorry."

I did nothing... embarrassed, as I rushed to the bathroom to clean myself up. My legs were shaking, and there was a bruise on my thigh where Monty had gripped me. And I could barely clean myself because my hands were trembling so badly. It took everything within me to fight back the tears.

Did he love me? By hurting me? At least that's what it felt like at that moment.

There was a subtle knock at the door. "Lisa, I'm sorry," he murmured. "I just love you so fucking much. And the thought of losing you drives me crazy sometimes that I can't think straight."

I remained silent, leaning against the bathroom door. Softly, I cried to myself; my trembling hand muffled the sounds of my whimpers.

"Baby, please." He whispered.

I turned on the shower and climbed in slowly, allowing the hot water to scold my skin.

Time stood still again... I drowned everything out, numbing every feeling and thought.

I remained silent for the rest of the night, spending the evening in my room, and listened to R&B slow songs like Brian McKnight, Toni Braxton, and other songs from the nineties. After a while, I drifted off to sleep.

12:42 a.m. flashed on my alarm clock next to my bed on the nightstand. My vision blurred, but something in the pit of my stomach screamed at me to be vigilant as my eyes strained to adjust through the darkness. Monty sat in the chair across the room; his labored breathing stopped as he realized I had noticed him.

"I didn't want to wake you." He muttered with a smile. "Not just yet. You look so beautiful."

He walked over to my bed... fully naked, and sat next to me. A part of me loved to see his body. As a football player, he was in great shape. It had been a year since he seriously started working on getting drafted in the NFL, so he'd been working harder than ever in the gym.

I remembered it flattered Katie that he still wanted to keep seeing her, even after deciding to join the League. To her, that meant things between them were real.

"Lisa," Monty lowered his head. "I'm so sorry that I hurt you. I've just been so stressed with the team and my last year in school... There's so much pressure on me and so many eyes watching me; it gets overwhelming sometimes. And then there's the thought of losing you. The thought of you even talking to someone else drives me crazy."

I was still so mad at him, and I didn't want to hear what he was saying.

Monty leaned over and switched my reading light on, illuminating his intimidating stature with a dim light.

"Monty, I'm tired," I responded. "And I'm sore. Can we talk about this later?"

He reached for me and pulled the covers down before tracing his finger around my nipples underneath my nightgown. His eyes had that look that he got when he wanted more than just kissing and fingering. He wanted sex. I was in pain and tried to stop him. But since he'd started his senior year, I'd seen less and less of him.

I didn't want him to stay... But I didn't want him to go...

I knew if I protested, he would only make me feel even worse than I did and would say that I made him fall in love with me, only to hurt him by breaking his heart. And that broke my heart. Monty had a way of disarming me. Sometimes he'd make me feel like this whole thing was my idea so that I couldn't back out of it. Or he would tell me that although he knew it was wrong, he couldn't help falling in love with me.

"When we're together," he confessed, "it feels like this is the only time I can be myself. That the dark things inside me can find a home with all the darkness within you."

I thought to myself. *The darkness you planted inside of me... The darkness you nurtured. Every time you touch me...*

He shifted his body, positioning himself under the covers with me. I knew what he was looking for — permission, some expression on my face that told him I was still his girl.

"You're my forbidden fruit," he exhaled, kissing me. "I knew that to taste you would damn my soul, but I had to have you so badly that I didn't care. Your body is a drug to me, and I'm hooked."

I felt his knee wedge in between my legs; his hand stroked his erection. I didn't care anymore at that moment and just yielded to what he wanted. In some bizarre way, not fighting made me feel like I had some choice in the matter. I loved and cared about Monty, or at least I thought I did, but our passion was filled with desire, pain, and we always had to keep it a secret.

The pain was indescribable as he entered me; after that incident on the couch, it was torture to have him inside me, claiming me as his once again.

I cried, but he kept going, pushing into me harder... deeper, pinning my arms against the bed so I couldn't move and moaning into my ear. And retreated into myself and went away again. I'd gotten used to being outside of my body, detaching my feelings from whatever was going on around me. I'd gotten used to his love and gotten used to feeling like there were two parts of me — the one that people saw and the real person who only Monty saw.

Nothing was real… It was just a dream…

Soon, it would be over, and I would be me again, or some version of me.

Time slowed to a crawl, but even now when I think about it. The painful memories of his lessons and displays of love were all I remember…

If love didn't hurt, then it wasn't real. At least, that's what Monty taught me.

****

Monday, March 21st, 2016

Walking into my office sometimes leaves me in awe. I'd worked my ass off to graduate from MIT. I worked so hard to build this tech company from the ground up. This place feels tainted now, after these allegations surface about Lamont and that reporter came to see me. Since then, Monty gave me the seed money that helped build this company, and all of my other accomplishments feel hollow now. He was paying for my silence, and although I saw it as an old friend just helping me out… I'm sure the public wouldn't see it that way. And it would ruin me.

I lean back against my chair, wishing I could disappear—hoping Monty and I had been more careful with our text messages and emails. But mostly, I wish that all of this would just blow over.

"Hey, Ms. Rose?" Russell pokes his head through the door immediately after knocking. "You have a phone call… from your sister… it sounds urgent."

My stomach falls to my ankles. Instinctively, I know whatever Katie's calling about; it isn't good at all. She never calls me at work.

"Tell her I'll call her back." I force a smile. "Thank you, Russell."

By noon, I'm still sitting behind my desk, staring out the window at the adjacent building, when I flip my phone over. There are several text messages from Katie, Dante, and a number I don't recognize. My body goes numb as I watch the alerts crawl up the lock screen of my phone.

My hand trembles, clicking into the message from Katie:

Katie: I need to talk to you tonight, Lisa.

Me: Is there something wrong?

Those three dots pulse on the screen.

Katie: I'd rather talk to you in person. I'm coming over.

Me: Talk about what?

More dots…

Katie: I'm coming over tonight.

Then I read Dante's message:

Dante: Hey, L, are you okay?

Me: Yes, why?

Dante: I've just been hearing things.

Me: Like?

I stare at the dots, knowing what's coming next.

There's an alert.

Dante: There's a post on some blog about Lamont being involved with a teenage girl while he was in college... I don't think anyone realizes it's you, but...

The three dots pulse in a bubble.

Dante: It's out there now.

Me: Thanks for the heads up...

I don't touch the phone for the rest of the day, not wanting to think about the devastating effects this might have on me. I stare at my MacBook for so long the battery dies, but finally, I work up the courage to go on the site and look at the posts myself. And there they were, for all to see. Sexting messages between Monty and me. The text was from Monty. His nickname throughout college and his NFL career is 'Magic Monty.' He once mentioned it was his nickname because he would make impossible plays.

And my nickname in the text was Witchy Charmed after the T.V. show Charmed, which was my favorite show when I was younger.

For years we texted back and forth while Monty was away at college or away games, and even a few years after they drafted him into the NFL.

Then my Yahoo alert chimes; I maneuver the arrow with the mouse pad and click on the message.

To:lisa.rose@yahoo.com
From:CR@gmail.com
Subject: Please read

Dear Lisa,

This is Chloe Roberts; we met in your office a few days ago. First, let me apologize to you. I wanted to share your story BUT keep your identity private, and I'd hoped that it would help encourage the other women to speak up and share their own stories. After we spoke, my work computer was hacked, and someone posted everything I had on a website. My guess is because someone knew that I was working on this article and wanted the story first.

I'm so sorry for any pain or distress this has caused you. The posts don't display your name specifically, but I can't say for sure this won't lead back to you somehow. Again, I'm so sorry... this wasn't how I wanted any of this to go down.

Please call me at my personal number and email, because I don't trust the computers at my job anymore.

I'm sorry if this victimizes you for a second time; that wasn't my intention at all.

Chloe R

I'm useless for the rest of the day. I respond to emails. Answer phone calls. But I'm on autopilot. I'm not okay, and I don't want the day to end, thinking about any and every excuse not to go home to see Katie there waiting for me. I can't bear to face her right now.

My phone vibrates against the glass surface of my desk, and my heart sinks, and my hands tremble as a BLOCKED number appears on my phone.

It's him... I know it's him.

"Hello." My voice shakes.

On the phone, Monty says, "What the fuck, L? My fucking agent just called me about some post found on some website."

"Do you know anything about this?"

"I just found out about it this morning." I groan. "I don't know who leaked the messages."

"These messages are going to fuck me, and that's a fact. They don't need proof... I'm fucking finished."

I get up, walk around my desk, and quickly shut the door. I glance through the vertical blinds to see if anyone notices or is even staring in my direction. The cubicles that my employees work behind provided perfect cover for them and me.

"What do you want me to do? The last time I checked, you had my old phone, and I gave it to you when I went off to MIT." I hiss, cupping the microphone with my hand as if someone else is listening. "I've been evading and denying questions that have to do with us for years. Even when the teachers, the police, and everyone started grilling me about what happened with Derek, asking me if there had been any other boys I'd been with, I said nothing."

I don't want to have this conversation now, but I know it is just the warmup for whatever Katie wants to talk about later. And need to stop running from this and stop carrying this burden around with me. I need to let go. And need to search for some kind of normalcy and happiness. I'm so over this.

"So, what you really should ask is, where the fuck did you leave that phone, and who has it?" I snap. "Because after you asked me for it, I washed my hands of the whole thing. Let's not forget, I have something to lose as well here."

"I thought you might have made a copy or something," Monty says. "For some kind of leverage later."

Really… He thought I would betray him?

After everything, he did. After all, he put me through. I'm offended by the accusation… I'm reminded every waking second of what we did… the affair, and the people we hurt. But he lives his life as if he's done nothing wrong. Monty has been living his dream — hell; he gets to live other people's dreams too. He's rich and famous. Every time he steps on the field, people chant his name like he's a god.

I'm the one waking up in cold sweats from the nightmares, and I'm the one living in shame. The one who's fucked up.

I'm the foolish girl who got caught up…

I exhale a breath. "I've never come forward. And I never will. But don't lie and play the victim with me, Monty. These other women who are accusing you only want one thing… justice." I sit down in my chair again, feeling the rage swelling inside me. "I don't give a fuck about these girls; I just want my name kept out of the mess that you've made for yourself."

"So, you want me to go to prison?" He asks, almost sounding hurt by my boldness.

"No," I reply. "I just want to forget you, as easily as you forgot me."

"I love you," he claims. "You're my forbidden fruit… my sweet fruit. I could never forget you."

Your fruit has soured… I think to myself.

"I have to go."

I hang up the phone before he can respond. Before I lose my resolve. Before I break down.

When I leave my office at four-thirty, the taxi I order is waiting outside for me. Dread fills me while riding in the backseat, watching buildings go by in a blur—a metaphor of how my life is feeling at the moment. Everything is spinning out of control, and it's only a matter of time that everything comes crashing down around me.

TEN

Once I'm home, I head to the kitchen, dropping my messenger bag on the couch as I grab the Crown Royal and some Diet-Coke. I sit on the couch, sipping the cool amber liquid as it stings my throat. I glance over at my phone periodically and obsessively, waiting for a text from Katie. After a minute these is a text message from Dante asking me if I read the website post and seeing if Katie had arrived:

> **Dante:** Are you okay?

Dumb question…

I grab the phone and type feverishly:

> **Me:** I'm anxious. I don't know if I can do this right now
>> with Katie.

> **Dante:** You don't know if that is what she wants to talk
>> about.

Of course, it is…

> **Me:** Why else would she want to come over with such
>> urgency. The last time she was this upset, our father   had died.

I stare at the three dots…

> **Dante:** Do you want me to come over and be there for
>> support?

He's too nice to me sometimes.

Me: Maybe after she leaves... this conversation is long

overdue.

Dante: Okay, but just know I'm here for you.

Me: Thank you. I'll call you afterward.

By 8:30, I get a text from Katie.

Katie: Hey, are you home yet? I'm crossing over the bridge right now and will be there in ten minutes. Please be home. I'm not in the mood to wait outside for you to get home from whatever bar you frequent. We need to talk.

Me: I'll be here, Katie.

I reach into my messenger bag, retrieve my laptop, turn it on, and return to that website. So far, the post about Monty's text—has over 28.5k comments. I read a few of them. And they range from disbelief and anger to darker comments and sick fantasies. Reading the series of text messages between Monty and me takes me back to those moments when I wrote them. I think about how naïve I was back then. I was really in love with Monty. But now, I just feel like a fool.

When my phone buzzes with a call from Katie, I watch it vibrate against the cushions of the couch, debating on whether I'm going to answer it. The first call goes to voicemail. But she tries again immediately, and this time I answer it—a sense of sickness, a feeling of despair and shame, washes over me. I've been avoiding this moment for what seems like a lifetime, and now it's here. Maybe I'll tell her the truth. Perhaps I'll just keep lying and protect him. I haven't decided. Nevertheless, I wrestle with the dilemma until she reaches my front door.

The knocking against the door nearly stops my heart. Opening the door, Katie stands there, focusing on her phone, typing a message to someone. She walks in without even acknowledging me.

It must be for work; celebrities can be so needy sometimes.

Afterward, she puts her phone on silent, shoves it deep into her Louis Vuitton purse, then looks up at me, finally making eye contact.

"I called you twice." Her voice is low and direct. "I was afraid that you would not be here on purpose."

She knows I hate confrontation.

"Okay, what's wrong, Katie?" I sigh. "I'm sorry, I haven't called you since our dinner; I've been busy with work and other things."

"I understand you are busy," Katie snaps. "You know that's not why I called you."

"Okay, let's hear it then." I gulp the rest of my whiskey. "What do you want?"

"The truth."

That's bullshit; no one ever wants the truth. I think to myself. People may say they want it, but it's a lie. The truth is dangerous... It's holding the mirror up and seeing all the blemishes that we try to hide.

"About?" I ask, pretending to be ignorant of what she's alluding to. "Katie, I've had a rough day. So, can we not play this cat-and-mouse game?"

"Alright," she sits down on the long section of my L-shape couch. "I've been following the news reports and articles on the accusations against Lamont. Did you know they suspended him from the league until after the authorities conduct their investigation?"

I shrug my shoulders, pretending to be uninterested.

"Then, I came across some posts on a website."

Katie pauses.

"And?" I cross my arms over my chest.

She rolls her eyes, and abruptly stands up, heads into the kitchen, and pours herself a drink. "WitchyCharm, Lisa? I remember you being obsessed with that show for years."

"Okay?"

"So," she gulps a glass of liquor, slamming the glass on the countertop. "You're going to stand there and continue to lie to me about Lamont?"

"What do you want me to say, Katie?" I swallow my tears before they escape my eyes. "You're right. I was obsessed with Charmed. And I saw the posts too."

"I need you to tell me the truth, Lisa," she says, tears streaming down her cheeks. "Please... I need you just to tell me what happened. Did something happen? Or am I feeling guilty for nothing?"

Feeling guilty?

"Why would you feel guilty?" I ask. "You've done nothing wrong."

"I ignored my instincts," she exhales heavily. "I felt that something was wrong, but every time I would bring it up, Lamont would reassure me he saw you as a little sister and nothing more."

I watch Katie; the pain in her eyes is great. Her head hangs low as she sits back on the couch. I don't look at her at first, and I don't move. I stay on the couch in silence until she speaks again.

"Lisa, please." She cries in a full ugly cry. "It will stay between you and me, I swear. And I won't get angry, and I just need to know the truth."

I can't take it anymore.

The secrets.

The lies.

The hiding.

"It's true," I murmur in a tone that's so low, I'm not sure I said anything. "The texts are between Lamont and me."

There's an awkward silence that is deafening and uncomfortable between us.

All I can think about is all the times Katie innocently asked Monty to pick me up and watch me when she had to work a more extended shift or when she had to run errands for my dad.

"Oh, Lisa." Katie inhales sharply.

I shrug my shoulders in an 'I don't care' demeanor.

"When did you suspect something?" I finally ask.

"After Sara Croce came forward about Derek."

Ah, Derek Page… The boy who single-handedly fucked my life up.

****

Friday, February 16th, 2001

It was February, the Friday after Valentine's Day for all the couples out there. I'd been invited to a birthday party at Ashley Page's house. I welcomed the invite-only because Monty was coming for the weekend, and I was still mad at him for some stupid reason that I couldn't remember. The party was great and turned into a sleepover; five girls stayed over... Jennifer Whitman, Amber Cummings, Sara Croce, Rachel Smith, and myself. We all drank beers and watched movies while Ashley's parents were gone for the weekend. Usually, my dad wouldn't let me go anyplace where there weren't any parents around. But I had lied and said Ashley's parents would be there all weekend long.

Later that night, around 1:12 a.m., everyone was asleep in the living room or passed out from too much alcohol and pizza. I was lying in the far corner, slightly a few feet away from the other girls, near the bathroom, so if I had to go, then I wouldn't disturb anyone. The room was dark; the only illumination was from a light at the end of the hall.

Suddenly, I felt someone next to me. My eyes sprang open in a jolt, and I saw Ashley's older brother Derek gently tugging on my blanket. He startled me, but I cupped my mouth to muffle the scream.

"Sorry," he whispered. "I didn't mean to scare you."

"Derek," I snapped, keeping my voice low. "What are you doing?"

"I want to talk to you."

"Now?" I hissed. "This late?"

"Yes," he said.

Looking into his eyes, I saw the same dark hunger that would be in Monty's eyes when he came to me in the middle of the night. But I was slightly drunk and brushed off the uneasy feelings.

No...

"Derek, it's late, and I want to go back to sleep."

"Wait... wait." He whispered, grabbing my hand. "Come with me."

He didn't wait for me to answer, pulling me to my feet by my wrists and then guiding me down the hall alone toward his room.

At the moment, I didn't want to be there, and I wanted to go home. But I did nothing.

Derek led me into his room, shutting the door behind me.

I was trapped.

Derek was tall and skinny, not athletic, like Lamont was. His face was thin, and with his dark black hair, he appeared more like a Goth or skater boy who listened to way too much Marilyn Manson. He was definitely not attractive to me at all. He was just Ashley's nineteen-year-old brother to me.

He pushed me on the bed and moved my underwear to the side after removing my pajama shorts. Then slid two fingers inside me. I froze. After that moment, all the fight that I might've had drained from me. I was still a little woozy from all the alcohol. I knew I didn't have the strength to fight him off. Even worse, for some reason, I didn't want any of the other girls to know that I was in his room at all.

"Derek, please don't." I inhaled sharply, reacting to his touch. "Let me go back into the living room."

"Wait," he said. "I will, but first, just let me touch you."

"No... Derek." I replied. "I can't."

"Then let me put the tip in."

I didn't want to... I never did. I'd been there so many times before with Lamont. In that state of confusion and conflicting emotions. And I'd learned a long time ago that what I wanted didn't seem to matter to anyone. It was the first time I felt like a sex object and not a human being.

Derek pulled my shirt over my head, not waiting for me to reply or object. He flipped me onto my stomach, pressing my face into the soft pillow. Then climbed onto me like he was mounting a horse. His hot breath swept against the back of my neck as he tried to penetrate me with his hard erection. Before my body could react, before I knew it, he was already inside of me.

It wasn't like how it felt when I was with Monty; it was rough and hard. More forceful and degrading. Still, I climaxed quickly, and Derek said he felt it as I did. And he took it as reassurance that I wanted him to. I hated myself more and more with each thrust. I hated my body for betraying me the way it did.

"I knew you would like this." His breath inhaled sharply. "Just relax, and I will do everything. I'm going to fuck you so hard."

Derek pushed my head so deep into the pillow that I could barely catch my breath, and it muffled the sounds of my moans. After the sex was finished, he got up and opened the door, disappearing for a minute while I pulled my pajamas over my sore limbs.

"Don't get dressed yet," he said, reappearing. "Everyone is still asleep. We have time to go again."

I crossed my arms over my chest, covering my breast. I was shaking from the chill that traveled up my spine.

What if Lamont finds out that I cheated on him? It was the only thought that lingered in my mind.

Before we had sex again, Derek took the time to slip on a condom. As he pushed his way inside me, he cupped his hand over my mouth and said, "Shh, be quiet; you don't want anyone knowing what we're doing."

Again, he pounded into me, hard and fast. It felt like my insides were going to break under his brutality as my limbs went limp. My eyes stared at the alarm clock next to the bed, blocking everything else out. I just went numb and went away. I didn't want to cum again, but I did — more than once.

"Does that feel good?" He exhaled and grunted. "Because you feel so good to me."

After he was done, Derek checked to see if the other girls were still asleep before allowing me to leave the room. I quickly headed to the bathroom and cleaned myself off. I wanted to wash every place Derek had touched me. But was afraid that running a shower would draw unwanted attention from the other girls. As I stepped out of the bathroom, my eyes met Sara, looking up at me from her sleeping bag on the floor.

Fuck…

A week later, Sara asked to spend the night at my house. At first, I objected, but Katie agreed so that she could get some more alone time with Monty. The night was as awkward as I feared. Monty spent the night trying to ignore me. And for some reason, that annoyed me more than Sara's intrusion into my personal life. Sara and I had been friends since I arrived at Penn Foster. She was one grade higher than me, but didn't treat me like some stupid freshman. I enjoyed hanging out with her from time to time — at school, but not at my home.

That night, Sara walked into my bedroom and shut the door behind her, giving us some privacy. She asked if she could talk to me for a minute. Sitting on my bed, I watched her walk over and sit next to me on the edge of the bed.

"What's up?" I asked.

"I want to talk about something serious," she said. "I just don't want you to get mad at me. But I have to ask you a question about Ashley's birthday sleepover."

"Okay?" I murmured.

"You've been avoiding me, and I really don't understand why." She lowered her gaze to the floor. "Is it because of what happened?"

I shrugged my shoulders.

Sara exhaled deeply and said, "I saw Derek take you into his room."

At first, I went into panic mode, trying to figure out several excuses and rational explanations that would explain what she saw without telling the truth.

"Oh," I said. "That was nothing... Derek just wanted to show me some of his artwork."

Sara observed the reaction and expression on my face.

"He wanted my opinion as a fellow artist."

That was weak... I thought to myself.

"In the middle of the night, Lisa?" she asked.

I shook my head. "I couldn't sleep, so I didn't mind."

"Bullshit."

I didn't know how to answer her because I didn't know exactly what she knew or how long she'd been awake that night. And I didn't know if she'd heard anything while I was in Derek's room. Sara shrugged her shoulders like she was trying to navigate through the discussion carefully. Then she looked at me with a concerned look in her eyes.

"Did anything else happen in the room?" she asked.

"Why do you ask Sara?"

"I just got a feeling, that's all."

"What kind of feeling?" I snapped, in full defensive mode at that point.

"Lisa, I know that something happened," she said. "Did Derek assault you? Or touch you? If he did just know, none of it was your fault."

My eyelashes fluttered, smothering the tears. "What are you talking about, Sara?"

"Lisa—I know. I was up the entire time. You were in there with him for a long time. Then I saw Derek come out to see if everyone was still asleep. I pretended to be, but I watched him go back into the room. Another thirty minutes went by before you left the room and darted into the bathroom. You looked upset, and I saw it all."

"That means nothing, Sara. We were just talking."

"Bullshit," she said. "I know Derek; he's obsessed with sex... watches porn all the time, and has a reputation around school. You can tell me, and it's okay. I don't think you did anything wrong, and he took advantage of you."

I shook my head dismissively. "It was nothing."

"Lisa, listen," she said. "Derek's a predator. I've heard rumors and stories. He's a creep. They suspended him for a week for sexually harassing a girl last year. He pulled his cock out in class and made her touch him." She leaned forward and whispered the rest. "He's even tried to get with me."

"That doesn't mean he did something with me," I said, watching the confusion wash over her face.

"I don't believe you," she quickly replied. "if you're scared, it's okay. But if he hurt you... or assaulted you... then you need to report him. Before he hurts someone else."

Sara stared at me with pity in her gaze.

"Leave it alone," I said. "It has nothing to do with you. And I'm not responsible for other people, and I'm not going to say what happened because it's none of your business, and it's no one's business... so back off."

Sara didn't push the issue anymore, and we tried to get through the rest of the night, but that following Monday back at school. She seemed different, and I noticed her staying after class and speaking with different teachers, which wasn't like her.

On Tuesday the 27th, when I was in the middle of band class. A student knocked on the door and came in, handed Mr. Fletcher a note, and looked at me.

"Lisa, you're needed at the office... bring your things," Mr. Fletcher said. As I walked across campus to the office, I did not know what this was about. Sara had been avoiding me all day, and every time I'd seen her around, she was speaking with a teacher or in the office.

Monty's words echoed in my mind. Deny everything. Don't tell them anything. If they had actual proof, the police would be there to question you and not anyone else. We had a plan, and even though I doubt this had anything to do with Monty, I had planned to stick to what he said.

In the principal's office, behind closed doors, Mrs. Susan Harris, the principal, sat behind her desk, waiting for me. Also in the room was Ms. Mayo, my English teacher. As I sat in the uncomfortable chair across from her, chills rippled up my spine.

"You wanted to see me, Mrs. Harris." I flashed a smile.

She sat up in her chair and cleared her throat; it was hard to read her face or know what she was thinking. Then she nodded at Ms. Mayo, who spoke.

"Lisa, it has come to our attention that there was an incident that might have occurred a few nights ago," she said, sitting in the empty chair next to me. Immediately, I felt a sense of relief, knowing this wasn't about Monty at all — it was about the sleepover.

Posturing beside me, Ms. Mayo continued, "We just want to clear some things up and check to see if you want to tell us anything. And if you were okay?"

Mrs. Harris chimed in and stated that there had been other rumors about this person they're referencing, but nothing like this accusation. I knew she was talking about Derek, but I had nothing to say. Nothing that I wanted to say.

"Something has been brought to our attention, and because it's been brought to our attention," she added, "we're obligated to do some investigating."

"So, did anything happen at Ashley Page's party the other night?" Ms. Mayo finally asked. "You can tell us… you don't have to keep something like this inside."

I shook my head—no.

"Lisa, you're safe. It's okay."

The lies they tell—I wonder if they believed them themselves—the road to Hell was paved with good intentions. That was something that I knew for sure.

Ms. Mayo leaned back in the chair, never taking her intense gaze from me, studying my expression. "Someone has come forward. Someone that was there that night, and we're just trying to make sure that you were okay."

More lies… I thought.

"I know who you're talking about," I murmured. "Sara has already asked me these questions, and I already told her that nothing happened."

Ms. Mayo looked at me. "Is that right?"

I nodded, then looked away, squeezing my books tighter against my chest.

Ms. Mayo grabbed a piece of paper off the desk. It was a letter in Sara's handwriting, and she started to read what was on it.

"I was at Ashley's birthday. It was a sleepover. Everyone was asleep, but I couldn't get comfortable, so I was still awake. It was around two in the morning when I saw Derek Page pull Lisa into his room. They were alone in there for almost an hour in total. Later on, Lisa left the room and headed to the bathroom…

She appeared to be very upset about something, and her sleeping clothes were barely on her body. Then she snuck back into her bed. I suspect that Derek Page, who is nineteen, did something to Lisa. Although, she won't tell me."

She handed me the piece of paper, and just then, Katie entered the room.

Fuck...

"Katie Rose, where's your dad?" Mrs. Harris handed her a copy of the letter too as she entered.

"He's on the road until Friday," Katie murmured, focusing on carefully reading the letter. Then she paused and looked over at me. "Is this true?"

"No," I said, shaking my head, feeling like I was going to throw up. "It's just a rumor, and Sara is just assuming things."

"Rumors tend to come from somewhere, L," Katie snapped. I couldn't tell if she was more upset about the letter or something else entirely.

Ms. Mayo raised to her feet and cleared her throat. "Lisa claims nothing happened, and as a school, we can't press the issue any further, but if you could, please have your father contact us as soon as he can. It's required for us to inform the parents when something like this comes up."

Fuck you, Sara... your concern was fucking up my life. Now, the school had to call my father, and that was all I needed.

"I will have him call you Mrs. Harris." Katie smiled. "As soon as he comes back from the road."

In my gut, I knew there was going to be a more significant fallout as soon as I got home, especially when Monty found out. And that thought terrified me.

ELEVEN

On Thursday, as I walk into Dr. Nichole's office, she looks up at me over her glasses and can instinctively tell my world is falling apart.

"Lisa, what's wrong?"

"I'm okay." I lie from the habit of doing so for the last few days. Katie said little after I confessed to her about Monty. She simply walked out of my apartment, avoiding eye contact with me as she left. I know Katie's in shock or disbelief, but she didn't call me a liar, which is a good thing, I guess. I just wish I knew what she's thinking.

"Don't lie, Lisa; you're not doing okay."

I sit down on the chair's soft leather as Nichole sits on the sofa across from me after placing a cup of tea on the coffee table between us.

"Tell me, what's going on?" The doctor asks.

I press my lips on the rim of the mug, allowing the hot beverage to sting my tongue. "Katie asked me about being abused as a child. She knows that someone else other than Derek Page assaulted me before. Someone close to our family. It seems lately that all these accusations about Lamont Johnson have her asking questions about all the times he was over at our home."

I want to confess everything to the doctor. I want to talk about Monty, but I'm not ready to tell her he's the man I've mentioned in our previous sessions. I once loved the man more than life itself until I realized that our relationship wasn't just forbidden like Romeo and Juliet, it was illegal.

Nichole pulls the frame of her glasses away from her face. "Oh my God, that's huge. Why does she seem to think that Lamont did something to you?"

"Intuition," I reply. "Monty and I were close. Very close."

The doctor waits for a moment and exhales deeply while she collects her thoughts. I know she's waiting for me to continue. And I know that she's smart enough to have put two and two together, knowing Lamont is the person I had a relationship with as a teenager. But I'm still not ready to admit it out loud.

I take another sip of tea, calming myself before continuing. "This week has been Hell. Dante is back in my life, which is confusing things. On the one hand, I'm glad he's here with me. But on the other hand, I am afraid that I will fuck things up again and hurt him. I'm in the final negotiations with Apple for my tech at work, and they want to meet for a presentation. Now Katie is questioning me about the past and things that hurt too much to bring up again."

"Wait a minute," she interrupts, surprised. "Dante Kingston is back in your life?

"Yes… And Lamont has been calling me more frequently." I lower my gaze, feeling the weight of this secret becoming too much to bear.

"Why has Mr. Johnson been calling you?" Nichole lifts her eyebrow, focusing on the one topic that I'm trying so hard to avoid.

I can't take it anymore. The burden. The secrets and guilt. For weeks now, I've been barely able to keep my sanity. I'm spiraling out of control, but at least now I'm aware enough to recognize it.

You can't protect him anymore—my subconscious sighs. You have to let him go… for your own survival.

Nichole's eyes are trained on me, waiting for further explanation. And looking at her breaks me to the core of my being, and I'm ready to say it out loud.

"I lied before. Lamont is the one I had a relationship with from the age of thirteen to my early twenties," I blurt out, before my brain can stop the words. "I had a crush on him at first; then it evolved to just having a secret connection between him and me. Then it turned into a sexual relationship. In the beginning, I didn't think it was wrong at all. I felt he loved me. With all these new allegations, I feel somewhat responsible for these women's pain. And I can't handle it. What's worse is that Monty gave me the seed money to start my business and—"

"You're afraid that people will find out and come after you like they are attacking the other women?"

"Exactly."

"Lisa, you told me bits and pieces about your relationship in the past. However, this is the first time you've admitted that it was Lamont Johnson that you were in a relationship with. But I need you to elaborate a little more, so that it can help me decide which way is best to proceed to help you," she says.

"Okay?" I sigh.

"So, you were underage?" She scribbles something down in her notebook.

I nod, finishing my tea, wishing it was whiskey.

"How did it start? When was the first time things got intimate?"

I shrug. "A few weeks after my thirteenth birthday. I had mentioned it before, although I didn't tell you it was Lamont."

"Yes, I remember," Nichole says. "Did you ever see it as rape?"

Again, I hate that word. To hear it, sends a shiver that ripples through my body, and a lump gathers in my throat.

"He was my first," I murmur. "My first crush. My first love. The first man I ever had sex with, I mean. And my longest relationship. Monty was so instrumental in the person I am, and I would not be where I am now without him."

Her eyes flutter. "Okay, I understand now."

I've felt bad for so many sessions because Nichole tried to help me, but didn't know the entire story. It's like she was trying to put a puzzle together without having all the pieces.

I take my phone out of my bag and hand it over, allowing Nichole to read the text messages on the website and the messages that Monty has been sending me since this all started.

"Oh, wow. So, you were his original victim." Nichole exhales, sinking in the couch's cushion. "Now, it seems... he wants to know if you will still protect his secret."

I nod, not able to form words at the moment, feeling like I'm back in the office with Mrs. Harris and Ms. Mayo, and all eyes are on me. I feel like a helpless child.

"I mentioned him being a friend... but I've only told a few people the truth about him."

"Does Dante know?"

"Yes," I reply. "It's why we initially broke up. Dante couldn't understand why I was still in contact with Lamont or why I had said nothing for all those years, and he couldn't understand how I could sit there and just take the abuse."

Across from me, Nichole leans back, scribbling more notes. "That was the reason you two broke up? Dante actually said it like that?"

"Yes, I'm sorry," I say. "I know it's a lot. I told you about Derek Page and that whole fiasco when everyone found out what happened; I just couldn't bring myself to talk in-depth about this, too."

"It's okay, Lisa, therapy is here to help you, and you weren't ready... and I would not push you." She reads the rest of the text. "After everything you went through when your friend told the school about Derek, it's understandable why you wouldn't say anything about Lamont. They vilified you, accused you of lying about what happened with Derek. Then you were forced to go over what happened repeatedly. And even worse, you said that you were just labeled as that girl who had sex and then cried rape."

"Yes." I nod my head, remembering the harsh way my life fell into chaos as I think back to that time when everything fell apart.

****

February, 27th 2001

It was the day everything changed...

I stepped out of the principal's office after being confronted with Sara's letter. And the second the door shut behind me, and we left the office together, Katie paused and glared at me. At first, she didn't say a word as we walked through the empty halls of the school toward the exit of the building.

"Why are you staring at me?" I murmured.

But Katie didn't answer.

Once we exited the school's front doors and entered the parking lot, the tension was nauseating. I could hardly take the silent treatment from her while we walked.

At that moment, I remember wishing she'd just yell at me or say something. Katie's eyes were dark and filled with rage or pain; it was hard to discern the difference. I stepped back, pressing my palms against the cover of my books, putting a little distance between Katie and me. As we got to the car, I noticed Monty was waiting for us, and panic surged through me like lightning. Every nerve within me was on edge, and I was raw with emotions.

"Why is he here?" My voice was small.

"He's here for me."

"Katie, please don't tell him about this?" I said, lowering my head, feeling embarrassed... ashamed. "It's so embarrassing."

Katie raked her fingers through her hair and exhaled in frustration as she halted abruptly. "Just tell me the truth right here and now. Don't lie to me Lisa; I mean it."

She pulled my arm, forcing me to a stop. "Did something happen at the party the other night?"

I didn't say the words but nodded my head subtly, never once looking her in the eyes — yes.

"Did Derek Page touch you?"

I nodded again, reluctantly confirming.

"Did more than touching happen?"

A final nod, small yet profound... because I had been ignoring the reality of what happened for days now.

"Did he rape you?"

"Katie," tears swelled in my eyes; my voice was low and trembling. "Please don't make me say it."

Katie's eyes widened. "That fucking son of a bitch. He won't get away with this."

"Katie, please," I pleaded. "I just want to forget about it. Forget about the entire night."

Katie pulled me towards the car, saying nothing as we climbed in and pulled away. Every cell in my body was in a complete panic as adrenaline surged through me. I didn't know what Katie was thinking, and she wouldn't look at me.

During the entire ride home, no one said a word. The tension inside the car was so thick that it could be cut with a knife. And I was left sitting in the backseat, crying silently, while staring out the window at the blurred imagery.

This was a mess.

Once we got back to the house, Katie told me to go to my room and do my homework. I didn't argue because I was too afraid to. I went to my room, closed the door, and cried some more. And then I heard Katie through the door telling Monty to watch me for at least an hour while she went somewhere.

126

"Tell me what happened," Monty said, coming into my room once we were alone. "Why is Katie so upset? Did you tell her something? Does she know about us?"

Of course, he would make this about him.

"No." I shook my head.

"Then what the hell is going on?" He murmured.

"It's personal."

He almost seemed amused by the words. I pulled my books out of my backpack and sat at my desk near the window. I remember feeling so guarded and violated at the same time. And at that moment, I didn't want Monty to be there with me at all.

"Lisa, tell me what happened. Are you okay?" Monty asked as he leaned against my desk, staring right through me; it felt like I was invisible.

"I'm sorry. I didn't want Derek to touch me." I blurted out. "I said no. but he...."

Lamont's eyes widened, his nostrils flared as the anger visibly boiled within him. "He touched you? What else did he do?"

I shook my head, not wanting to say.

"Did he fuck you?" He yelled. "Did you like it?"

What the fuck? I thought. *How could he ask me that?*

"No!" I screamed. "I hated every second of it. I told him, no... But he wouldn't stop, and he wouldn't let me leave the room."

"Oh, sweetheart," he said, pretending to be calm. "Did you fight him?

"He scared me," I confessed. "He scared me to my core. I froze and couldn't move. I'm sorry."

"I could fucking kill him," Monty growled.

Katie entered the room, noticed me crying, and looked at Monty. Instinctively, I stood up and explained why he was in my room alone. "He heard me crying and came to see if I was okay, and I told him no and what happened. I just needed to get it off my chest."

Katie's head turned slightly, but it wasn't anger but relief that appeared on her face. "Thank you for being here with her while I was out." She looked at me. "Lisa, come to the living room with me."

I lowered my head, looking down at my trembling hands. I didn't want to see her expression. Nor did I want to see Monty's, either. I just wanted to run away and be alone.

"Come with me, Lisa." Katie finally said again, leading me by my hand.

In the living room, a police officer named Sgt. Thomas was lingering around the front door, waiting. The officer explained that Katie went to the police station and reported what happened. But they wanted to get a statement from me. Even worse, Sara went with her and wrote a statement.

Monty stood in the doorway, looking casual, but I felt him staring a hole in the back of my head.

I tried to conjure the courage I displayed back in Mrs. Harris' office, but I was beaten. If I protested making a statement, both Katie and Monty would think I was lying. And even though I could lie, for some strange reason, I couldn't. I felt even more like a victim at that moment, with no control over what was happening to me or around me.

What hurt, even more, was that Monty would believe that I would see anyone other than him. Even though he was often away at practice or his football games, Monty's presence seemed to remain long after he was gone. I felt like I couldn't do anything, fearing that he might find out.

I fought the urge to run into my room, lock the door, and hide from the mess that was my life.

"Lisa…"

The officer stepped further into the living room and sat down on the couch in front of me. Katie sat next to me, holding me so tight, reassuring me. I buried my face in her neck, unaware that I was trembling until she steadied me. I felt safe there, at home, with my sister.

"It's okay." Katie smiled, hugging me. "Just tell the officer what happened. Just tell the truth… that's all I ask."

"Well, I was at the party last weekend." I reluctantly began. There were five of us girls there… Jennifer Whitman, Amber Cummings, Sara Croce, Rachel Smith, and me. We were all having fun at Ashley Page's sixteenth birthday, the night started out okay. We ordered pizza from Dominos. The other girls drank a little beer in the refrigerator, and I had two cans of beer along with them. We watched a few movies like American Psycho, Traffic, and another. And finally laid down in the living room around midnight."

I paused, not wanting to talk about what had happened next; I was not ready to think about it, let alone speak about it. Once again, I felt helpless, as if all my control and power to decide what was best for me was being overlooked.

"Then what happened." The officer urged me to continue.

"I was asleep for a while, and that's when he came and woke me up."

"Derek Page?" Katie interjected, "Ashley's nineteen-year-old older brother?"

I nodded my head... yes.

"Okay, what happened next?" Sgt. Thomas scribbled Derek's name on her notepad.

"Derek grabbed me by my arm and led me into his room. He didn't tell me why; he just told me to be quiet."

Katie squeezed my hand for reassurance and didn't let go.

"It's okay, Lisa." She fought her tears, and her pain was so visible that it was heartbreaking. "I know this is hard, but we need to get through this. He has to pay."

"Do we have to do this now?" I asked, burying my head in her embrace.

Going to the police was never a choice I had, nor did I want. But when you're a teenager, everyone seems to think they know what's best for you without even consulting you. And they know everything. To them, you know nothing.

"No, I can't." I pulled away. "I don't want to talk about this."

Especially in front of Monty... I thought to myself.

"Lisa, everything will be okay."

No, it wouldn't... I knew nothing would be okay after that night. I knew that was a lie, even before I was called into Mrs. Harris' office. Once a secret is out, you have no control over who hears it or how far it will spread. That's what Monty always told me. It's a rolling snowball that would roll downhill and spin out of control, only getting bigger and more destructive as it moved.

"What time did he wake you? I just need all the details you can remember." The officer added.

I frowned, feeling that my feelings and objections were being completely ignored.

"It was around 1 a.m.; he thought everyone was asleep. He didn't know Sara was still awake. Derek said he wanted to talk... I told him I wanted to stay in the living room, but he didn't listen."

Saying the words aloud made me aware of how naïve I had acted that night. I knew, deep down, Derek didn't want to talk, but I didn't make any noise, scream, or do anything. And the guilt was mounting within me.

"Okay," the officer scribbled more notes. "Did you ask to leave?"

"Yes, but Derek was blocking the doorway."

"Why didn't you scream? Or wake up the other girls?" Monty interrupted.

He was angry; that was visibly clear... I just didn't know if it was more at Derek for what he had done or the fact that someone else had touched me.

"It doesn't matter," Katie snapped, giving Monty an intense glare of disapproval. "You don't have to be here. You know... if it's too much for you."

"You're right." Monty threw his hands up. "I'm sorry, Lisa, that was uncalled for. I'm just so pissed that this guy violated you."

Monty's posture changed, and the tension seemed to telegraph from him like an image on a projector. I tightened my grip on Katie's hand for reassurance before continuing.

"He pushed me on the bed. Then he pulled my pajamas away... and removed my underwear. Then slid two fingers inside me. And I was so scared, I froze."

"Did he threaten you?" The officer cleared her throat nervously. "Did he say anything?"

"No, but I felt threatened." I lowered my gaze. "Derek towers over me and is very scary. His eyes were so dark; it felt like nothing was behind them."

"Had you been drinking?"

"A little, but I wasn't drunk... Derek gave beer to all the girls. But I felt like I couldn't say no to having one."

"Okay," she scribbled more words on the paper. "Continue."

"I said 'no,'" I added. My voice was barely above a whisper. "I said it several times. But Derek pulled my shirt over my head and flipped me on my stomach, pinning me to the pillow."

I paused, bracing myself for the painful memory of what happened next.

"Before I knew it, he was already inside of me." I exhaled heavily. "It was rough... hard... forceful and degrading. When I tried to scream, Derek silenced me."

All the emotions rushed through me now; I felt every feeling I felt that night. And I could no longer control my tears, allowing them to fall down my face freely.

"It's okay, Lisa," Monty said, placing his hand on my shoulder, quickly withdrawing it when I flinched at his touch. "I'm sorry."

It was clear he wasn't mad at me, just at what happened to me. And I felt a sense of relief wash over me.

"When Derek finished... the first time." I reluctantly continued. "He left the room to see if any of the other girls were awake, but when I tried to get dressed, he came back in and stopped me."

"And he assaulted you again?" Katie asked, now crying along with me.

I nodded my head — yes.

"I feel so guilty," she said. "You didn't even want to go to the party."

We sat in silence for a few moments while Sgt. Thomas finished her notes.

I thought I'd be relieved after speaking about what happened, but I felt worse. Once the charges were pressed and the investigation started, I could do nothing. Now it was out there, and I'd seen Law & Order SVU.

I was helpless, knowing that my life would spin out of control, with no end in sight.

TWELVE

Wednesday, April 2nd, 2016

I feel a little better after seeing Nichole. She recommends increasing our sessions to three times a week, at least until this mess with Lamont blows over. But today, I have more pressing matters on my mind. Today is when everything will change for the better, or everything I've worked at for the last two years will fall apart.

Pulling up to the Apple offices on 11th Penn Plaza, near New York's Madison Square Garden and Penn Station, is intimidating, to say the least. I head to the building's 14th floor, feeling nauseous as I watch the numbers roll on the screen, and the elevator cables pull me towards my destination. I take a deep breath as the doors slide open.

The receptionist sitting behind the desk gives me a subtle glance over her Apple desktop computer.

"Can I help you?"

"My name is Lisa Rose; I have a 10 a.m. meeting today." I smile, fidgeting with my black Calvin Klein button-up suit I spent way too much money on.

Immediately, the woman perks up, flashing a smile as she pushes away from her desk.

"Miss. Rose," she gestures with her hand for me to follow. "Please follow me to the conference room, if you please."

I firmly grip my messenger bag before following her down the long hall into the conference room at the end of the building.

"Here you go, Miss Rose. You can set up your presentation here, and the others will join you shortly. Good luck."

"Thank you," I say, shaking the nerves. Once alone, I take a deep breath, pull out my laptop, and set up my presentation on the edge of the conference table. When I'm satisfied with everything, I take a moment to glance out of the large windows overlooking the streets below.

Just breathe...

This moment feels surreal. After years of hard work, I will soon be face-to-face with the top members of the most prominent tech company in the world.

Although no one has connected the text messages to me, the fear is still at the forefront of my thoughts. I couldn't sleep last night, and I haven't eaten all day, fearing that I might vomit. Somewhere in the back of my mind, this thing with Lamont lingers.

Focus, Lisa.

"Lisa Rose?" A male's voice rumbles from behind me.

I turn sharply, startled. An older gentleman, appearing to be in his mid-forties, walks up behind me. He has thinning brown hair, dark brown eyes and is wearing an expensive Giorgio Armani suit and a flashy Rolex watch that is visible one his wrist as he approaches and firmly shakes my hand.

"Paul Anderson." He introduces himself. "Senior Vice President of Communications and Technology."

"Please to meet you, Mr. Anderson."

"No, please call me Paul."

"I'm a bit nervous." I smile, concealing the fact that I feel like I'm about to faint, and my mind is trying to remember if I put on deodorant this morning. "I've spent so many years just to get to this point."

"Don't be nervous," Paul says. "I've read your proposal and the schematics of the prototype of your app... it's revolutionary."

He pauses, taking in the view from the window.

"Just present your invention. The patents for your concept, the technology, and the real-world applications. After that, I'm confident that you will have offers thrown at you."

"Okay." I smile.

"You'll do fine. Just remember, you've done all the hard work already, and you have your foot in the door; now all you have to do is just walk in."

I smile again and nod, knowing it's true, but still feeling like I'm going to be sick.

"I know you're nervous, but you will be amazing."

My mind is swirling with many thoughts, but they're not about this meeting. I promised myself that I wouldn't let this thing with Monty affect me, but I haven't been able to concentrate on anything else since the news first broke.

I've been texting Katie for a few days now, but she hasn't responded. My life is a mess right now, and I have to pretend that I have all the answers for this meeting.

As the Web app Engineering tech, Software Engineering president, and the others slowly make their way into the conference room, Paul eagerly introduces me to every one of them. And then my world falls apart in one moment.

"May I introduce you to our project manager, Jason Colwell?"

Shit...

Jason's eyes fixate on me, with a look I can't describe. The room feels like it's spinning when I realize he recognizes me, too. "Well, Lisa Rose..." He forces a smile. "I'm sorry. You look like your name would be Jasmine to me."

Fuck... this isn't the first time a one-night stand has caught up with me. I had to switch classes in college because I picked up a guy who happened to be my Computer Design professor that previous summer.

"Nope," I smile awkwardly, trying not to run out of the room in complete embarrassment. "It's Lisa."

Jason subtly pulls me away from the others, and I genuinely don't know what to expect, but the room feels like it's spinning around me.

"You know, I've never woken up alone in a hotel room before."

"You were sleeping," I reply. "I didn't want to wake you. Besides, you told me you worked in real estate."

"True." He shrugs. "And you told me you were in New York for one night."

"Look," My voice is barely above a whisper. "We had fun, and both got what we wanted; let's leave it at that."

"Fine."

I put on my mask again as well as my walls, nod, and make small talk with everyone else. I laugh at their corny jokes and pretend that I'm in their league... and it seems to be working. Within ten minutes, I win the entire room over and have them eating out of my hands.

Each person takes their seats around the table while waiting for the CEO to arrive.

"Ryan is always fashionably late," Paul says, leaning back in his leather chair.

I smile, looking over my notes one last time.

I'm as prepared as I will ever be.

The receptionist pushes the door open, and in walks Ryan Wilson, head of Apple's New York headquarters.

He's intimidating, stepping in with confidence that draws the air out of the room. His blue suit screams money—and he says nothing as he walks around the conference table. No one else speaks, waiting for him to take his seat at the head of the table.

"This is Ryan Wilson," Paul says. "Ryan, Lisa Rose."

He smiles, but it's in a don't waste my time type of way. "Ah, I've heard about you."

"Good things, I hope," I say, cursing myself as the words leave my lips.

Ryan nods, switches his iPhone to silent, then places it on the glass table. "Miss Rose... the floor is yours."

I draw in a deep breath, click the mouse pad on my laptop... say a short and silent prayer and begin. "Well, communication is the staple of our world. But so is accessibility. We need it in our day-to-day lives, but sometimes certain circumstances will arise where we may need some help. Or we may need someone else to assist us."

I read the room and saw a lot of bored faces.

"So, I invented an app, called The Assist... With this app, our customers can essentially hire their very own personal assistant for a few hours... a day... or a week. To carry out certain tasks when they cannot. If you have broken your leg, for example, and need someone to pick up something from the store for you. With The Assist, You can go through our catalog of professionals and pay someone to run errands while you recover."

"Wait," Ryan lifts his hand, stopping me. "So, you're saying that with your invention, someone can presumably rent people for certain tasks and errands?"

"Yes, sir." I smile, feeling more confident. "Our Assist applicants go through a background check before they are allowed to offer their services and are rated by our customers."

"Okay, I'm assuming this is based on your location... PTA mom could use your app to hire someone to pick up cookies for the fundraiser because she forgot. And your applicants will come just to do that. It seems like a waste of time, and what if your customer wants to rent someone for like a one-night stand Or some illegal activity?" Jason interjects with disdain in his tone.

It's clear he's feeling some type of way about me leaving him in the hotel room that night.

"Yes, and I've thought of that." I smile, scanning through my notes. "That's why we designed restrictions in the Assist App; customers have to describe specifically what they need and enter an agreement with our applicants. Both parties can back out and cancel the service for any reason. After the app connects the right person for the customer, our applicants are tracked through our app, and we have placed an algorithm on estimating the time needed to carry out the jobs. The customer can choose the sex of their assistant... if they need someone with a car and many more personal preferences to get matched to the right person."

"So, you can track the movements of your applicants," Paul interjects, now paying full attention to every word I say. "You can go to the app, select that you need someone to pick up groceries or dry cleaning, etc. And your app estimates the time that will be needed to complete these tasks."

"Yes." I smile. "That's precisely what I'm saying."

The room erupts with inaudible murmurs and whispers. And Ryan leans back casually into the seat and adjusts his silk tie into his blazer.

"Interesting, and you own—"

"I have my own company," I add. "It's small, but I have people who wrote the code for this app. And others who helped me design the concept. I had my lawyer put in all the patent applications in..., and I used my own money for the 3D mock-ups and real-world applications. I own everything."

"Impressive." Ryan flashes a smile. "And how did you get the funding to do all of this?"

"Several private investors." I lie. Monty was my only investor, but I pushed that thought down.

"Wow."

"This person or persons must have deep pockets." Ryan continues.

"My investors wish to stay anonymous," I reply sharply, wondering if he's fishing for something or knows something. "I have the paperwork that proves this invention is all mine."

I'm sure that Ryan has done his homework on me. If he dug deep enough, he would've certainly stumbled across the fact that Katie was dating Monty a few years ago, right before he signed a sixty million dollar eight-year contract with the NFL.

"Alright, please continue."

I'm feeling frazzled. I've replayed this presentation in my head for hours now, but I can't seem to formulate the right words or regain the confidence I had a few minutes ago.

"As you see, we design the Assist app with a built-in GPS tracker. Real-time customer service. And the site is easy to use. The pay is determined by the job's tasks and the distance or mileage used. And the amount of time that will be needed."

"May we see your app layout and design, please—"

"Yes, of course." I hand Ryan the designs, and the prototype that I've installed on my phone.

He tries to hide the fact that he's impressed, but I can read the room... they are all impressed.

I stand in silence as each of these high-powered men examines my work. It took a team of people to make this possible, and they are all counting on me to secure this deal. The pressure of that alone is enough to make me crumble, but I'm determined to keep pushing forward. If Apple isn't interested in my business, I'll go to Samsung. Looking around the conference room, everyone stares at Ryan and me.

Ryan glances down at his Patek Philippe watch, then his phone, and places it back on the glass. "It seems that you are a very driven woman, with good business sense and one hell of an impressive invention here."

But... My mind sighs.

My heart pounds against my chest as I expect him to pass on my proposal. I prepare myself for the worse... Him telling me he's going to pass. The devastating feeling that will come with being rejected. The long ride home, where I try to figure out how to explain that I failed to my team.

"I think it will benefit everyone to explore this further. And see what else your software company is working on." Ryan finally cracks a smile. "Please leave a copy of everything that you have with us, and someone will contact you within the coming weeks... congratulations, Miss. Rose, I'm impressed."

Finally, a win... my mind celebrates, doing cartwheels around my consciousness.

We talk about the specifics for a few more hours, including a decent dollar amount for my work. Everyone nods in agreement, clapping over my presentation. Well, everyone but Jason, who's scowling at me like I stole something from him.

Ryan looks me in the eye. "Well done, Miss Rose."

"Lisa," I smile, shaking his hand once again as the meeting concludes. "Call me Lisa, please."

"Well, Lisa, congratulations again. I'll have my people send your office our official offer within the next week or two. Let's schedule a Skype call in the following weeks for a follow-up and nail down the logistics. If everything checks out, you will be the face of the future in communications and services."

"That would be fantastic, thank you."

We've spent many nights combing through every detail of this app to get to this moment. I wait a moment as everyone files out of the enormous conference room before calling Adrian Brown, my project supervisor. Since I moved to New York, he's been with me since the beginning.

"We did it," I squeal into the phone, letting Adrian know. Immediately, he asks a million questions about the details and all of that.

"Later." I smile into the phone. "Go out and celebrate tonight and tell the team, will ya?"

"Yes… yes," he laughs. "I'm definitely celebrating tonight, and I'll see you in the office."

I also text Katie even though she's still not talking to me:

Me: Meeting went well… they're interested and want to move forward and make me an offer on the app.

Just then, an alert chimes on my phone.

BREAKING NEWS on ESPN:

"Lamont Lee Johnson is under investigation by the FBI because a fifth woman coming forward and the recent posts on the website that will not be named. In light of these recent events, Mr. Johnson can no longer represent the NFL."

NFL League chairman Burt Donald made a statement earlier... stating that the National Football League takes these accusations seriously.

Oh my God, they fired him... The news sucks all the joy out of my moment, and I just want to cry.

THIRTEEN

The following day, after a night of drinking, I awake, unable to concentrate on any work at all. I called in sick from the office, stating that I celebrated too hard and had a massive hangover. Since I'm the boss... who's going to object. Pulling my face from the fabric of my pillowcase... after sleeping in for another hour, I decide to get up.

Glancing at the screen on my phone, I see several texts from Katie—there are five missed calls from Monty's blocked number... And two missed calls from Dante. I slam the screen back down on my comforter. I feel suffocated and need some air. And feel like the world's problems can go fuck themselves for just a bit longer.

It's nearly noon when I finally step outside; I walk to the end of the block. Then a little further to the next block. I keep walking mindlessly for what seems like a few minutes, but in actuality is a few hours. Once realizing it, I curse myself for leaving my phone at home.

This is how people go missing in New York... I tell myself.

I rest on a bench near Rockefeller Park River Ter & Warren Street and stare out at the Hudson River.

"What a mess you've gotten yourself into, Monty." I exhale.

I sit for a few more minutes, feeling more tranquility here than I've felt in weeks, staying here until the sun lowers just enough to guide me home.

Rounding the last corner to my apartment, just as the sun sinks in the sky, I see Dante leaning against his BMW i8, feverishly tapping on the screen with his thumbs. He rolls his eyes and jogs in my direction when he notices me.

"Lisa?" he breathes, "What the hell? I've been calling you all day. When I didn't reach you... I even called your office. Then Katie... She's looking for you, too. Why the fuck haven't you been answering your phone all day? Where have you been?"

Dante calms himself as his anger is replaced with relief, and he wraps his muscular arms around me gently. He smells so good that I feel my body tingle with excitement just to be near him.

"Are you okay?"

"I'm fine, Dante. I just needed to clear my head." I smile. "I honestly didn't mean to stay out this long."

He glances at my disheveled appearance.

"Have you even eaten today?" He asks, suddenly feeling more concerned and eager to help. "You're cold. Let's get you inside."

"Okay."

"Then we will order in some food." He adds, ushering me to my apartment as if I am too fragile to walk myself.

I don't argue. I'm just happy Dante's here.

I take a shower in the apartment while Dante orders some food from Dian's Kitchen. It's my favorite place to eat. The water cascades over me; scorching water scolds my skin, washing away all the dirt and sweat of the day. I feel better once I settle in, wishing to stay in the shower and not come out again.

As I step out of the bedroom wearing a black T-shirt and shorts, Dante is in the kitchen, standing in front of two wine glasses.

"I brought this a few months ago," he says, looking at the black box with pink lettering on the front. He lets out a weak laugh. "I hoped we could celebrate your new deal with Apple."

"What is it?"

"1996 Dom Perignon Plenitude Rose."

"Wow, Dom Perignon?" I run my fingers over the box. "Fancy."

"Well, I wanted to impress you." Dante smiles, his blushing cheeks tell on him. "You know I like to pull out all the stops for you. Remember that time I closed down the restaurant just for us."

It was the night that he proposed... how could I forget.

"I'm sorry, I hurt you, Dante."

"It's in the past. I'm here now." He smiles, popping the cork from the bottle and pouring us both a glass.

He raises his glass in the air. "Here's to your deal and being one step closer to being almost as rich as me."

We both laugh, clinking the rim of the glasses together in a toast. "Thank you."

The cool liquid tastes as expensive as it looks, going down smoothly as I take a sip.

"Wow, this is great."

He laughs, mirroring what I'm thinking.

The Dian Kitchen arrives in record time; I settle on the couch as he serves me a plate.

Dante sits on the couch next to me, his skinny black jeans pressed firmly against his thigh muscles as he rests the hot plate on his thighs. He seems so different from the Dante I knew six months ago, and yet there's a familiarity to him that puts me at ease.

"So, how is work?" I ask, stretching out my sore limbs while shoving a pan-fried dumpling into my mouth. I'm starving so severely that simple etiquette has gone right out the window.

"Work is work." He takes a bite of his noodles. He never talks about work with me, and I don't mind. I asked him why once, and he simply said, "when I'm with you, all I want is to be with you... no distractions...nothing else matters."

"Are you going to call Katie back?"

"Not tonight."

He narrows his eyes.

"May I ask how therapy is going?" Dante changes the subject.

"Fine... why do you ask?"

He places his noodles on the coffee table and looks at me. "I'm just wondering how much your therapist knows."

"Dante," I roll my eyes, upset that he's ruining a perfectly excellent dinner. "She knows about what happened with Derek Page."

"You know that's not who I'm talking about."

My stomach turns, threatening to expel this delicious dinner and expensive Dom Perignon. My thoughts race through my mind, thinking about the five missed calls from Monty. I'm sure it's more by now, and I still haven't glanced at my phone since I got home.

"She knows about Lamont too, if that's what you're getting at," I murmur. "I told her during our last session together."

"What?" he postures and focuses on me. "What did she say?"

"That's confidential."

He pauses, sensing my defenses are up again.

"I'm mean," I clear my throat, reluctantly continuing. "Understand, I'd been around Lamont for so long. And after everything that went on after the state pressed charges on Derek, it traumatized me all over again. I couldn't possibly say anything after that. But I'm not excusing or defending him... not anymore."

"I understand, Lisa."

"I just wanted to forget the whole thing." I shake my head. "I don't want to go my entire life feeling like a fool that fell in love with someone like that."

"Has Lamont tried to contact you... since they fired him?" He asks.

"Yes... that's why the phone is still in the bedroom... and I haven't touched it all day."

This is too far, but I know he's just concerned.

"Well, that's impressive." He smiles. "And for the record, I understand why you never reported Lamont."

"Why bring this up?" I hiss. "Why open old wounds? Why can't you just leave it in the past?"

"Lisa, you don't think that this isn't affecting you now? That the man who raped you repeatedly for years and got away with it doesn't matter at all?" Dante narrows his eyes, studying my face for an answer. "It bothers me because he hurt you for so long, and no one knew. You've had to live with this cloud looming over you for years, and the man still won't leave you alone... even now."

"Dante, I understand... why you want him to pay, but isn't he paying now? They fired him, and they have labeled him a monster and predator. And that's all before they have filed any charges against him."

I pause, feeling almost sorry for Lamont.

"In the eyes of the public, Lamont is guilty... my story won't make a difference."

My thoughts drift, but only for a moment. I feel guilty that I wasn't the only one, and because I didn't dare to accuse the most popular player in town, other women got hurt. I will have to come to terms with that and live with it for the rest of my life. But telling my story isn't important to me. Not now, not ever; I just want the pains of the past to dissolve and go away. I just want to be normal and not have nightmares every other night.

I don't know if I'll ever be ready to face what happened to me. I'm always conflicted because I hate Monty as much as I love him.

"Look." I shake all thoughts of him away. "They forced me to press charges and talk about what happened before with Derek, and I won't go through that again."

I stand up quickly, placing my plate in the kitchen, completely losing my appetite.

"Lisa," Dante follows me. "I'm sorry."

Damn it, Dante...

I don't answer him, maneuvering past him to head into my bedroom. I'd tell him to leave if I were angrier, but I don't want to be alone tonight. Last night I was too close to harming myself. As a teenager, cutting and starving myself was a way I used to cope with everything that wasn't in my control. I've worked long and hard to overcome those urges, and last night — I almost slipped.

I'm scared.

"Lisa, you want me to go?"

"No," I reply coldly. "I just don't want to talk about this anymore."

Dante exhales deeply, lowering his hands to his side. "I know I overstep sometimes, and I'm working on that... I swear. I just want to protect you and be here for you."

"You don't know how it was for me, Dante." I clench my jaw, feeling the tears stream down my face. As I look into his eyes, I see the pain in them, too. "When people found out what happened to me... what Derek did to me. Three things happened: They didn't believe me... They'd blame me and avoid me... Or they'd try to fix me like I was some charity case."

I wipe my tears away.

"I hated it, and I hated them for seeing me differently... for treating me differently. Derek denied the whole thing ever happened and said I came onto him. Even with the evidence and Sara's eyewitness account... he got three years' probation."

"What?" Dante says, with a look of disgust on his face. "The motherfucker only got probation... that's it? Oh, I'm so sorry, sweetie."

He finally understands.

"Dante?" I laugh weakly through the tears that are freely falling from my eyes. "I know you want to do more for me. But being here with me is all I need from you. You don't have to rescue me... we're long past that."

His expression is one I can't read, and it scares me.

"Is that what you think? That I'm here to play Superman and save the little lost girl?"

"Yes, in so many words."

"Stop it, Lisa." There's a slight sting in his tone that's unfamiliar to me. "I didn't show up six months after we broke up for me to save you."

I watch him rakes his fingers through his head, then curses under his breath. "Fuck. I'm here because I'm the one who needs you. I'm here because I need you... not just physically or sexually... These last months were the worst months of my life. I did everything to forget you. Went to the gym twice a day. And traveled around the world. I even moved because everything in my apartment reminded me of you. I'm just a better person when you're in my life."

"What?"

I wasn't expecting that. Here all this time, I thought Dante being here was for me, and it never occurred to me that the feeling was mutual. He isn't just using me... for company or sex, which scares me more because I don't know what else I have to offer him.

"Even after you told me what happened to you." He adds. "I never saw you as damaged... or used... or a victim. You were just my Lisa, and I loved you even more. You didn't let those motherfuckers break you. You're strong. The boss of your own company, and you're barely twenty-seven years old. Beautiful and smart."

My heart flutters in my chest, wanting to accept everything he's saying. I just don't see myself as strong or beautiful. When I look in the mirror, all I see are my flaws. I see the cracks in my reflection like a broken mirror that has been put back together. That's what I see when I look at myself, only the broken fragments. My past. What Lamont molded me to be his forbidden fruit. The truth is, I hate what I see. I feel weak… used… and hollow.

"Dante, I—" My voice cracks as I get choked up by my emotions.

"Look, I want nothing more from you than to just be in your life." He exhales. "As a friend… Or a lover. Or something more. I don't want to be in a world where you're not in my life."

Fuck...

This six-foot-three hunk of chiseled perfection can sure get soft sometimes. It's sweet, almost to the point of being cheesy. I'm taken aback; I've never seen him this vulnerable before. I've never seen any man in my life be this vulnerable. Can't he see that I'm a mess? I mean, I almost self-harmed last night over the guilt of what's happening with Lamont. And that scares me because even after all of these years, Monty will always have some kind of unnatural hold on me.

"Sometimes, I feel you don't see me at all."

"But I do." Dante smiles. "I see you better than you see yourself."

Damn, he's good…

"Thank you," is all I can get out. "No one has ever said anything like—"

"That's *their* problem." He growls. "I know what I have in front of me... I'm no fool."

But I have been for all this time when it came to him...

I look down, fidgeting with the fabric of my T-shirt. Dante tilts my chin up, shaking his head. "Don't hold your head down like YOU did something wrong."

When we sit back on the couch, I finish the bottle of champagne. And pull Dante close to me, wanting to just be near him. Where did he come from? What does he see in me? I can question these things all night, but I don't want to. He holds me tightly against his chest as I finally let go of all the emotions that I've been holding in all day.

"You never have to hide from me, Lisa," Dante says. "Nothing you say or do will change the way I feel. You went through something horrible, but you're stronger now...you aren't helpless anymore."

I want to argue, but he's taking the wind out of my sails, and I have no more fight in me.

I straddle him, positioning myself on his lap. Slowly, my fingers fiddle with the buttons on his Solid Trofeo French-Cuff dress shirt, unbuttoning each of the black buttons... one by one. He doesn't move, and I relish every moment.

I don't want to think about Lamont or Derek; I've allowed them to have enough of me.

Leaning in, my lips brush against Dante's lips. Despite that, he allows me to kiss him first, even though his erection tells me otherwise.

"Please." I breathe against his neck.

"Tell me what you want, L." He smiles, cupping my face, looking deep into my eyes, and penetrating my soul with his gaze. "Please, what?"

It's a simple statement, but the words mean so much to me. In his own way, Dante's telling me I'm in control. I have the power here. And he wants me to know that. At this moment, I feel closer to him than I have ever felt to anyone.

"I want you to please touch me. Take me into the bedroom and —"

"Make love to you."

God, I want him so much right now...

"Yes."

Dante doesn't hesitate, kissing me passionately. Our lips crash together like two objects colliding. All my walls are down, and I have no mask to conceal the 'real' me. This is just me, naked... raw, in front of a man that cares for me deeply. To taste him and feel him drives me wild — I crave him more than air itself. I want all of him and want to give him all of me.

I moan softly against his lips.

"Are you sure?" He pulls back for a minute, catching his breath. "Your emotions are pretty raw, and I don't want you to feel worse afterward or that you have to have sex with me tonight."

But I want to... I think to myself.

"I want you," I repeat in a much more assertive tone. "Take me into the bedroom."

Dante smirks, shifts his weight, and clasps his hands under my ass, lifting me with minimal effort.

"I want you more." He says as I crisscross my arms and legs around him, and he carries me into the bedroom. "I want you so badly; I feel like I'm about to bust one right now."

"Me too, baby."

"I want to feel all of you tonight, Lisa."

A ripple shoots through me as he places me on the edge of the bed.

Dante kneels in front of me; his fingers sweep up my bare thighs until he reaches my sensitive spot. He smiles and rolls my shorts down, discarding them on the floor beside him.

"No underwear tonight, Ms. Rose," he smiles devilishly. "I'm very pleased."

Slowly, he slides two fingers inside me, and I nearly unravel from the touch. I want Dante so badly; my body is aching for more of him. I quiver; my body screams for merciful release. His lips kiss my inner thighs and trail downwards as he licks my clit. It's enough to send me over the edge.

"Please, Dante."

"Patience, baby, I want to taste you and take my time," he says. "I've been thinking about what I would do to you all day."

He smiles, playing and teasing me for a bit longer until I can barely take it anymore. "I think you're ready for me now."

"Yes." I inhale sharply, feeling the room spin around me.

I watch him posture, unfastening his pants, lowering them down to his knees. I feel his erection spring free from the binding of his clothes, take it in my hand, and slide him inside of me.

Finally... my mind screams.

He hovers over me and falls deeper into me. Filling me so completely that it feels right... real. Emotions surge to the surface, almost consuming me. My mouth quivers as I melt for him. Dante lowers, kissing me passionately. Our tongues twist and play together.

Oh, God...

I arch my hips into his frenzied pace; each thrust is wild and uncontrolled as the sensation of his sex claims me from the inside out.

"Oh fuck, Dante."

"That's it, baby." He concentrates, nearing his climax. "Cum for me. Let go."

He drives into me deeper, picking up speed. His body crashes into me like waves on the sand, leaving me desperate for more of him. As another orgasm swells within me, I cling to him, trying to steady myself.

"Had enough?" his voice is hoarse, slowing his strokes as he waits for me to answer.

"No."

"That's my girl."

Suddenly, he postures up and then turns me face down on the bed, positioning my ass in the air. He eases into me again, grabbing my wrists and pinning them to my back.

"Is this okay?" He breathes, adjusting himself.

"Yes," I moan, feeling him deep inside from a different angle.

"Are you sure?"

"Yes." I consent again, entirely sure.

The subtle sting takes my breath away as he mercilessly plunges into me. Pumping in and out of me, as his body slams into my ass, again and again, I quiver uncontrollably, feeling him steadily speed up his strokes.

"Dante, I'm—"

"Me too."

My moans grow louder and louder, every muscle tenses and tightens, and I'm driven over the edge of ecstasy. I moan into the sheets as Dante releases my wrists. I'm grateful the cotton fabric is muffling my screams at the moment. Dante grunts, his body stills as he releases and folds.

He lays next to me, holding me and cuddling me as we both struggle to steady our breathing. I'm grateful that again, I don't go away, staying in the moment with him next to me. I want to stay in this moment forever...as long as I'm with him.

"Are you okay, Lisa? I didn't hurt you, did I? I lost control a little in those last moments."

"I'm fine."

And I mean it... for once.

I want to go again, but my body is begging for a break.

"Rest, L." His fiery breath sweeps against the nape of my neck. "I'm not going anywhere."

****

It's morning, and I'm still in bed, trying to wrap my head around last night and all the things Dante said to me. He loves me, and even though I can't explain it... I'm grateful. I have the bed to myself for a few minutes while he's taking a shower. When he woke up, he told me he wanted to take the day off from work and spend the entire day with me. I don't object, wanting to spend more time with him, too.

Just as we finished getting dressed and walked out of the bedroom, Katie walked through the front door and into my apartment, using her emergency key. Dante straightens immediately, adjusting his black button-up shirt. He has an 'Oh shit' expression on his face, the expression a boyfriend would have if we'd been caught doing it by my parents.

It's cute...

"Katie, what are you doing here?" I ask, adjusting my clothes as well. "And why are you busting through my door like you were the cops or something?"

"You haven't been answering your phone. I got so worried." Katie sighs in relief. "What the hell, Lisa? You promised you wouldn't disappear like this after the last time—"

Then she finally notices Dante standing there and freezes.

"Katie, you remember Dante?"

Dante smiles, visibly embarrassed, as he waves subtly.

"Dante," she says, too angry to be embarrassed, walking in and dropping her purse on the couch. "Nice to see you again... I didn't know you and Lisa were talking again."

Dante towers over her petite five-foot-eight frame as he shakes her hand.

"Actually," I clasp my arm around his. "We're seeing each other again."

Dante looks at me; his expression is mixed with shock and happiness as he flashes me a subtle smirk.

"It's a recent thing," he smirks.

A ripple of warmth shoots through me, hearing him verbally confirm it out loud.

"I guess that would explain why you aren't picking up your phone, then." Katie rolls her eyes. "Still, you could've let me know you were okay."

I clench my jaw. "Katie, you've been ignoring my voicemails and texts for nearly a week now. Don't take that high and mighty road with me."

"Um," Dante says, sensing the tension building in the room. "I'm going to go to Blue Spoon and get us some breakfast."

I nod, acknowledging him.

"Would you like anything, Katie?"

"No, thank you." She forces a smile, never taking her eyes from mine. "Take your time. I need to talk to my sister for a minute."

"Sure." He smiles, leaning down, kissing my forehead before collecting his things and leaving.

In the meantime, I make a pot of coffee in the kitchen as Katie plants herself on the stool next to the island.

Since our last talk, she hadn't spoken to me; I don't know what to expect, but one thing I know. I'm done apologizing.

"What do you want?" I ask, sitting on another stool across the island from her, facing her.

Katie looks up at me, fire blazing in her dark brown eyes.

"Are you serious, Lisa?"

I take a deep breath, preparing for the worse.

"I needed some time," she lowers her head, gliding her fingers over the surface of the counter. "At first, I was so mad at you. And that you'd been keeping this from me the whole time Lamont and I were together made me feel stupid and even angrier. For some reason, you felt you couldn't tell me, and that hurt."

My jaw tightens again; my stomach drops a few inches as my heart flutters in my chest so hard that it's difficult to form words at all. "It's in the past, Katie," I say. "I didn't want to think about it... let alone talk about it."

"Well, you should've told me," she huffs. "Why didn't you ever say anything?"

I sigh, getting up and pulling the hot pot of coffee, pouring the brown liquid into two mugs, and passing one to her.

"I was ashamed. Lamont convinced me we were protecting you... Even worse, he convinced me you would hate me for taking him away. I was a teenager, and I loved my sister... and I was in love with my sister's boyfriend. At first, it was a small secret, then it felt like a burden that was so big I couldn't get from under it." I reply, guilt dripping from every word. "I felt disgusted with myself for so long. You can't even imagine."

Katie looks up at me, stopping the mug short of touching her lips.

"Lisa, you think I'd ever blame you for this," she sighs, focusing her gaze on the countertop. "I'm angry at myself. And I'm furious with Lamont."

"Why?"

"Because deep down, the signs were there," she reluctantly continues. "Deep down, something always felt off between you and Lamont. And instead of listening to my intuition, I made every excuse that I could think of to convince myself that I was wrong. The truth is, I loved the status that came with being Lamont's girlfriend, and now I am wondering if I traded my sister's innocence for that status."

"I'm sorry, Kat." The words are long overdue, but are still a struggle to get out. "I should've come to you... trusted you."

"Why didn't you?" Her eyes look directly into mine. "I understand not saying anything when you were a teenager, but after you left for MIT, you could've told me. Or anytime after that."

"It was too big of a secret. At least that's what it felt like at the time. And even when I realized what we were doing was wrong, and what we had wasn't love, I felt like I was in too deep." I blurt out. "Lamont had me convinced that it wasn't a big deal. That what we had was love. It was my secret. Our secret. And my darkness, and I didn't want any of it to touch you."

Katie sinks onto the stool even lower. And for a moment, I fear I may have crossed a line. The pain in her eyes is something I never wanted to see, feeling far worse than I ever imagined. I often forget that Lamont was her entire world for a long time, and she was in love with him beyond words. And now that she knows the truth, her world has shattered just as much as mine has. With every revelation, I feel like I'm sticking another dagger into my sister's heart.

"Lisa," the tears run streaks through her makeup. "You don't get it. You say that the secret was yours, but the shadow of what he did to you lingered and seeped into every other aspect of yours and my life ever since you were forced to keep it. Secrets like that aren't meant to be kept. Secrets like that eat away at you like acid."

Shock ripples through me as her words process in my brain. "I never thought about it that way before."

"I've spent the last few days thinking about everything," Katie says, pausing for a moment to sip the bitter coffee.

"Lamont always wanted to come over to our house," she blurts out, tears swelling in her eyes. "At first, I thought it was because he didn't want to be in his dorm room, but now I realize the truth. He loved babysitting you and spending time with you; I thought it was to help me out with work, but no... and then there were more signs that if I'd just paid attention to, it would have been clear to see."

She pauses again.

"And I feel like a fool." She stares at me, her face devoid of all of its color. "I feel like I let you down, too."

I'm already done with this conversation. The day started so well, and now I'm forced to let Lamont and the past ruin another happy moment for me.

"When did it start?" she asks, her voice shaking. "Tell me, please."

"A little after my thirteenth birthday." I avoid her reaction, focusing on anything else. "That was the first time we —"

"What the fuck? Where was I?" Katie shakes her head like she's trying to remove the twisted and depraved images from her mind.

"You were sleeping." I sigh. "Your sleeping pills, remember? He would sneak into my room a lot after you'd take them and fall asleep."

"Oh, Lisa," Katie says, her face sinks into her hand. "I'm so sorry that I wasn't there for you. His popularity and his charm blinded me. But that's no excuse."

"It's okay; I'm not completely innocent in this," I say. "I should have said something. And I've never blamed you... it was my shame."

She takes a breath. "I want to kill him, and I want to hurt him for what he has done to you."

I exhale, finish my coffee, then walk around the counter to sit next to her on the adjacent stool. "Lamont's paying for it now... In a way."

"It's not enough, Lisa," Katie bursts into tears, slamming the mug down so hard that I'm afraid it would shatter on the counter. "These girls came forward, and I commend them for that, but Lamont got to live the dream... for a while at least. He got away with it for so long. Hell, even now, the media is vilifying these girls like they were the ones who did something wrong... it makes me sick."

Again, I say, "It's okay, Katie. I'm seeing a therapist, and now that Dante and I are trying to work things out, I'm doing okay."

"But you weren't okay for so long before this." Her voice trembles. "The cutting. The eating disorder... and the one-night stands with strangers. You have been paying for my ignorance and blindness for far too long. In a way, Lamont has still been victimizing you this entire time."

"Katie, I don't know what to say." I hug her tightly.

She's right; I've been punishing myself for so long. For so many years, I wanted her to ask me all the questions she's asking right now. I used to imagine her walking in when Lamont was touching me and her reaction to having the truth flaunted in her face — knowing he wouldn't be able to explain or lie his way out of it.

"I understand," she sighs, wiping her tears. "After what you went through with Derek — I don't blame you for not saying anything."

I shrug my shoulders. "It's okay, Katie."

She blinks, reading my expression. "I just have one more question — when was the last time Lamont contacted you?"

"He started calling and texting me once the allegations became public. And ever since he's been fired, he's called me nonstop for the last two days," I confess. "Which was another reason I hadn't picked up the phone."

"What?"

"He reached out to me when the first girl, Kira Davis, first accused him." I continue. "He assured me it wasn't true. He said she just wanted money from him, and he refused to pay her. So, now, she was making up all these horrific stories about him."

Katie plunges her head into her hand again. "I brought this monster into your life. And I will never forgive myself for that. Mom would be ashamed of me if she was still alive — dad too."

"You didn't know." I kiss her forehead. "Don't let this eat you up."

"You've been dealing with this secret for half of your life, and you still are." Katie sniffles, wiping more tears from her cheek. "You shouldn't have had to go through this alone... no woman should."

The jiggling of the keys in the doorknob alerts us that Dante is back. As he walks in, he searches for Katie. Katie retreats into the bathroom to clean herself up as I pour a fresh cup of coffee for him this time.

"Is everything okay?" He mouths to me. "Are you okay?"

I nod and smile.

Everything is fine... now.

FOURTEEN

After another thirty minutes goes by, Katie leaves. The day continues perfectly; it feels like a dream. Dante and I spend it just being tourists of New York. We visit the Oculus, walk across the Brooklyn Bridge, and have lunch in SoHo.

As evening rolls in, I am on cloud nine. But Dante has to go home for an hour or two to pack an overnight bag, planning to stay over for the rest of the weekend. Once alone in my apartment, I decided to do some actual work and send a few emails, checking the seventy emails I'd missed for the last two days.

Suddenly, my phone vibrates on the sofa cushion next to me, sending ripples throughout my body. *UNKNOWN* number flashes on the screen, and I freeze in my tracks, debating whether I should answer it. Lamont has called at least seventeen times in the last two days, and I didn't want to answer it while Dante was here, knowing it would upset him. But now that I'm alone, something more than curiosity is compelling me to answer.

Monty…

It's nearly 9:45 at night. Dante texts, saying he will come over in about an hour, so I decide to answer. Once the line clicks, my tone is distant, finally accepting what I know to be true. The rumors — the accusations — the things these women are saying he did to them. It's all true. I can't ignore it anymore because he did it all to me. And I have to accept that.

"Hello?"

On the phone, Lamont exhales, "Where the fuck have you been? I've been calling you for days. Why haven't you answered my calls?"

I'm getting déjà vu vibes... from when I was fourteen again. It's like I hear his voice, and I'm that little girl all over again. I can't explain it, and I hate it so much. But he makes me feel like a child again as all my resolve leaves me.

"I've been busy." My tone is distant.

"Too busy for me?"

"Yes." I sigh, slamming my laptop shut.

"Can you believe it?" he asks. "They fucking fired me. The League wants to take back my signing bonus and everything. And now I'm being investigated by the feds. This is fucking messed up. I did nothing wrong, Lisa... I swear, I'm innocent. These bitches wanted to be with me. They practically threw themselves at me, and now they just want to destroy my reputation and my life. You know it's not true, right?"

I don't answer, listening to his denial that the end is near for him. The saddest part about this is that Monty has convinced himself he's the victim in all this, and he still believes wholeheartedly that he's done nothing wrong.

"You believe me, right?" He continues, almost sounding like he's crying on the phone. "I still have you on my side, don't I? Lisa, I love you... always have and always will. I'm not the monster they're portraying me to be. My wife, Natalie, has left me. My agency has dropped me, and I fear the police will kick down my door any day now — I need you."

The desperation in his voice does not affect me; in fact, it makes me sick to my stomach. He used to be God to me. And now, this mighty man, who thought that he was untouchable, feels his world crashing down around him — like mine once did.

Standing up walking towards the window, I look at the city. The moon is rising over the skylines and skyscrapers. It will be a full moon tonight, and I think about how I used to love the moon growing up. And how it casts a white light over everything...The moon sees everything, I used to say as a little girl. And now I'm reminded of that fact once again.

"Lisa? Are you there?"

"I'm here, Lamont."

"Why are you so quiet? We have a connection; you know that, a deep connection. I need you. Tell me, I haven't lost you too." He says, puffing into the phone with an unfamiliar panic in his tone.

I'm done... I need to let go. It's Lamont or me, and at this moment... I'm picking myself. I choose myself, for the first time in my life...

"Katie knows what happened between us." I blurt out the words before realizing that I had said them. "And my boyfriend knows, too."

"Your boyfriend?"

It's not surprising he only picks up on the second part. It bothers him more that I have a boyfriend than the fact that his ex-fiancé knows about our dark little secret.

"Yes, Lamont," My voice falls flat. "My boyfriend."

"I don't know what you want me to say about that. You're my girl. Always have been, and you always will be. You mean everything to me. Lisa, I don't know what this is. My life is over. And it feels like you're abandoning me, too."

"You know what you did." The coldness in my tone reflects my mood. "I know what you did, too... you can lie to everyone else, but don't lie to me."

He's quiet. I've never talked to him like this before, and I know he's trying to figure out how to respond to what I just said.

"I know it's all true," I say. "I won't be blind to that fact. And have ignored the fragile truth between us for so long, mainly because I loved you."

The silence is deafening... all I can hear is my heart pounding in my chest.

"They meant nothing to me," he finally confesses. "I'm sick. I have a problem. Sometimes I drink too much, and I can't help myself. And when you're famous, all these girls just throw themselves at you... I couldn't help myself."

"What did you do to them?" I ask. "The same things you did to me?"

"To you? You wanted me to do those things to you, and it was special and beautiful." Lamont cries into the phone. "Why are you trying to make it sound perverted and disgusting? We were in love, and I love you."

Love?

"How could you do this?" I fight back the tears, feeling more guilty I could've stopped him long ago if I'd just turned him in.

I remember when I was going through the chaos with Derek; Lamont was so distant and cold with me... Blaming me for what Derek did to me. He was intentionally mean for weeks after I filed my police report. And when we were intimate, he made sex with him hurt on purpose, often making me cry as he punished me for letting someone else touch what he perceived was his.

"What do you want me to do, Lamont?" I ask. "I haven't come forward with my stories of what you did to me."

"What I did to you?" He exhales, offended by what I'm implying. "We made love, and we were in love. I gave you my heart. My body and my soul."

"I was thirteen, and I had a school-girl crush on you." My voice cracks, thinking about the pain. "And didn't have a clue of what I was doing."

"I never raped you, Lisa. You wanted me just as much as I wanted you. Don't play innocent in all of this."

I don't respond, still not wanting to admit what he did... or what I did.

His voice is low. "I love you, Lisa. I've always loved you more than Katie. More than my wife, Natalie. You have always had my heart — "

I hang up the phone quickly, cutting him off. Now Lamont knows he's lost me, too. A part of me wants to call him back or send a message to him somehow. But I simply place the phone back on the couch, walk into the kitchen, and make my concoction of Crown and Coke.

Dante knocks on the door just in time, distracting me from breaking down; I've just said goodbye to the longest and most significant relationship that I've had. I'm scared, and I feel empty inside now that Lamont isn't occupying his place within me. I don't know why

I'm so upset, but I am — and who am I without him? What will my life be like without him in it?

As Dante enters the apartment, he kisses me, and it reignites the fire in my belly for his presence and touch. He seems to reassure me that everything will be okay with one kiss and I will be okay. I push Lamont out of my thoughts, focusing on the here and now.

My last thought is the memory of Monty abandoning me when I needed him, so we're even now.

It's over…

****

Tuesday, April 3rd, 2001

In quiet moments, the memories still haunt me… the dark times when everyone abandoned me, even Monty.

I remember being so angry the following weeks after everything with Derek was made public. Ashley and the other girls practically blamed me for what happened that night. Each of us got in trouble for drinking beers, and they were mad that I admitted that, even though we swore we would keep it a secret. They collectively concluded that I slept with Derek and then cried rape.

Ashley even spread rumors I slept with everyone, from football players to random students from other schools. Some of my so-called friends would put notes in my locker nearly every day. Some would call me a slut, or tell me to kill myself. Or called me a whore. No one would talk directly to me, but had plenty to say about me. Derek was the victim, and I was the villain.

Being home was even worse after a fight with Katie about going to the police without my permission. I stayed in my room. Dad got a call from Mrs. Harris and heard about the police report. But refused to talk about it and avoided me every time he was in my presence. It scared me to even come out of my room when he was home because I didn't know what to expect. I was utterly alone. Constantly feeling anxious and afraid. And felt like the worst human being on the planet. I couldn't understand what I had done wrong, even though everyone around me seemed to have an opinion about it.

My room became my sanctuary – my haven – my tomb. What was worse was that Monty wouldn't reply to my texts or emails. When he came by the house, he did his best to ignore me in front of Katie. And when we were alone, he blamed me for Derek, even though he would pretend to be loving and caring in front of Katie. Every night I would stay in my room and sketch pictures on my sketchpad, and I fought the tears that were mounting. I couldn't understand why Monty was being so mean. Why was he ignoring me? Why was he blaming me? Why did he abandon me like everyone else? He was supposed to understand.

Most nights, I stayed up silently crying to myself, contemplating suicide. It was all I thought about for weeks. And I dreaded waking up each day if that meant I would have to endure another day of Hell. I lost weight from not eating, and my life fell apart around me. I simply wanted to disappear, and I didn't think anyone would care or notice if I did.

I thought about Monty and our relationship up to that point. Him sneaking into my room at night after Katie went to sleep, sliding into my bed. Fingering and fondling me under the blanket and then sliding his sex into me repeatedly... now I feared Monty didn't want me anymore, and it broke my heart because if Lamont didn't want me anymore, then who would?

Without warning, there was a knock on the door that tore me out of my train of thought. Katie stood in the open doorway without coming in. I wasn't even aware that she'd returned from school. She was just a shadow to me now, like everyone else in my life.

"Are you hungry?"

I shook my head — no

"Still mad at me?"

"No." I lied, thinking, *what's the point?*

I was mad at her, but not as angry as she thought. I was mad that coming forward and pressing charges had sent my life spiraling in uncontrollable directions. And furious at the way people were reacting toward me. It upset me, feeling alone, even in a crowded room. And every person I once called a friend either betrayed or abandoned me.

"I'm sorry that I didn't talk to you before going to the police," her gaze lowered as she looked at her feet. "When you told me, I reacted without thinking. My only thought was to make that fucker pay — I didn't even consider what you were going through. Or how you were feeling."

She came in and sat on the edge of my bed. "I'm sorry, Lisa, that I took the choice from you."

"Then why did you do it?" I mumbled, still sketching on my pad. "This is ruining my life. You don't even understand how bad it is, and you aren't here all the time."

Katie looked down, playing with her fingernail for a moment, and sighed. "When I was a freshman in high school, one of my friends—Elizabeth Colton, told me her father had been raping her since she was very young. No one knew about it, and the secret was killing her. She told me every sick detail that her bastard of a father did to her—then made me swear not to tell anyone. And I swore to her I wouldn't say anything. At the beginning of my sophomore year, we were informed that Elizabeth had committed suicide three days after the new school year started. In her suicide note, she revealed she could no longer take her father's abuse and ended it all."

Katie placed her hand on mine. "I still can't help but think that if I would've said something or tried to help her—she might've hated me, but she'd be alive right now."

I closed my sketchpad, feeling guilty about the way I'd blamed Katie and Sara when it was Derek who did this. "I'm sorry."

"Lisa," she sighed, wiping a stray tear from her face. "Every night since you told me what Derek did, I've had reoccurring nightmares that one morning I'm going to open this door and discover that your dead—I've even gotten up in the middle of the night and checked on you while your sleeping. I can hear you having nightmares about him, screaming in the night. And I just don't want you to end up like Elizabeth. She felt like she had no one, and soon her secrets and shame destroyed her."

But I felt alone... and even with all of her good intentions, Katie couldn't possibly know how this felt. I was wandering in the darkness without a flashlight, and the black abyss was drowning me.

For a minute, we stared at each other; Katie's eyes searched for any hint that I was close to being pushed to the edge like that. She wanted to ask me but was afraid of the answer—and I felt at that moment how much she'd been worried for me.

"Have you ever thought about—"

"No." I lied, fighting back the tears.

Most days, flashes of images would appear in my mind like waking dreams. Images of what Derek did to me that night. They were so vivid that they would often take my breath away, and I would panic. It felt like I couldn't escape these waking nightmares, no matter where I was or what I was doing.

"I just wish things could be like they used to be," I admitted. "I wish I could be the person I was before."

"I know that something like this changes you," Katie held me close, "but it doesn't define you—this isn't who you are—it's what was forced upon you by someone else."

She hugged me tightly for the first time in days. Ever since I told her what happened, Katie had been treating me like I would break if she came too close to me. Now I realized she just wanted to give me time and space... A part of me was grateful, but another part of me didn't want her to let me go.

"I know things are tough for you at school, but if Ashley and the other girls are blaming you, even after

Sara confirmed your story… then they were never really your friends." Katie added, "Fuck them. You will always have me, and you can come to me with anything."

That night was the first night in days that I came out of my room and rejoined Katie in the living room. We had a sister bonding night, watching cheesy romance movies, eating pizza and popcorn. We finished the night with Rocky Road ice cream, my favorite, while watching The Wedding Planner with Jennifer Lopez. Slowly, my walls came down, and I started feeling like myself again.

FIFTEEN

Tuesday... April 5th, 2016
Present Day

Despite everything I'm feeling. I'm grateful for the first time in my life. Ever since these accusations surfaced and the media have been all over it, I've seen Dr. Nichole Owens twice a week on Tuesdays and Thursdays. Now, I'll have to find more time to add another day and make it three times a week. All the emotions and guilt poured out of me during our sessions, and it's been a lifesaver. Today she's wearing a white blouse with a gray knee-length skirt and, of course, her four-inch heels.

I should take notes about her fashion sense... I think to myself.

"How have you been since you met with Apple," she asks, "That has to be an enormous weight off your shoulders."

I nod — *yes*.

"Has Lamont contacted you since that night?" Nichole asks, diving right into the main topic. "The night you confronted him with the truth and said that you won't defend him anymore."

"No," I lower my head. "I abandoned him — hurt him. I don't expect him to want to talk to me after that. And promised him I would never say anything about us, and I broke that promise."

Nichole stares at me with a bewildering expression on her face. She leans back against the cushions of her sofa. It's her signature move when she's really taken aback by something I've said or done. As if she's trying to wrap her head around it... analyze it, and process it all at the same time. "It wasn't a promise that you should've had to keep, Lisa."

"I feel sorry for him, okay? I can't explain why, but I do." I cross my arms over my chest, shrugging my shoulders. My defensive walls spring up almost instinctively as the words leave my lips, and I disassociate out of instinct.

Nichole scribbles something in her notes. "I understand — how you can feel that way, but Mr. Johnson brought all of this upon himself. He made his bed, and he's a predator. And now his life is sinking faster than the Titanic. Don't let him drown you, too."

Sipping some water from a bottle, I pause before continuing. "I was so mean to Lamont, and all but called him a rapist? I told him that Katie knew everything."

"Wait, what? Lisa, that's huge," Nichole says, removing her glasses for a minute, "why gloss over that like it's nothing."

"Because I never wanted her to know."

"I know," she says. "But secrets made in the darkness will always find their way into the light."

"That sounds like something from a fortune cookie," I murmur, leaning back against the leather cushion of the couch, glancing out the open window. "Or something that Yoda would say in Star Wars."

I'm such a nerd...

"Perhaps," Nichole smiles at the reference. "But it doesn't make it any less true."

There's an awkward pause while Nichole takes a cloth from her desk.

"Have you given any more thought about coming forward and telling your story?" she asks, cleaning her glasses with the cloth. "For your benefit and no one else, I mean."

The thought had crossed my mind so many times before this happened. But I can't do that to Lamont now, no matter how much he's hurt me. It feels like kicking a wounded horse. Lamont is more than likely going down for sexual assault... rape... and abuse. My story wouldn't change anything; just add more years to his sentence... if he even gets sentenced at all. And the media would only accuse me of jumping on the bandwagon of hate for him. Believe it or not, Lamont still has many supporters on the internet.

"No, I'm still reluctant to come forward," I reply. "I don't want to."

Nichole sighs.

"I'm sorry," I look down, feeling the weight of my shame creeping in and sensing the doctor's disappointment. "I just want to forget what happened and move on... that's all I've ever wanted."

"Forgetting is not moving on," she exhales heavily. "Lamont took your childhood. Your virginity. Your innocence. He twisted and manipulated you to make you fit his sick fantasies. And convinced you it was love. The damage that he did to you can never go away. He took something from you that you can't get back. There is no way to forget that."

"I know," I murmur.

"You don't have to be silent anymore," Nichole continues. "All the people that are close to you and care about you... already know. The only person you are protecting now is him."

"I still feel like I need to."

I tell her how Lamont used to call our love forbidden fruit because it was so special, and he called it a love story, like Romeo and Juliet. Even though we weren't supposed to love each other... we did... and for a time, I believed him.

"I do love him... even now." I cry, knowing how fucked up that sounds. "He molded me into the woman I am now, and even though I'm sometimes a walking disaster. I can't deny him. And will always be that thirteen-year-old girl who had a crush on the football star. We're bonded together. No matter how hard I try to deny that. Lamont is a part of me. Sometimes, I can close my eyes and hear his voice."

"He's your abuser, Lisa, nothing more," Nichole says coldly. "No matter how much he tried to romanticize that. The truth is uglier and darker, and the truth IS that no adult should ever creep into a child's room in the middle of the night... or touch them... or have sexual intercourse with them. Ever!"

I shake my head as images of him touching me. Fucking me. Loving me, rattles in my brain.

"He was your gateway to adulthood, but he's also a monster."

"I know," I say. "You are right."

"You know?" Nichole repeats. "You're still traumatized, and he has programmed your mind to accept what he did to you as love. But that's not what love is... it doesn't even come close to it."

Nichole sighs again, leaning forward slightly, resting her forearms on her thighs. "What he did was twist and manipulate your mind and body to fit his needs and fetishes—then used guilt to keep you quiet—then claimed it was love to excuse it all. None of it was your fault. You were a child, but you're not a child anymore, so you can take back the power that he took from you all those years ago."

I've never understood that phrase, "take back your power..." what the fuck is that supposed to mean? What's done is done and cannot be changed. Every night I dream of Lamont; he's in my every waking thought. And every day, I fight the urge not to text him or call him, just to hear his voice. I'm secretly falling apart, and the good doctor tells me to take back my power.

It's fucking annoying sometimes... I know Nichole's trying to be positive and reassuring, but some days, I just want to be pissed and wallow in my misery.

I talk about everything else that's going on in my life, from seeing Dante again. To the nightmares I have about Derek and Lamont almost every night. I confess drinking numbs the pain and gets me through the nights. And how my anxiety and depression are reaching a boiling point. I tell her that mostly, each day, I'm struggling to keep it together, afraid that if I fall apart, I'll never be able to pick up the pieces again.

I'm afraid of that the most.

"Do you think I should continue writing it all down?" I ask, finally. "I used to journal all the time to get the thoughts out of my head, but I've been so busy lately that I have written nothing down in a while."

"You'd have to be careful with that... writing it down could further traumatize you if you don't deal with the emotions, or it could help you."

"I understand that, Nichole."

She sighs. "Lisa, the reason men like Lamont get away with these things is because we allow them to... their victims are too ashamed — embarrassed or afraid to say anything. The women would rather suffer in silence than be labeled a 'victim.'"

I know she's right; it's just hard to hear her say it... damn, she's good.

"I think writing it down will be stressful, at least at this present moment," Nichole adds. "I worry it won't help because you're not willing to let go or admit that he even did anything wrong with you."

She pauses.

"You're still blaming yourself instead of placing the blame where it needs to go... on him."

She's right... even though I hate to admit it. I do blame myself each day. I always have, and I'm afraid I always will.

"I feel like I'm suffocating and can't sometimes breathe," I wipe my falling tears. "I never saw myself as his victim, but I feel tremendously guilty that he's been hurting someone else."

"He's your abuser... he's the only person who should feel guilty in this situation, not you."

"Right," I exhale deeply. "You say Lamont brainwashed me. He controlled me. Abused me, but I didn't feel any of those things at the time. I even climax during sex with him, and no one other than Dante has ever made me do that."

"That's just your body's reaction to the friction," she interjects. "It's involuntary, like when a person closes their eyes when they sneeze or keeps laughing after they're tickled. Having an orgasm doesn't mean you wanted it."

I roll my eyes.

"Don't do that." Nichole snaps, closing her notepad. "Don't dismiss what you went through like you deserved what he did to you. You deserved a real childhood and to lose your virginity to someone you loved. Or at least on your terms."

Nichole gives me an intense look filled with sympathy.

"It's hard for me," I say, "And I struggle with it every day. Before Lamont, I was invisible, and he saw me when no one else did and made me feel special. I was supposed to be his girl. What we had... our moments of love and kindness. I craved that and sometimes missed it. Now it's all tainted, and it's so hard."

"What's hard, Lisa?"

"To admit that there were times I didn't want him inside me! That a lot of times, I felt like I didn't have a choice. And sometimes he hurt me and used Katie to keep me quiet." The words trip and stumble their way out of my mouth. "He said I seduced him. But a lot of times, what we were doing felt wrong, and I ignored those feelings just to please him."

"He used love and fear to keep you quiet?"

"Yes, he used my love for Katie, and my love for him, as well as the embarrassment of being found out, to keep what we did a secret."

As I say it, tears stream down my chin uncontrollably. Nichole nods subtly, understanding where I'm coming from.

"Things changed between us after Derek, though." I wipe the wetness away with my sleeve, ignoring the box of tissue right in front of me.

"Tell me how?" Nichole asks, posturing with her pen at the ready as she opens her notepad once more.

****

July 24, 2001

After the whole Derek thing, the summer came and went in a blur; I spent most of the days in the house when I wasn't working... I was nearly sixteen and felt more like an adult. I had my own bank account and a part-time job at Denny's. Lamont came over a lot more at the beginning of the summer.

He had bought an apartment closer to my house, and it was only a few minutes away. He would encourage me to come over to see him a lot more... for privacy. Monty would say that it was vital now more than ever that we were careful. He was almost paranoid that people like the paparazzi and tabloids were watching him after he signed his multi-million-dollar deal with Nike and had been drafted.

Katie seemed to be constantly working, too; she even picked up a second job to save more money. And they hardly saw each other but still said they were dating to anyone who would ask.

I remembered my first time in Monty's condo; I stayed the night before after I got off work. When I got up and walked into the enormous bathroom. There was a jacuzzi tub and a walk-in shower, and using it was heavenly. I had my own space where just my things went: my washcloth, toothbrush, and other feminine products.

Even the rumors at school had died down by the end of the school year, allowing me to be excited to go back in August to start my junior year.

Looking in the mirror and brushing my teeth, I worried Lamont would forget about me now that he was a big-time football player. I was not the little girl that he used to know. And was almost five feet nine inches tall. I had my driver's license and drove a Toyota... more boys were interested in me now that I'd grown into my breasts. Even though I paid none of them any mind.

I just feared that Monty would tire of me any day.

While he was away at practice, I'd sit and watch Law & Order SVU and CSI all day on my off days. I remembered there was one episode on SVU where the victim was giving her statement to Olivia, and she was crying about being abused repeatedly as a child. She felt guilty because her father started abusing her younger sister after she left home, who later killed herself as an adult.

The woman cried to Olivia, "I survived, but I left her with that monster." Then the music swelled, and it got all dramatic. I didn't know why that stood out to me... It was just a stupid episode, but that scene lingered in my mind for a while, even after the show ended.

I shook my head and turned cartoons on instead.

Women were suffering every day with the fact that someone had raped them, so why would I be the exception? I thought to myself.

It took months for Lamont to finally forgive me for what happened with Derek, and that was all that mattered to me. He bought me gifts again and responded to my text, no matter what he was doing. He even put extra money in my checking account and helped me buy my car. And for a while, I was happy... we were happy.

I continued flicking through the channels until Lamont texted me, saying he was on his way home. Then I turned off the TV and headed for the shower. He liked me to be clean and ready when he got home.

Once he arrived, I could immediately tell Monty was in a bad mood and had been drinking. His breath reeked of hard liquor like he had downed a bottle of gasoline, but I didn't ask what was wrong; I was too afraid, staying quiet until he spoke first.

"I saw him today," Monty growled drunkenly. "He was just walking along the street like he didn't have a fucking care in the world."

"Who, Monty?"

"That son of a bitch... Derek." Monty was almost red with anger. "I can't believe that motherfucker only got three years' probation."

The irony wasn't lost on me that Lamont was furious about this.

Oh shit. I thought to myself. Here we go...

Just as things felt like they were almost getting back to normal, this happened and made waves in my tranquil life.

"Fuck him." I snapped, drinking a cup of juice.

Without warning, Lamont knocked the glass out of my hand, and before I could react, his hand was around my throat, squeezing me tightly. "You did that already, remember?"

I couldn't breathe, but he didn't let up on the pressure he was applying to my windpipe. The room spun around me as I struggled under his grip.

"I can't believe you," he murmured, nearly lifting me onto my toes. "I can't believe you let him fuck you."

"Monty," I choked, tears swelling in my eyes. "I didn't."

He let go, seeing the fear in my eyes. I wanted to yell or push him out of the way and tell him to go fuck himself, but I fell to my knees, gasping for air, sucking up as much as my lungs could handle.

"I'm sorry," he said, snapping back into reality like he just woke up from a daydream. "Baby, I didn't—"

"What the hell, Monty?"

"I'm sorry, I would never—" He stuttered. "I wouldn't—"

"Hurt me? You keep saying that." I choked over my breath.

My mind drifted, thinking about when Lamont told me a bit about his mother.

"She was an alcoholic who would sleep with anyone who gave her a second look," he once said. "I hated her."

He once told me she would beat him and lock him out of the house all day long, not caring if he ate or was okay. And the men she brought home would sometimes—well, he never came out and said it, but I knew at least one man abused him sexually.

But his mother died when he was thirteen or something. He never went into detail. Afterward, he stayed with his football coach, who molded him into a successful athlete. When I was fourteen, and he told me his mother had died, it was one thing that made our connection much deeper because my mom died in a car crash when I was younger. But lately, all the connections we once shared seemed tainted.

"Lisa," he cried, "I'm so sorry... I don't know what came over me; I lost control. Please forgive me."

He took my hand and led me to the living room. Then lowered me to the floor, pulling off my jeans and underwear. The floor was hard and cold and sent chills up my body. I was shivering. And after what he just did, I didn't want to make love. Those nights were what I called the 'bad nights,' when Lamont was more violent and out of control, especially when he was drunk or mad. He would fuck me like I wasn't there at all... like I meant nothing to him.

I remembered laying on the floor, staring at the shadows dancing on the wall as he shoved himself inside of me so hard I yelped. And retreated into my mind, with tears streaming down the corner of my eyes, while he grunted and thrust, not caring if it hurt. I didn't think he was there either. It was like he was trying to fuck his own pain away and reassert his control... over himself... over me... over everything.

"Take it," he breathed. "Take it."

His strokes were fast—and hard as he forced my body to slam into the floor violently. I felt the wind being knocked out of my lungs as he relentlessly pounded into me like a jackhammer.

It hurt... that's what I remember the most...

During those moments, I would distract my mind with anything but what was happening at that moment. Then, Monty paused abruptly, and he flipped me over onto my knees... more thrusting... more pounding. I couldn't bear it, but I was afraid that if I said something, it would only make him angrier, so I took it.

Relief washed over me when Monty was finally done, nearly forty minutes later, according to the image on the clock. He poured himself into me, not caring if he would get me pregnant. But after Derek, my dad made Katie take me to the Gynecologist and put me on the pill.

Entirely spent, Lamont collapsed on the floor where he passed out for the rest of the night. I laid there watching the minutes turn into hours before I finally willed my limbs and sore joints to stand. I showered then left his apartment, not making a sound higher than a whisper.

The next day, he called me, not remembering the night before or anything that had happened.

I was hurt and furious.

But when he heard how upset he made me, and the details of the night and what he did to me... Monty wired $50,000 into my checking account as an 'I'm sorry.'

I had never felt so low... or cheap. I felt like the whore that everyone had been calling me at school.

I didn't talk to him until September after school started. *That's the end of my memories of that summer...*

SIXTEEN

Friday, April 8th, 2016

"My entire team has worked their ass off to make this Apple deal a reality, so to thank them, I'm throwing a party tonight." I say over the phone. "Will you be able to make it?"

"I wouldn't miss it," Dante replies. "I'll pick you up at 8:00 tonight then."

"I'll be ready."

Around 7:46, Dante picks me up in a Black Escalade, dressed in an elegant black Hugo Boss dress suit that matches my stunning black Hugo satin dress with a high slit that hugs my body in all the right places. The gorgeous plunging neckline with a low v-back accents my features perfectly. The minute Dante saw me at the apartment, his mouth fell in awe, telling me this dress was the right choice.

"You look stunning, L." He grins.

"Thank you."

The Red Flamingo is the perfect place to hold a party in Manhattan. Part restaurant and dance floor, it's classy and high-end. They decorated the hallways with elegant attire. Dante escorts me through the expansive enclosed dancefloor to our table and my body tingles with excitement just thinking about being here with him tonight. The room alone is breathtaking, with fifty-foot floor-to-ceiling windows from the top floor of the building, offering spectacular views of the entire city. I'm impressed that the decorators put all of this together so quickly.

We walk to the balcony overlooking the skylines, and I pause for a moment to take in the view.

"It's beautiful, isn't it?" Dante whispers in my ear. "Sometimes I forget how beautiful this city can sometimes be.

"It's overwhelming." I stare out at the night sky. "I can't believe that I'm here with you celebrating this deal... and happy."

He stands behind me, pulling me tightly into his massive arms. I turn to face him, looking into his emerald eyes. They burn with love and desire for me with an intensity that I'd only read about in romance novels.

"I'm so happy I'm here with you and can celebrate your success." He brushes his lips over my neck and plants a warm kiss on my skin. "You make me happy beyond words, and you deserve this... I'm so proud of you, Lisa."

My heart skips a beat as I snuggle into his warmth. The other guests slowly filter in, but I'm lost in this quiet moment with the man I love, reveling in this god-like being that's holding me in his arms.

A familiar voice breaks through the moment, bringing me back to reality. I hear my name in the distance and sigh at the fact that we've been discovered. Adrian Brown, arm-in-arm with Mia Wells, approaches and joins us on the balcony. Adrian, my project supervisor, looks smooth in his blue Hemsworth suit, and Mia is wearing a flowing beige satin gown that suits her petite frame.

I smile, taken aback at the sight of them outside of the office setting, until Mia leans forward to hug me and kiss my cheek.

"Hello, Lisa. You clean up pretty well." Mia smiles. "It's weird seeing you in anything but a business suit... but you are pulling this off, boss."

"Thank you. You look beautiful as well, Mia."

Dante smiles, shaking hands with Adrian, and greets him warmly.

"This is Dante Kingston, my —"

"Your boyfriend, yes." Blood rushes to my cheeks as Adrian smiles and looks at me. "I'm glad you finaly found someone who can keep up with you."

"I try." Dante jokes, winking at me.

Adrian clears his throat. "Well, we are going to mingle and say hi to everyone else that's arriving... don't stay out here too long, boss... you are the woman of the hour, after all."

"This night is to celebrate all of our hard work, Adrian, not just mine," I say quickly, not used to being praised and feeling awkward about the entire situation.

Mia laughs slightly. "How about Lisa and I make our rounds with the other guests, and you two get us some drinks?"

A moment passes.

"Sure." Adrian smirks. "Let's get these lovely ladies a drink, Dante. Maybe I can get to know you a little better in the process."

Dante grins and kisses my forehead. "I'm a private person, but I don't mind getting my girl her favorite drink."

Adrian laughs to himself and pats Dante on the shoulder as the two walk inside and out of sight. Mia gently grabs my arm and walks me back inside and into the swelling crowd that has formed.

"It's been a crazy few months, hasn't it?" She slowly struts to a nearby waiter, lifting two glasses of Dom Perignon champagne off of a silver tray, handing me one.

"Well, that's why we are having this party tonight, isn't it?" I say nervously. "To celebrate everything this company has accomplished."

"Of course. This deal with Apple has been stressful for every one."

"And you have had to carry so much stress on your shoulders. Adrian says you've spent many nights working on getting the App just right and going through the code over and over again."

"Yes, the algorithm had to be tweaked a little. We needed to adjust for the increased volume of traffic, but Adrian has been a godsend." I smile, scanning the room for Dante, but I can't seem to locate him through the sea of faces.

"This deal will open so many doors for the company. I'm sure you have more ideas for apps and ways to expand."

"I do."

Mia smiles, sizing me up in her gaze as if she wants to say something more or is fishing for something else.

"Adrian admires you, Lisa. I know he really cares about you. But he is worried about you…I'm worried too. Sometimes he says you scare him and I remember how I felt during those dark times in high school, when we first met. We all depend on you and need you to continue to lead us, and God forbid if anything happens to you… It would devastate all of us. No one wants to hear that you might — do you understand?"

I choke down the last of the champagne, hoping she couldn't see through the walls I've put up. Few people knew I tried to hurt myself a few months back, but Adrian was the one who found me half-dead in my apartment. I know Mia is coming from a place of concern, but that doesn't lessen the blow of what she's hinting about.

"I'm much better now. I—I have a better hold on my personal life. And I appreciate your concern, but I'm fine."

Mia grasps my hand in hers and gives it a gentle squeeze as she flashes a warm smile. "Lisa, I've known you since high school. I know you don't talk about what's going on with you often, but I thought that if things got too much for you... you would've at the very least reached out to me. I just want to know you're okay. Especially with everything going on with Lamont."

Feeling the weight of this conversation, I look for any distraction and see one when Katie arrives in the restaurant.

"I'm fine. My sister just arrived, Mia. Will you please forgive me? I have to go and greet her."

I cross the room toward Katie. She's wearing a gown with a shimmering sequin fabric that hugs her figure all in the right places. Its beautiful deep plunge neckline with an open back is eye-catching. She smiles, recognizing my discomfort.

"Lisa, whoa! You look absolutely gorgeous."

"Me?" I blush. "Look at you."

She turns and gives a slight twirl.

"Lisa, I think you know Jason Colewell, right? He works for Apple."

Oh shit…

"Yes, of course."

"Congratulations, Lisa."

Jason's eyes scan my body with a slight smile as his gaze soaks up the view. I want to run from embarrassment but can't. In fact, I am surprised he's here at all. I only hope he doesn't try anything in front of Dante… for his sake.

"Thank you, Jason." I smile, searching for another glass of champagne. "I didn't know you would be here this evening."

I glance at Katie and realize that she doesn't know what went on between Jason and me. Since my presentation, I haven't spoken to him, and I have no interest in striking up a conversation now.

"I just thought I'd pop in and say hi." Jason smirks, "And I met your lovely sister outside… it's good to see that beauty runs deep in the family."

Vomit…

"Yes, my sister is very stunning."

"Come on, you guys are going to make me blush." Katie slaps him and laughs. "Well, Jason tells me you killed in that meeting, but I had every faith that you would wow them."

The moment can't get any more awkward, but thankfully, Jason's focus shifts from us to someone across the room.

"Well, I can't take up all of your time. Enjoy the party?" He says in a hurry.

Katie hugs me and leaves to mingle with everyone.

Suddenly, I hear his voice again, drawing my attention. Jason smiles, walking behind me, catching me alone for the first time.

"Lisa, there is someone —"

"Lamont?" I interrupt; my eyes dart around the room, hoping no one recognizes him and wondering why he's here at all. The party is strictly 'invitation-only.' What in the hell is he doing here? My feet feel wobbly as Lamont stares at me. Inside, my body is in full panic mode, and my heart beats hard against my chest. I want to throw up, but feel like I can't breathe at all.

"What the fuck are you doing here?"

"How else was I supposed to get your attention?" he murmurs. "You weren't answering my calls or texts."

Jason grins, and at that moment, I know he knows about Lamont and Katie. I clench my jaw and try to keep my composure and not make a scene or draw any attention to us. It's my worse fear coming to life; Jason must have done some digging into my past. But he is the last person who needs to know about my history with Lamont or the things that went on between us.

Never in a million years would I ever think I would see Lamont here. I'd hoped he would lie low somewhere far away from me. I feel my body going into a full-blown panic attack with every second that creeps by.

I haven't been in Lamont's presence in years, and now that I'm near him, I just want to disappear.

"Let's talk." He says, pulling me to a distant corner of the room.

Lamont doesn't let go of my hand. Panic washes over me as I jerk my arm away from him. I tense up, crossing my arms over my chest.

"Lisa, why are you doing this?" he says, leaning so close his scent fills my nose.

He's drunk…

Being near him sends mixed emotions and pain through my body. Years of staying out of my life, Lamont has only been a ghost of the past that I've been running from ever since he let me go. He's supposed to be a voice on the phone, and a haunting memory, not here physically.

"Why are you doing this?" I tremble, keeping a distance between us. "You can't just show up here and interfere with my life like this."

"I needed to see you. I can't stay away. And just wanted to see you. To just talk. And when Jason told me about this party… I just had to see you."

"What do you want from me? I don't want to see you or speak to you, Lamont… Why can't you understand that?"

"You can't quit me." His eyes dart around, looking to see if anyone is watching us. "You wouldn't have any of this if it weren't for me… you owe me… you can't abandon me now."

I search around for Dante or Katie, but I can't see them through the crowd. I'm alone… alone with him.

I know he can't do anything. But even though we are in a room full of people, I don't want to raise the alarm.

"Lisa, you are my everything. At night, all I think about is you and the first time we made love."

My body is trembling uncontrollably now as the flash of his face penetrates my thoughts and memory. I shut my eyes, trying to block it all out, but everything is rushing to the forethought of my mind.

"You were so perfect... so tight. And you wanted it to. You came for me every time I was inside of you."

I try to walk away, wanting to find security, but he grabs me again, pinning me to the wall and blocking my escape.

"You can tell yourself whatever you want, but you know that you still love me, and you still want me. I was your first. I will always be inside you... a part of you."

"Lamont, you're drunk. Let me go. Now!" I say, still trembling uncontrollably. There was a time I wanted to be near him, but that's not what I'm feeling now.

When I can't take another second of being near him. Lamont finally lets me go, once he realizes that someone has noticed us.

"What the fuck are you doing here?" Dante growls, rushing to my side. "I should fucking kill you."

"I just wanted to see Lisa." Lamont smirks drunkenly. "And congratulate her on all of her success."

I step away as Katie appears by my side. I want to run and just vomit in a corner somewhere. Everything is spinning around me, and I can't focus. Dante stands there with nothing but pure rage in his eyes. I know he wants to beat Lamont to death, but I grab his arm, steadying him.

"Dante, please don't." I plead. "I just want him to leave."

"How dare you come here?" Katie hisses, circling me with Mia closely following behind her.

Sheer panic fully grips me as the tears fall.

"Lisa." Katie throws her arm around me, her eyes filled with concern. "What happened? Are you okay?"

Lamont slinks away, leaving out of a side exit before anyone can cause a scene. Both Dante and Katie swarm me, ushering me outside to the balcony and away from the sight of the other guests. I know I should feel relief, but I don't.

"Are you all right?"

That's a dumb question...

"No." I shake my head. "I can't believe he would just show up here."

"That motherfucker," Dante holds me close; my body is still trembling in his arms. But the room is no longer spinning around me.

I bury my head in his chest. And just try to breathe.

Lamont must be desperate, coming here to see me, knowing that both Katie and Dante would be here tonight.

Dante holds me so close, not wanting to let me go, even when I try to sit down on the bench next to the ledge.

"What did he say to you?" Katie asks again a moment later after she makes sure Lamont is really gone.

"It doesn't matter." Dante's voice is comforting and brings me back to the moment. I don't want to make eye contact with him, but when I do, all I see is his concern for me, and I want to cry. I close my eyes, wiping away the tears.

"It's okay, Lisa." He whispers against my ear. "I'm here… and I'm not going anywhere."

"I know," I reply. "Just don't leave me again."

"I'm sorry, baby." He kisses my forehead gently.

Mia appears next to me with a glass of water in her hand. "Lisa, here, are you okay?"

"I just had too much champagne." Feeling sick, I nod and smile, pulling it together enough to take a sip of water. Dante stands with me, steadying me.

Katie hugs me, and I feel her body trembling along with mine. I can't imagine what she's feeling right now. Especially knowing the truth about Lamont.

"Dante, please take her home," Katie instructs him.

Dante nods and ushers me back inside.

"Come on, sweetie."

"Yes," I exhale, visibly shaken. "Take me home, please."

Fuck Lamont, he always does crazy things when he's desperate.

****

September 31st, 2001

My junior year in high school felt like a fresh start. I was still not speaking to Monty, and as much as I missed him... I was still angry at him. The last text from him said:

Mighty Monty: Have a good first day of school. I hope you miss me as much as I miss you... I know I fucked up, and I'm sorry. Please come back to me. I love you.

Witchy Charmed: Thanks...

I was relieved as I walked through the vast walls of the school. Over the summer, they had re-carpeted the classrooms and hallways and put a fresh coat of paint on everything. I fussed over my wardrobe for two days before school started. Not wanting to dress too flashy, but also dressing my age. I settled on a pair of dark-blue denim Levi jeans, and a black button-up shirt from Express.

Once in first period, I watched the other students pour into the classroom, making their way to their desks. Averting my eyes from making any direct eye contact with anyone, I felt others gawking at me. I didn't know if it was because they remembered what happened with Derek or because I looked so different from the year before. I was taller. Thinner. And I cut my hair short a few days before school started.

It took me three tries to figure out the combination to my locker after not using it for three months. I placed my new textbooks inside it, silenced my cell phone, and pulled out my Chemistry book. A few boys passed me and whispered about how different and sexy I looked. They couldn't believe I was the same girl from the semester before.

"Looking good slut." One of them said to me. "Even I might wanna fuck you this year... but you might say I forced you."

They all laughed and walked off.

Assholes... I thought to myself.

I slammed my locker door, furious. Derek pled guilty, so it was clear that I didn't make it up, but some people, mostly friends of Derek or Ashley, still thought that I slept with him and then cried rape. I didn't want to come forward or press charges in the first place, but they made everything my fault. It wasn't fair, but I sat there and said nothing... putting all my walls up again

All-day boys stared, but I made it through the day with no drama. Ashley transferred to another school, and the other girls who were at the party all graduated last year. Including Sara Croce, so already the year felt like it was going to be better for me.

After the first week, I made friends with Mia Wells. She was a new student but had already caught the attention of almost everyone. But she was different; not interested in being popular or being caught up in any high school bullshit. She had a boyfriend in college, so she had no interest in dating 'boys.' She was classically beautiful. Tall...Her raven-black hair stretched halfway down her back, and she looked like a runway model.

Mia smiled at me as we walked to French class.

"Did you study for this test?" she asked, shifting her stack of books from one arm to the other. "I started to, but then Brett called, and I lost track of time. Before I knew it, it was nearly 1 a.m."

"I studied for a few hours but then fell asleep with the book on my chest." I joked.

"Well, at least you studied," she laughed. "I tell you relationships can be so hard sometimes."

Tell me about it...

I shrugged my shoulders and smiled. "I think you'll do fine with this test. You take more notes than anyone else I know."

Mia laughed to herself. "I'm glad you have confidence in me, at least."

We entered the room before most of the other students arrived. Mr. Joe Dion, my French teacher, was out of the room for the moment and we were alone.

I barely got a chance to pull my notes out before Mia leaned over in my direction

"Hey," Mia whispered, looking around. "I have a question."

"Okay."

"So, I heard a rumor," she said. "And I'm not one to listen to them. I like to go to the source and get the facts...you know?"

I nodded my head, knowing where she was going with this.

"You don't have to tell me anything," she added, "And I don't judge, but—"

She gave me a look.

"I heard you had sex with some boy," Mia said. "And then tried to have him arrested when you felt bad about it. Is that true?"

"No."

"I didn't think so."

I was grateful—she didn't just believe the rumors and flat out asked me for the truth. Despite that, I had a hard time talking about it or thinking about it. Thinking about Derek made me think about Lamont... and that just made me sad. I just wanted to pretend it never happened at all.

"You don't have to go into details," Mia added. "But what really happened?"

I stared at my notes as I struggled to answer. I could lie, but I didn't want to. But the truth was too painful too. The rumors were way off—I didn't willingly sleep with Derek and then just change my mind at the last minute.

"I was at a sleepover," I chose my words carefully. "One of the girl's brothers took me into his room and—I didn't want him to do anything but—."

"So, he forced you?" She asked. There wasn't a hint of judgment in her voice; it was more concern than anything else like Mia didn't want me to convince her; all she wanted was to know the truth.

I nodded my head.

"I wanted to keep it a secret," I continued. "But one of the other girls saw what happened. She told a teacher, and everything spiraled out of control."

"I see," Mia whispered. "And everyone blamed you."

"Yes."

"People suck sometimes." She snapped, slamming her notebook open. "I'm sorry you had to go through that."

I nodded again, forcing a smile. At that moment, I could appreciate her genuine concern and sympathy; it didn't feel fake or condescending.

My eyes followed the other students as they walked into the classroom, and finally, Mr. Dion walked in. Just as the late bell rang, class started.

"Wish me luck," Mia smiled, winking at me as the tests were being handed out.

Later in the day, during World History, Mia whispered she had something to tell me. It caught the attention of Ms. Shannon Waters and she separated us when we were caught talking during the movie that was playing. I was forced to sit at an empty desk in the back of the classroom. I was annoyed because I was sitting next to Bradly Cummings and couldn't stand being around him. He gave me a strange vibe that I couldn't explain but knew I didn't like. I stayed quiet, paying attention to the movie when Brad threw a note on my desk:

You look like a hot piece of ass. It said... Will you give me a BJ in the gym after school? I know you know how to... slut.

I wanted to make a scene, throw the note in his face and let everyone know what he wrote. But I didn't, balling up the paper. I threw it inside the desk, mouthed 'fuck you' to him, and focused on the movie again.

A few minutes later, I felt Brad's presence uncomfortably close to me. He was invading my bubble space and I didn't appreciate it. He took my hand, guided it underneath the desk, and placed it on his penis, which was sticking out of his pants. The room was dark, and only the light emanating from the television illuminated the room. No one noticed what he was doing.

"Take it," he whispered. "You know you want to."

I froze. But not entirely, forcing myself to do something...anything.

Abruptly, I stood up, collected my things, and rushed out of the classroom, avoiding eye contact with everyone, and ignoring Ms. Waters's objections.

Fuck...

I didn't look up from my notebook as I rushed through the halls towards the bathroom. I felt like I couldn't breathe, only feeling slightly better once alone in the stall.

A moment later, my phone buzzed in my pocket.

It was Mia.

Mia: What happened? Are you okay?

I texted back:

No... I think I'm having a panic attack.

Mia: Where are you?

Me: Bathroom...end of the hall.

I didn't know how much time had gone by, but the door of the bathroom swung open. "Lisa? It's Mia. Are you still here?"

"Yes," I said, slowly pulling on the stall door, walking out to meet her.

"What happened?"

"Bradly." I hyperventilated, handing her the crumbled note.

She read it, then crumbled it back up. "What the fuck? This is gross. That motherfucker."

I looked at her — her expression was full of disgust and shock. My breath slowed and returned to normal, after another few long seconds.

"Are you okay?"

I shook my head — no

"He tried to make me jerk him off," I said. "His dick was out... And he took my hand and tried to make me touch it."

"He pulled his dick out in the middle of class?"

"Yeah."

I glanced up at her.

"What the fuck? I would have run out of there too, but not before I punched him in the balls."

"I thought about it." I smiled.

Mia laughed. "Wanna get out of here?"

I had never skipped school before, but.

"I thought you'd never ask." I smiled.

Outside, in the school parking lot, we sat in the car, trying to figure out what we were going to do next.

"I would take the note and give it to the principal," Mia said as she smoked a cigarette in my car. I zoned out, thinking about what would happen if I did that.

I had stayed up late the other night texting with Lamont, and I finally told him I forgave him. We made plans to meet late Friday night while his team has a week off and he didn't have to play on Sunday. He told me he would do anything to see me again and make things up to me.

If I turned Bradly in, I feared it will just stir everything up again. And I didn't want to do that. It was best to just keep it to myself. I'd found that most people wanted to remain blissfully ignorant about these things.

"Mrs. Harris and I have history." I said, "Telling her anything will just make my life difficult again."

"She knew about that boy who—"

"Teachers and Principals must investigate and report those types of things," I murmured. "I don't know about sexual harassment, but I think it falls into that category too."

"I understand."

Mia finished her cigarette, tossing the bud out of the window. "Hey, are you hungry? I could go for some In and Out burgers right now."

I nodded, starting the car, and pulled off…little did I know that scrawny girl would be with me all these years later. I confided many things to Mia, although I kept my relationship with Monty a secret.

We've been inseparable ever since.

SEVENTEEN

Monday, April 11th, 2016

Back at work, I can't seem to concentrate on anything. All I can think about is the party the other night and what Lamont did. And all the things Dr. Nichole said in our last session. It feels like there is a war within me, and I'm being pulled in two different directions. Every sponsor and deal that Lamont had been connected with dropped him days after his firing went public.

I pull out my laptop, not wanting to risk using the work Mac computer in my office, just in case someone monitors it. Everyone else is out to lunch, leaving me in the office alone.

The fact that Lamont's world is falling apart just as mine finally seems to come together makes me feel slightly guilty. A part of me feels like he's finally getting what's been coming to him, but I'm also imagining what the women who accused him are going through.

Are their lives falling apart too? Are their friends and family members blaming them? My mind wanders thinking about the possibilities of the many outcomes that may happen for everyone involved.

I hope to complete a deal with Ryan within a matter of weeks. Since the Apple meeting, he's been emailing me questions about the software and interface of my design. He says my prototype is good, and he wants to make it revolutionary. I don't know what that means, but it sounds promising. No one has connected the texts and emails between Lamont and me...back to me. However, I'm still concern about exactly what Jason knows and have an unsettling feeling that looms in the pit of my stomach — especially about Lamont's stability and mentality.

Suddenly my iPhone vibrates against the desk, I don't recognize the number, and my heart drops as I reluctantly answer the call.

"Hello?"

"Hello, Lisa? Lisa Rose." A squeaky female voice says.

I rush to the door, quickly shutting it as I look out my office window and draw the blinds.

"Who is this?" I ask, feeling my stomach dropping.

"Is this Lisa?"

Immediately, I think about hanging up, exhaling, and letting go of the breath I didn't even know I am holding.

"Please, don't hang up," the voice says as if she's reading my mind. "This is Chloe Roberts. I spoke to you a couple of weeks ago. I wanted to apologize again for bombarding you at your office and the fact the documents were leaked onto that site. I no longer work for the magazine, but I'd still like to work with you and get your story out there."

I say nothing. Not knowing exactly how to respond to this. If Chloe's not working for the magazine, then why is she calling? Why does she still want to talk with me?

My throat feels dry as I speak, "I told you already that I have nothing to say. I haven't spoken to Mr.

Johnson since he cut ties with my sister." I lie. "And coming forward will only complicate my life."

"Okay," she says. "I understand where you're coming from."

"Do you? Because you keep calling me... emailing me at home and now at my work."

"I know," she says. "The other women don't want to talk to me either."

I roll my eyes at the phone as if she can see my face.

"One victim—Kira Davis, had to be hospitalized, did you know that?" Chloe adds. "She tried to kill herself after people started coming after her on social media. It got worse after the NFL dropped Lamont. Reporters are trying to poke holes in her story. She's even thinking about dropping her case altogether. The media has painted her as some gold-digging slut. She's gotten death threats—I'm sure you can relate to some of that."

"What are you implying?" I ask, "What does any of that have to do with why you are calling me?"

I hear the wind blowing through the phone. She must be in her car or outside or something. "Lisa, I've done my homework on you," she sighs. "I know about Derek Page. And what happened when you came forward about what he did to you. I can imagine that you went through a similar experience that Kira is going through right now. You could help her through it. Be there for her."

"Who the hell do you think you are?" I lose my cool. "What makes you think that you have the right?"

My tone stuns her.

"These are people's lives, and it's traumatizing beyond words." I snap. "Unless you've experienced it, then you have no fucking clue,"

There's silence on the other end for a few seconds.

"You're right..." Chloe's voice lowers, dripping with shame. "I'm sorry to put this on you like it's your responsibility because you were his first, and you've known him for so long. I can't imagine what you've been through. And I know I sound insensitive or that I just want a story. But I don't. Women like you and the others, are abused by powerful men and then disgraced and discarded. No one ever hears your voices."

She pauses, picking up her phone.

"I didn't just work for the website. I'm also a freelance writer, and I'd like to write about you and what you went through."

"What?" I ask. "Why would I agree to that?"

"Because your story needs to be told," she says, "I wouldn't publish anything you didn't want me to, and I'd change the names to protect you and your love ones."

My phone buzzes again; glancing at the screen, I see one message from Monty and one from Dante.

I exhale, feeling my face getting hotter by the second.

Calmly, I say. "Can I think about it?"

"Yes, of course," she says, her tone cheers up, "I'll wait for your call, and if you still say no, I'll move on to one of the other victims and see if they're willing to talk."

So many thoughts race through my mind. Too many to process right now. And it's all giving me a severe migraine.

"Okay," I exhale, feeling defeated. "I'll think about it and let you know."

The phone clicks as I disconnect the call. I exhale as a surge of blood drains from me, and I nearly faint, having to hurry back to my seat. I feel sick like I'm on a merry-go-round ride that's spinning out of control — I'm dizzy — want to throw up and want to get off.

I check my text messages:

Text from **Dante**:

Hey beautiful, thinking of you... How about dinner tonight at my place for a change. The address is 522 W 29th Street #10B, New York, NY 10013.

I type:

Okay, I'll see you after work, sexy. And we can explore what exactly you've been thinking about.

I don't know why I text that, but it sounded sexier in my head.

I'm corny sometimes, but I'm out of practice...

My thumbs hover over the screen of my phone, as I stare at the second alert... text from Monty:

I don't dare to press on it, closing out the iMessage and then my phone altogether.

"Hey Lisa, are you well?"

Looking up, Adrian is standing in my doorway... I'm not sure how longs he's been there.

"Yeah," I say quickly, slamming my phone down, hiding the screen as if he'd just caught me watching porn on it. "I'm just finishing up for the day. Answering some emails and finishing up before the weekend."

He smiles.

"Any plans?" He asks. "Or are you just going to work all night too?"

"Yup, seeing Dante tonight."

A look of relief washes over his face.

"He is a mysterious yet intriguing man — I realized that at the party the other night, I see why you like him."

"Well, he keeps me on my toes?" I smile, fighting back my tears. "What about you?"

I try to pay attention to his answer, but the thought of Lamont's unanswered text is rattling through my brain like an itch I desperately want to scratch.

I spend the rest of the day monitoring my emails... sending more out. Work keeps my mind off of Lamont...off of Kira. Off of Chloe. As the day draws to an end and night closes in, my smartphone buzzes a few more times — more texts from Lamont. There was a time I'd jump to hear from him. Longing to listen to his voice on the other line.

Even after he married his wife, Natalie, he called me almost every day. He even called on their wedding night. And I used to love how much I was on his mind. But now — I don't want to see him — hear him or think about him anymore.

At 5:49 p.m., I step out of my office building to a warm surprise. With a single red rose in his hand, Dante's waiting for me, and the passenger door is open, inviting me in for a ride. Seeing it immediately makes me feel better. And all I can do is smile as I approach him.

"I missed you too much, and thought I'd give you a ride." He flashes his perfect smile. "Did you miss me too?"

"More than you know."

****

Walking in Dante's condo, I'm impressed with the meticulous design. I say little as we drive through the city. Once at Dante's place, we take a private elevator, exiting out and entering his enormous foyer.

"Impressive," I smile, trying not to show just how impressed I am. "How many rooms?"

"Four bedrooms and three baths." He almost sounds embarrassed.

"Why so many rooms for one person?" I flirt, exploring the place further. "And you teased me about my apartment?"

"I know."

There are expansive floor-to-ceiling windows in the living room that overlooks the city and an elegant gas fireplace with a marble slab.

Everything is so spacious, and there's a terrace with spectacular views of the entire city. It makes me question why he'd come to my apartment when he has this to come home to.

"Why—"

"Why, what?" He steps closer.

"Why did you spend all of those nights at my place? When—"

"Because it's where you felt the safest." He kisses my forehead gently. "I didn't want you to be uncomfortable."

We step into the massive kitchen, and Dante has a bottle of wine.

"What is this?" I'm shocked at the lavish display before me.

The dining room table is beautifully set up for two with candles and silverware. The enormous room is dimly lit, and the soft sounds of Kenny G are humming in the background.

"I thought that after the other night, you could use a little spoiling." He smiles. "With fewer unwanted interruptions."

"Are you cooking" I kiss Dante's cheek gently, grateful for his thoughtfulness as his arms wrap around me tightly, pulling me closer to him.

"Oh no, I would make too much of a mess. Chef Marco is cooking a five-course meal for us... dessert included."

"Hmm," I tease. "I love dessert. And I'm sure we'll have dessert after Chef Marco leaves."

Dante's eyes grow dark with hunger, but for me and not food. He pulls me closer, kissing my lips hard and passionately. His erection already presses against me within a few minutes of being in his arms.

"Careful now. If you keep that up, we won't make it through dinner."

"I know." I smile, catching my breath.

A knock at the door interrupts the intimate moment; I get comfortable as Dante opens it, allowing Marco to enter with several bags of groceries in tow.

We settle down at the table as Chef Marco pours us two glasses of wine, and I help myself to several glasses before the appetizers are served. I take a bite of the Pan Roasted Sea Scallops that are perfectly cooked.

"Wow, I think this is the best scallops I've ever had?" Dante says as if reading my thoughts as he compliments Chef Marco.

"How was work?" I ask, knowing the answer.

"It was a good day." He smiles. "I made some good profits."

I devour the rest of the appetizer, surprised that he even answers me.

"How was your day?"

"It was a day," I smile, not wanting to get too much into it.

"I understand."

The next meal is soon served… Butternut Squash Glazed Black Cod.

"Well, what do you think?" Dante smiles, cutting into his Cod. "Did I do good?"

"More than you know," I answer. "I skipped lunch, so I am grateful."

Dante shakes his head, thinking about the many reasons I might've missed eating all day long. But usually, I don't eat. My diet consists of the menu at Dead Rabbit and the variety of beers and liquors on their shelves.

"You need to take better care of yourself, Lisa. What you're doing to yourself isn't healthy." He lowers his head.

"I'm a work in progress."

"Aren't we all?" he smiles.

I finish my last bite of the Squash, feeling completely satisfied.

"I got a call from that reporter, Chloe Roberts." I finally confess, speaking low enough that only Dante can hear me. "She wants to write a book or something about my 'story.' she also told me that one of Lamont's victims is in the hospital."

"What?" Dante's gaze fixates on me. "That's terrible. Is the woman okay?"

"I don't know." I lower my gaze from his. "I hope so."

He sits back, gently placing his fork and knife on the plate. "What about the other thing the woman talked about... the book? What about that?"

"I don't know, Dante," I sigh, wiping my mouth with the napkin and leaning back. "I've spent my entire life running and trying to ignore my past. And all the things that have happened to me. Derek... Lamont... and the other sins of my past. I don't know if I want people to know about that."

I pause, sipping on more wine.

"I didn't want to come forward or get involved with any of this mess. I know I'm all fucked up, even though I appear that I have my shit together, and I'm not sure that I want to broadcast that."

"I understand that, Lisa. But what if your story can help someone else?" Dante wipes his lips with his napkin. "What if there is someone out there who's going through something similar and reads whatever this girl Chloe writes, and it helps them get through their trauma?"

I know he's right... but I'm just not there yet.

"I didn't turn her down." My body sinks into the chair's cushion. "I told her I would think about it."

"And will you?"

"You can ask her to leave you out of it, make it anonymous, and change the name of the characters. Promise me... Promise you will actually think about it... for me."

I exhale, rolling my eyes. "I promise, babe. Now, can we stop talking about this?"

We finish dinner, complimenting Marco's excellent work.

We've barely finished all of our meals before Dante ushers Marco out of the front door, thanking the chef for a wonderful meal as the elevator doors close.

The lights are still dimly lit as he walks into the dining room. Once alone, he turns towards me, his eyes looking at me with such hunger; I stop pouring the glass of wine, knowing what he wanted. I finish pouring two drinks and follow.

"Thank you for this beautiful dinner." I hand him a glass.

Dante takes a sip, barely giving the wine a moment to breathe, before placing the glass on the table. At that moment, all I can think about is how good he looks. His muscles pressed firmly against the black fabric of his button-up shirt. His face is still, but the intensity that fills his eyes calls me, telling me he wants me. His emerald eyes shimmer, projecting the sexual delights that are swirling in his mind. He licks his lips, drawing me closer.

"Come here." He murmurs. "I want you."

"You have me."

We will not discuss how our workdays were. Or talk about much of anything right now. All thoughts dissolve the moment his fingertips travel up my thighs and rest on my ass cheek. The way his eyes stare deeply into mine speaks volumes. He wants me, and I want him too; nothing else matters.

Now we're barely inches apart; my heart flutters, being this close to Dante, wanting him as badly as I do. My body melts under the heat of his touch. This man... my man... stands here before me like a beautiful Greek god. Towering over me, muscular and breathtaking.

All I can think about is taking him into the bedroom and adequately thanking him for dinner. For improving my day. For making me better. I reach up towards Dante's face, sweeping my fingertips over the short stubble on his chin. The muscles in his jaw tighten as his eyes grow darker, acknowledging the invitation.

"I want to fuck you," he says. "Right here... right now. I barely made it through dinner; I wanted you so fucking bad."

His eyes tell me how sincere his words are. He turns me around, leaning my body against the edge of the table, as he slowly unbuttons his shirt and pants.

"You drive me so crazy." Dante's voice is low. "You're making it harder and harder for me to be a gentleman right now."

"Who said you had to be a gentleman?" I smirk. Deep down, I have to admit, I don't want to be handled gently, and I sure as hell don't want a gentleman. Dante has been trying so hard not to hurt me and not lose me again, even when I tell him I won't leave this time.

I know it's still a fear of his.

He pulls off my blouse; I don't see where it lands, nor do I care.

"Kiss me." I lean in closer, and without hesitation, his lips crash into mine as he pulls me closer, and our bodies ignite together.

My heart pounds against my chest as our bare skin touches, and after another moment, I lose control over my body as it reacts to being near him. My desire causes my mind to fog. Everything about the day fades into the further regions of my mind, Chloe... Kira... the deal with Apple. It all means nothing. All that matters is my man and the pleasures about to come.

"Let me thank you for such a wonderful dinner." I smile.

I look up at him through my eyelashes as Dante traces the outline of my face with one hand. He smiles while undoing my bra, and my breasts spill free. His massive hand cups my breast, massaging them and playing with my nipple gently and sensually.

I moan softly in response to his touch. My breath inhales sharply as I bite my lip. Without warning, he lifts me up effortlessly and walks me into the living room, gently laying me on the couch.

"I want to fuck you so hard."

"Then what are you waiting for?" I ask playfully, slipping off my skirt and allowing it to fall on the floor.

Before I can say another word, this strong and powerful man lowers to his knees before me submissively, and I feel him remove my panties. His eyes never leave mine.

"You're so beautiful," he says.

The anticipation is almost too much to bear, feeling Dante taking control of me, seizing my thighs as his head disappears between them.

I beg for more, and he skillfully gives me what I want, pleasure. His tongue sends shock waves pulsing through me. My body tenses in response.

Muscles tighten as I can barely take it anymore. He is driving me fucking crazy, and he knows it.

As I climax, tidal waves of sensations and emotions bounce from every cell in my mind and body. I can hardly breathe as Dante steadies his grip on my thighs, holding me and keeping me in position on the couch.

"Dante!" My breath is shallow.

"I know, baby," he smiles, looking up at me. "I know."

He rises to his feet and postures in front of me with a noticeable erection. Then leans over me and kisses my breast with his scorching lips, knowing that I want more.

"You taste so good to me."

He breathes against my skin.

"Dante, I—."

The words can't seem to form sentences as he continues caressing and fondling me.

I fight the intrusive dark thoughts trying to creep their way into my forethoughts and ruin this moment. I fight to stay in the moment there with him. And erase all the doubt in the pit of my chest. The fear of intimacy is a constant struggle. Sometimes I can overcome it, and sometimes...I can't.

"I'm sorry."

"Don't be," he pauses. "Do you want me to stop?"

I hesitate a second, just to collect myself.

"No."

"Are you sure, Lisa?"

"Yes."

I concentrate on him and only him, and soon the thoughts retreat into the darkest corners of my mind.

"I'm okay, Dante." I sit up, kissing him softly, thankful that he can control his dominating tendencies like a light switch when I need him to. His lips consume mine. And the taste of his tongue pulls me right back into the moment once again.

There are moments when Dante can be too much and too controlling, but he only pushes me to the edge and never crosses the line. I like it when he takes control, even when it makes me feel uneasy. It's like his twisted mind knows how to tame my twisted mind just enough to fulfill my dark desires.

"Are you still with me, baby?"

"I'm still here."

Dante grins, unzips his pants, and discards them on the floor next to the couch with my consent and reassurance.

Then he positions me on the edge of the cushion, with my legs wrapped around his waist.

"Are you ready for me?"

Without question, my body screams, 'yes.'

He straightens, then slides his hard sex into me, slowly inching deeper inside of me.

"That's it," He exhales as if a sense of relief washes over him. "You feel so good."

I close my eyes, inhaling sharply as my body accepts him, stretching with each slow and deliberate thrust. I feel the shock of heat rippling from between my legs as it spreads outwards through my body.

I cry out from the sensation of Dante picking up speed, sliding in and out of me with a quickness. Before I know it, I'm moaning and screaming out in uncontrolled and unbearable pleasure.

"Dante..."

My muscles tighten, trying to stay in the moment, distracting myself from the terrible thoughts of my past that are trying to creep up once again. I know it's only because I saw Lamont, and I don't want him tainting this moment. But it's harder today than it has been in a long time. And I hate it.

"Lisa, should we end this?"

"No," I blurt out.

Dante leans closer, pulling me towards him. His eyes search mine for reassurance again. I know he wants to continue... I do too, but I cannot.

"Don't stop Dante, please."

Dante does not move, still inside me, but hesitating.

"Lisa, I don't—"

"Dante... please, just fuck me."

Dante swallows hard and pushes inside of me again, reluctantly regaining his rhythm. My throat tightens, but I fight through it. I close my eyes and focus on the voice in my head telling me I'm safe and Dante won't hurt me... telling me to let go and allow my body to orgasm.

And I do just that.

"Dante, I'm cumming."

"It's okay, baby, let go." His breath is ragged as his thrusts increase to a punishing pace.

"Please..." My plea is weak. "Don't stop."

"I won't."

Every inch of my body ignites as I lose control of it.

This is precisely what I want, the pleasure... the release. It's what my body needs. I quiver and weaken under the pressure, no longer fighting to push back my dark thoughts. My muscles let go, and so does my mind simultaneously. No more struggling.

"Lisa, I'm—"

I gaze at him as Dante reaches his limits of pleasure and releases himself into me. His muscles tighten and stiffen as he struggles to catch his breath.

"I love you, Lisa."

I open my eyes, meeting his gaze; I love him too; I want to say it back, but at that moment, I can't.

He lowers, kissing me as if he understands the internal struggle that's swirling inside of me. Our lips sweep over each other, our tongues dance in a tango. And as the guilt sets in, I wonder if I will ever love Dante the way he loves me. I want to, but I'm so broken that I don't know if I'll ever let anyone in.

"I love you too," I say the words, knowing it's the right thing to say back, even though they feel hallow to me.

EIGHTEEN

My Nightmare:

It's Monty's birthday... He's having an extravagant birthday party and invites me, and as I get there, everything feels different and wrong. The music is deafening, reverberating through the walls of the house. Outside, the music can be heard from a block away. At least forty or fifty people cram into the giant four-bedroom condo inside.

With Monty's encouragement, I drink way too much alcohol and end up passed out in one of the spare bedrooms. But even with the door shut, the music vibrates and ripples against the walls. The air is so thick with the smell of weed and smoke that it chokes my lungs. I feel sick; the room is spinning. My body feels so heavy, and it's hard to move on the mattress. Nothing makes sense, nothing feels real, but one thing I know is that I want to go home.

Some time goes by, Monty wanders into the bedroom. He's furious that I'm leaving for college. I don't know where Katie is or if she's even at the party at all. I don't understand how angry he is until I feel the sting on my cheek from him slapping me. The force sends shock waves through me as he pushes my body up further on the bed.

"You can't leave me," he slurs, staggering towards me.

I try to get up, but there's no use. I'm too drunk, and he uses the force of his weight to pin me to the mattress.

"I'm sorry, Monty." My words slur.

"You can't leave me; I love you. You're mine. You're a part of me like I'm a part of you." He says. The words echo in the darkest regions of my mind.

But it wasn't like it usually was. Before I realize it, Monty is inside of me. He's not entering me vaginally, but he's in the other area, as my butt is in the air and I'm pinned down. There's nothing but pain, and I scream in agony, but the music drowns out my cries.

"You're mine," he says, drinking, violently pounding into me.

You're mine... you're mine... I'm inside of you. Feel me... I love you...

"Baby!"

I hear Dante's voice.

"Baby!"

The sound of Dante's voice pierces through the darkness and pain. Grabbing hold of me, pulling me back to consciousness. I jolt awake, fighting him, my arms flailing as I scream.

"Lisa! Wake up!"

"You're having a nightmare."

Dante raises his hands to protect himself from the frantic swings of my fists. My vision focuses; I see him sitting next to me, trying to comfort me and reassure me I'm safe. Even though I know he desperately wants to, he doesn't touch me.

"It's okay," he breathes in a panic. "You're safe... you're okay... it's just a bad dream."

I curl up towards the edge of the bed, grasping at sheets — the pillows — anything that will ground me and reassure me I'm awake.

"I'm sorry," I say, still in a panic but realizing I startled him awake too. "I'm so sorry."

My body is coated with sweat.

Dante, still holding his hands up as if he's trying to calm down a feral animal, tries to scoot a little closer.

"Please, don't." My body, still in fight-or-flight mode, hyper-reacts, causing me to gasp for air. "I can't—"

He respects my request, even though the confusion and pain are apparent in his bright emerald eyes. Slowly, he pushes his body away, giving me the space I desperately need. I watch him stand up, slip his boxers and T-shirt on, and sit in the chair next to the bed. The entire time, he never takes his gaze from me.

"Tell me what you need, Lisa?" Dante asks, raking his fingers through the tight curls of his hair. "What can't I do to help you right now? Let me help you."

He leaves the room for only a minute, returning with a glass of cold water, and sets it on the nightstand next to me. I eagerly and greedily gulp it down, nearly choking. Slowly, the images of my nightmare dissipate, and my current reality comes into focus.

The nightmares have worsened since all of this mess with Lamont started. The memories and pain feel so real that my body hurts.

After graduating a year early from Penn Foster and getting accepted to MIT, I spent two months in California before leaving. During my last year in school, Monty became increasingly possessive and increasingly violent. Thinking back to that night at his birthday party, all his rage seemed to pour out of him and purged onto me. When these accusations started, I thought I could handle them, but it's only bringing out things I want to forget… things about Monty… things about myself. Tears stream down uncontrollably.

Dante cautiously comes closer and gently wraps his arms around me. He doesn't squeeze me, just holds me. Grounding me. Comforting me. And at that moment, I crumble in his arms. Any strength or resolve I have is gone. My emotions are too much for me to deal with at this moment.

"I'm so sorry, Dante. I'm so fucked up and damaged and feel like all of this is my fault. What he did to those girls,   I—"

"No, baby," he says. "All of this is his doing."

"But if I'd just said something." My voice is dry and sounds hoarse from crying so hard, but I continue to sob. "I can't believe I let him—"

"Stop," he exhales. "You didn't let him. Lamont is a grown man… responsible for his own actions, just like the rest of us."

The pain is so intense my heart flutters in my chest. And it feels like it's tightening with every beat. The physical and emotional torment—trauma and humiliation are eating away at me like acid. I have ignored them for so long, and it's all building up within me.

Dante stays strong, being my anchor, my rock. His expression is dripping with concern, but I know he feels so helpless. And it's killing him.

"What can I do to help you, L? Just tell me. I'll do anything."

I can't speak through the tears. My head falls deeper into his chest.

"Please… tell me what to do."

It's a side of him I'm not used to seeing; as a Day Trader, he always seems so calm and in control. Now he sounds so unsure, almost like a child.

It's refreshing.

"Just stay," I breathe against his tear-soaked shirt. "Please, don't leave me... hold me until I calm down enough to fall back asleep."

I allow myself to feel the pain, crying and holding him tightly to me. I'm so thankful that Dante's here with me, but I'm embarrassed at having him see me this way. I've never been this vulnerable with anyone, feeling too afraid that I'd scare them off. But here he is, and it overwhelms me with more emotions than I can handle.

"You don't have to hide from me." He lays down on the pillow, cradling me as we lay there together.

"I love you," he says calmly.

"I love you." I exhale, feeling like I'm breathing for the first time, actually meaning the words as I say them. "You know that sometimes I can be difficult, but I'm trying to not push you away. It's hard sometimes."

Dante relaxes his hold, still keeping me close to him.

"I know. We all have our secrets and demons. But I am not going anywhere. Even if you ask me to. You're stronger than you give yourself credit for, Lisa. You've been through so much, and you're still here, trying to fight for happiness with me."

Tears flow again; I've been holding everything in for so long that crying almost feels foreign to me. I love Dante so much. He gives me strength, more than he knows. I don't want to let him go again.

"I swear, Lisa, no one will ever hurt you like that again." He squeezes me just enough. "I know I can't fix this with one fell swoop, but I will get you through this."

"I don't think I am fixable," I laugh through the tears.

"Then we will be broken together."

It's corny, but makes me smile for the first time since I woke up.

I breathe in, filling my lungs with his scent, calming my heart with each breath. My eyes hurt from crying, but the tears have stopped.

Our bodies intertwine under the sheets. Dante remains gentle and attentive to me and my needs. We lay there together... it's not sexual or tainted with any hint of sexual desire. It's just me needing him and him wanting to take care of me the way I need him to.

"I'm sorry, Dante," I whisper. "You deserve so much better than someone as fucked up as I am."

"Shut up." He smiles. "I'm here because I want to be."

He leans over, kissing my forehead with his soft lips, leaving a warm impression on my skin.

"Stop questioning why I am here." He sighs. "And stop thinking that I'm here because I want something from you. You will not scare me away. Don't hide from me...please. You aren't alone anymore."

He laces his fingers around mine as we drift back to sleep.

I love you, Dante...

After a few more hours of rest, I wake up again just before dawn. I leave Dante in the bed and walk into the living room. My phone has died because I forgot to plug it in after dinner and our sex marathon. Digging into my purse, grabbing the cord, I plug it in and check my messages. There are two from Katie and three from Adrian. And one unknown number.

Voicemail from Katie:

"Hey, I just wanted to call and see if you were doing okay. Please call me back. I'm here."

A text message from Adrian: I'm just checking in on the deal. Any recent news? I'm just anxious. Call me when you hear something.

I watch the sunrise over the buildings, showering the streets below with its rays of light. The images of my nightmare, still fresh in my mind, cause my emotions to feel raw.

"Hey, I got scared when I woke up, and you weren't there," Dante's voice echoes in the enormous living room. "Are you okay? Did you have another bad dream?"

He comes up behind me, embracing me and squeezing me against his bare chest.

"I couldn't sleep." I rest my head against him. "And you were sleeping so peacefully I didn't want to wake you."

"Oh, okay."

Dante spins me around, looking at me as if he's searching to see if I am really okay. "Are you okay?"

Last night scared him; I know it did. He felt helpless, and that's not something he's used to feeling. But I appreciate the fact that he's not treating me like I'm some fragile piece of crystal or glass.

"I'm fine," I smile. "At least I am now. I'm sorry for last night. I'm normally alone when I have my nightmares."

"Stop apologizing, Lisa." He exhales. "After what I saw last night. It just makes me admire your strength more. It was terrifying, and I can't imagine anyone going through that alone."

Even though he's understanding, I am still hard on myself for falling apart. It's hard for me to share anything with anyone, especially sharing a bed. Typically, I leave right after sex, not saying good night. It just feels too awkward for me. But I'm getting used to being here with him.

NINETEEN

Thursday, April 28th, 2016

It's been a few weeks since I last spoke to Lamont, and it's taking all the strength I have to not try to find a way to contact him. Or pick up the phone when I see an *UNKNOWN* number flash on my screen. His calls are less frequent in the middle of the last week of the month. I struggle with how I feel about that. There's a part of me who wants to know how he's doing. But the other part of me never wants to hear from him again.

By Tuesday of the following week, I realized there have been complete days that had gone by without a call from Lamont at all. Despite my anger for him, I'm saddened that he hasn't called. And a part of me worries if he may have gotten arrested. Or worse... By Wednesday night, I get an eerie feeling that stirs within me as I lie in my bed thinking about the last night we spoke in California.

****

June 7th, 2002

It was so hard to say goodbye…

I was all packed to leave and said my goodbyes to dad and Katie. They hugged me outside the house as I stood in front of my taxi. Katie whispered, "I'm proud of you. I can't believe you graduated an entire year early. And I love you," she cried as we hugged each other tightly.

I had to catch an 11 am flight to Massachusetts, and I would only have a week to get settled in once I reached the campus. Luckily, undergraduates were guaranteed four-year housing in one of MIT's dormitories.

I stared out the window of my taxi while riding to the airport. I wanted to soak up every moment I had left in the state. Slowly, a dull feeling came over me as I had an urge to see Monty before I left. We hadn't spoken since his birthday party, since he did those horrible things to me, and I'd been ignoring his calls. The things he did, was unforgivable. The pain he put me through...

Pulling up to his place, I got a feeling this was a bad idea, but I just had to see him one last time. Knocking on the front door, I felt like I shouldn't be there. But for the life of me, I couldn't explain why.

The door swung open violently, and Monty stood there with an icy stare. He looked like he had still been partying all week long. His eyes were bloodshot red, and there was a visible five o'clock shadow that he was sporting. His clothes were dirty, and it smelled like he hadn't showered in days.

I remembered thinking... He looked like hot shit.

"What in the fuck are you doing here?" He grunted.

"If you have to ask, then I don't know," I said to him, standing in the doorway. He doesn't invite me in, and I'm relieved. "I'm leaving for the airport now, but I wanted to see you."

Monty glared at me, staring through me as if I wasn't there at all. Then his bloodshot eyes looked behind me and down the street, searching for something or someone. He was completely paranoid. "Lisa, I've been calling you all fucking week. You didn't pick up, and now I don't want you here. What the fuck?"

"Fine," I said, turning back towards the taxi.

"No, wait, please. Come in, just for a few minutes. I'll take you to the airport myself." His voice sounded desperate.

After the last time, I was at his place. There was no way I would come in and be alone with him again.

"No, I should leave." I sighed. "This was a mistake."

Monty reached for me to grab my arm and tried to usher me inside, but I yanked my arm away from his grip. As soon as he realized I wasn't coming in, he slammed his hand violently against the door frame. I was still pissed at him for what he did, and coming into his place would only upset me again.

"God damn it, Lisa." He shouted. "Why? Why are you leaving me? Why do you have to leave now? Stay, and I'll buy you another ticket to Massachusetts tomorrow."

It was hard to say no, but I had to, for two reasons: I was afraid of him. And I didn't want to stay in this house again.

"I don't want to stay until tomorrow," my voice was flat as I took a step back in a defensive posture.

I stood my ground—feeling scared and like I'd made a mistake—but looking into his eyes almost made me lose my resolve. I crossed my arms across my chest, keeping my distance, while Monty glared at me. Leaning out the door. He looked around as if he was expecting to see someone jump out of the bushes with a camera. Then, quickly, he yanked me inside and slammed the door behind me.

Fuck...

"Look," he sighed. "I'm sorry."

"About what this time, Monty?" I hissed.

He shrugged his shoulders and rolled his eyes.

"Do you even know what you're apologizing for this time?" I asked, staying near the door. "Do you even remember what happened?"

"No... but I'm sorry for whatever is bothering you," his voice was dismissive. And he still wouldn't look at me because, deep down, I was sure he knew exactly what happened. "You haven't been answering my texts or calls for days. Now you're here telling me you're heading to the airport."

"You hurt me, Monty." I blurted out, tears pooling in my eyes. "You were drunk... too drunk to control yourself. You fucked me like I was one of your whores... like I meant nothing to you at all."

"What the fuck are you talking about?"

"Your birthday," I replied; my falling tears ran streaks through my makeup. "You pushed me on the bed, and... didn't care if I wanted it. And acted like I wasn't even there. You forced me... hurt me."

The words came out before I realized what I was saying. But that was the first time in our relationship I felt like a victim, and there was no love in the room that night. No love at all.

"You know that sometimes I lose control." The anger was visible in his voice. "Especially when I'm drunk. I was really drunk that night. I had a few too many shots of Hennessy. You know I go hard on my birthday. I was celebrating… but I was just so upset that you're leaving me. And I reacted badly."

"Reacted badly," I murmured, rolling my eyes at the fact that he was implying this was my fault because I was leaving.

I folded my arms across my chest once again, saying nothing.

"Oh, so what?" Monty blurted out, "Are you going to tell on me? Like you did with that other boy? Are you going to tell Katie and the police that I hurt you?"

The fact that he was even asking me disgusted me. There'd been so many times I had wanted to end things with Monty, knowing this was wrong. There were so many times my friends had asked me if there was something more going on between him and me. And I'd said nothing. So, for him to say these things to me was not only upsetting, but insulting.

"You know I won't say anything, Lamont."

"I'm just making sure that you know the consequences if you ever decide to." His voice was distant and cold. And the conversation sounded more like a threat than a warning to me. "Everyone will know what you have done. The police will get involved. News reports will post all the details all over the internet, and you will be tainted and branded for life."

Tainted for life? I thought. He's already tainted me for life.

"You'll be all over the news as well, Monty." I said in a low tone, carefully choosing my following words wisely, "Don't put this all on me. I'm not a little girl anymore."

Monty stared into my eyes; the anger intensified in his gaze. "I'm a famous athlete now... and rich. I have connections. If our secret ever got out. You will be the one who suffers... not me. Everyone always blames the accuser, not the accused. That's something I would've thought you'd learned after that mess with Derek. I'm sorry to say no one would ever believe you, Lisa."

Just to hear Derek's name sent a sting of pain to my heart like a hot iron poker. And the memories forced my eyes to close as I lowered my head in shame.

"How can you say that to me?" My voice was low. "I've never seen our relationship as bad. I love you... I always have and will. Even so, you treat me this way... even after you tried to convince me to stay."

I wanted to cuss him out, call him an asshole for treating me this way, for ruining me for anyone else. For years, I wanted to say that I'd walked around every day, scared that someone would see it. See the darkness he had implanted deep within me, marking me as broken forever. But I didn't because I had been a willing participant in this relationship since I was thirteen.

It wasn't fair to just blame Monty for all of this. He showed me things that I'd never experienced before and treated me like I was the most important person in his world. Now he was just scared because I was moving away, wanting the promise that I'd tell no one what we really meant to each other.

He wanted more with me, but knew that we would never have a future together. And in the end, he just wanted reassurance that what we did remained a secret in my life. But Monty was right about one thing. If the truth ever came out, it would ruin us both forever; nothing I do would matter after that.

"People will brand me as some kind of monster for loving you, Lisa," Lamont finally said. He looked down. "Because people just wouldn't understand. And I've worked too hard to get everything that I have now, and no one would understand what we share."

The tears fell freely from my eyes as I cried. It was an ugly cry as all the emotion, shame, and guilt escaped me. I looked down, quickly wiping away the tears, and tried to compose myself. But I couldn't. The truth was I love him, and I knew how fucked up that sounded, but I did. And I knew Monty loved me too, in his way.

"I will tell no one about us," I said in defeat. At that moment, he knew that he'd broken me. I had no more fight in me and yielded to his will... willingly.

"I just needed to hear you say it," he exhaled deeply. "And I'm sorry." He extended his arms, hugged me tightly, and kissed my tears.

My eyes were puffy, and my heart hurt. Knowing that I was still his, Monty wished me farewell. And told me he would visit me when he could. Deep down, I was so confused. I didn't know what had just happened.

One minute I was furious at him, feeling wronged and rightfully hurt by what he did to me. And in the next minute, I felt guilty and bad for leaving him at all.

"I love you, Lisa," he whispered in my ear. "No matter what happens, always remember that."

It wasn't until my third year at MIT that I saw him again. And that was when he told me he was getting married to Natalie Jennings, his fiancé.

****

Friday, April 29th, 2016

It's late and well into the night. My phone vibrates against the surface of the nightstand next to my bed. The noise jolts me awake; instinctively, I search for Dante, forgetting that he stayed at his place for the rest of the week. I lift my phone, seeing that it's 3:36 a.m., just as my phone buzzes in my hand. It's Katie. My heart sinks into my chest; the last time she called me in the middle of the night, it was to tell me that dad had died.

"Kate," I exhale, annoyed by the abrupt intrusion. "What's going on? Are you okay?"

"Have you seen the news, Lisa?" She cries uncontrollably into the phone.

"No, why?" I sit up in the bed, reaching for the lamp next to me.

"Turn on the news..."

I search through my phone, staring down at the screen, then inhale as I read the headline.

"Oh, no."

I press play on the newsfeed and listen, asking myself if I'm still dreaming. Or having a nightmare.

"I have to go." I quickly hang up.

BREAKING NEWS...

"Lamont Johnson has died after an altercation at a strip club, and shots were fired. Witnesses said they saw the former NFL star arguing with another gentleman inside the club, and once the fight spilled outside, someone Lamont was shot several times in the chest before the assailant sped away. The former NFL star, who had been recently accused by several women of rape and sexual assault, died at the scene."

"What the fuck?"

The tears fall before I even realize that I'm crying.

I stare at the screen, studying every word, praying that this is some sick joke. My jaw opens; I still can't believe what I'm reading. The authorities say that no one got a good look at the witness. And so far, no one has been apprehended. No one else was hurt in the altercation.

Murdered? Oh, Monty. I cry.

I don't know what to say. Or how to feel. The moment feels unreal. My mind can't form thoughts, trying to understand what I've just read. Guilt swells within me, wondering if I'd just picked up the phone and talked to him. Maybe this wouldn't have happened.

Soon Katie calls me again, still upset herself. I don't want to talk, but I know she needs me.

"Lisa, I don't know what to say." Her voice cracks. It's clear she's been crying too.

I swallow hard and exhale. Even though I want to break down, I am numb.

As she reads the news from the article word for word, I listen to her. I want to hang up the phone and shut it down, but I listen to her vent.

"They're saying that no one knows who this guy was who shot him... but Lamont was heavily intoxicated and rude to all the patrons at the club."

I try to listen to her, but Katie's voice seems to turn into background noise in my ears. And struggle to remember the last words I said to Lamont, but I can't. I just know they weren't pleasant.

He's dead? I can't believe it. My mind is racing with thoughts that are too fast to process.

Lamont is dead. My first love. The man who made me everything I am, both good and bad. This doesn't seem real. Nothing seems real. My heart doesn't want to believe what my eyes are reading or what my ears are hearing. I search the internet, praying that this is some kind of joke. But soon, the reality sets in, and I can't breathe as a sharp pain stabs my chest, and the room spins around me. I didn't want him in my life anymore, but not like this. Despite everything that they had accused him of and everything that happened between us, there were still genuine feelings that I had for him.

I stare into the space and the darkness in my room, trying to sort through what I'm feeling. A flood of emotions consumes me, suffocating me with each breath I take. I'm horrified.

I'm sad...

I'm angry...

And it's hard for me to admit, but I'm a little relieved...

The guilt of this new reality is more than I can bear, and as much as I thought the guilt and weight would be lifted, it feels heavier than ever before. As my eyes burn from crying and my heart breaks, all I want to do is talk to Monty one last time.

"Do you think they will catch the guy?" Katie's voice is low and stuffy. I realize that she's feeling what I'm feeling. Remorse and sorrow for a man who had been so significant in both our lives. "Do you think this has anything to do with the accusations against him?"

"I don't know." I sigh, letting out a breath I'd been holding in. "He'd been calling me for almost two weeks, ever since the party. But I ignored him. Then a few days ago, the calls stopped."

Katie sniffles and clears her throat. "I can't believe he's gone. This doesn't feel real. He did so much to help me when we were dating, more than anyone ever knew. Lamont paid for my college when dad couldn't afford it anymore because of gambling. And even after the shock... and anger I felt after you admitted what he'd done to you. As much as I hated him, I still cared about him, too. After all, Lamont was my first love, and you never get over that. I hate him, but I love him... how fucked up is that, Lisa? And those poor women that he hurt will never get their justice; it just doesn't seem fair at all."

Recalling the time Lamont told me. How much he was afraid of people finding out about him and the things that he'd done. It's fucked up, but I feel the same way that Katie does.

At that moment, I knew Lamont was self-destructing and spiraling out of control. So, it's no surprise he was drinking at a strip club and picking fights. All the allegations from these women were true. And I wonder, now that he's dead, would the media hate and persecute these women more now that he's gone.

"Are you going to be okay?" Katie finally asks, after an hour of crying into the phone. "I think I'm going to stay home today and sort through what I'm feeling. I haven't slept ever since I heard the news, and I'm in no shape to deal with my celebrity clients today."

"I'm fine." I lie. "But I don't think I'll be going into work today either. I'm just so tired."

Katie takes a deep breath. "I'm here if you need anything, Lisa. And I'm going to check on you a little later."

"Okay," I say, smashing the end call button quickly.

As soon as I hang up the phone, I immediately break down. All I can think about is how I don't care that it's barely morning; I need a drink. And after I go to the kitchen to pour myself a glass of Crown Royal, I climb back into bed, pull out my laptop, and search through every site I can find that mentions Lamont.

The story seems to stay the same; witnesses say Monty appeared intoxicated and was seen at a strip club. He stayed for a few hours until the owner kicked him out. Then, a few moments later, shots were fired, and they left Lamont dying in the parking lot. Slowly, more details filter in, and I read every sentence. I get halfway through the bottle of Crown before passing out on my pillow.

****

"Hey," a voice echoes in the darkness of my subconscious. "Baby, can you hear me?"

I will my heavy eyelids open, seeing Dante standing next to my bed.

"Oh my God, I just heard. Katie called me because she was worried about you and I've been calling you for hours. I see; you've been following the news."

"I'm fine." I wipe the crust from the corner of my eyes.

"I hated the asshole for what he did to you, but I wouldn't wish death on anyone. I don't understand any of it. Was it just some altercation or something else?" Dante sits on the edge of my bed.

"I don't know," I say, scrolling through the fifteen messages on my lock screen. "I don't know what to feel, but I'm okay."

"Bullshit, L." Dante leans in closer to me. "I know you're not okay."

I roll my eyes and stare at the emails on my screen. How can Dante know what this feels like?

"I'm sure you do," I snap back. "The truth is, I don't know what to feel. I'm just trying to get over the shock of it all."

"Well, I didn't know the guy." He exhales, "but my father physically abused me most of my life growing up, and I hated him for that. And yet when he died, I cried and was a mess for days...weeks."

He was abused? I think to myself.

It's completely new information to me. And now his domineering nature makes a lot more sense.
"I'm sorry that happened to you. But —"
Dante stands up.
"Christ, Lisa, don't tell me you are blaming yourself for any of this?"
"Dante, I don't want to talk about any of this —"
"Okay, but you will not sit here and feel sorry for that son of a bitch. Lamont made his choices, and he hurt you and so many others. I'm happy he's gone; maybe now he can't hurt anyone else. I'm sorry someone shot him, but I can't say that this isn't some kind of poetic justice."
"Dante, I said I don't want to talk about this. And I never saw Lamont and my relationship as something bad when we were together, so just drop it." I sigh. "I will not disrespect the dead; Lamont did so much for both Katie and me."
I sit up in the bed. "Now, if you don't mind, I need a shower, and I want to be alone today."
I know he wants to stay, but reluctantly, Dante leaves me alone. And the apartment feels cold and empty once again.
Damn you, Lamont. I should hate you so much, so why do I feel sorry for you? Why is my heart breaking? Why can't I breathe?

By noon, I'm good and drunk. Not wanting to talk to anyone, I turn my phone off. I never make it to the shower. I don't even manage to get out of bed. With the blanket firmly shielding me from the bright sun's rays, I lay in the darkness and cry.

I can't believe he's gone.

All-day long, the news of Lamont's death streams on the TV, from ESPN to CNN, to Twitter, etc. I ignore work and any incoming calls. I overlook the deal with Apple and all of my other responsibilities. A few months ago, I would've gone to the bar, picked up some random guy, and had sex just to fill the void, but I don't want to. I guess that's growth in a way.

One day goes by…

Two days…

Then three. And I'm still in shock over Lamont's death. I'm still so numb and dead to the world.

The clock on my phone says 4:23 p.m., and I've moved from the bed to the floor. I've set myself up on the floor next to my couch — with a bottle of Crown Royal, a two-liter Coke, and a glass. I pour myself glass after glass until the bottle is gone. Then stumble to the freezer and get another and repeat.

The news says the funeral is the following Monday. The coroner did an autopsy, but the report isn't in yet, nevertheless, they have arrested no one for Lamont's murder. I stare at my laptop, finally forcing myself to go over the details of my new contract with Apple. They're offering more for my app than what we discussed at the meeting. Ryan was a little off in his estimation of the offer. But I manage to go over all the paperwork and sign the contracts.

Suddenly, there's a knock at my door. The sound startles me, and I jolt.

"Who is it?" I yell out, looking through the peephole of my door.

"FedEx."

FedEx? I think to myself, questioning if I ordered something and forgot somehow.

I slowly open the door. There's a man in a FedEx uniform with a white envelope in his hand.

"Are you Lisa Rose?"

"Yes." My voice is dripping with confusion.

"Can you sign here, ma'am?"

"Sure." I scribble my name on the receipt.

"Here you go, ma'am," he smiles, handing me the large white envelope. "Have a nice day."

Examining the package, I assume it's from Ryan and Apple, and these are a copy of the contracts that I've signed. But as I read the postmark, it says from Lamont Johnson. My heart skips a beat, and the pain returns to my chest. It was sent out a week before Lamont was killed. Frantically, I tear open the envelope seal and remove the stack of documents inside.

First, there's a handwritten letter:

L,

I've tried to reach you for several days now. Even with my life falling apart around me, all I can think about is you. I know there's a darkness in me, and I will

250

probably go to Hell for all the things I've done. I'm a monster. But I loved you. I still do. And I always will. You knew all of me. You saw the darkness and still didn't run away. I'm so sorry that I hurt you and let my darkness consume you. And you still loved me, stayed loyal to me, even after I hurt you the way I did. I never saw what we were doing as a bad thing. To me, it was always beautiful and pure. My only regret is that I wish I'd never let you go.

Out of all the things I lost, losing you is the most devastating thing that's come from all of this. I'm sorry for all the pain I've caused you. And for what I did to the others...

Please, try to have a good life. Don't hold on to me or the darkness I've put into you. Enclosed are some documents for your eyes only.

Ever since I was drafted, I've been putting money into this checking account...for you. No one can trace it back to me, and I know this is far from making things right, but it's yours to do however you please.

I also enclosed a few other things. I don't know what will happen to me, but Lisa, I love you ... I only hope that one day you'll find it in your heart to forgive me, please.

Monty

The following document is a copy of his will and testament. Lamont left a checking account in my name, but he states that it's a charity in his will. The final balance reads north of eighty-five million dollars, reading the bank statements. Also in the package are old handwritten letters from me. He kept all these years, from when I was younger. His letter says it won't be traced back to him, so I'm safe, but why would he give this to me?

Oh, Monty... I can't believe he saved these...

I'm crying all over again.

TWENTY

May 12th, 2016

The following Thursday morning, when I walk into Nichole's office, she takes one look at me and says, "You're not doing ok. Are you?"

I try to raise my eyes to meet hers, but I'm so tired, and everything hurts. In truth, I don't even know how I ended up at the doctor's office. My days have been nothing but crying and drinking. I haven't spoken to Dante or Katie; I've only sent text messages so that they wouldn't drop by the apartment. Even standing in the doctor's office now, I'm unsure if this is real or a hallucination.

"It's been all over the news." Nichole's voice almost sounds relieved as she ushers me into her office and quickly shuts the door behind me. "I've been so worried about you, Lisa. I've left you several messages since the news broke about Lamont's murder, and I was getting so worried."

I try to speak, but my throat is so dry from the whiskey, and I'm so dehydrated. "I'm sorry. I didn't mean to worry anyone. I've just been so lost and confused."

She guides me to the leather chair, and I lower myself onto the cushions. "You're safe here, Lisa, you know that."

"Yes, I know," I say, almost in a trance-like state. "Thank you for seeing me."

Nichole sits across from me and waits for me to start; her eyes are filled with worry and concern as she inspects my disheveled appearance. I'm wearing sweatpants, and although I had a mind to shower, I did little else in personal hygiene. I'm usually well dressed, wearing a business suit with neatly pressed hair and flawless makeup plastered on my face. But I don't care today. I haven't cared for a few days now. Nichole has never pushed me before, but she mercifully takes the lead and starts the session today.

"Lisa," she sighs, placing her hand on mine. "I'm so sorry over what happened to Mr. Johnson."

I exhale, letting out a breath that I'd been holding for what seems like forever. "I can't believe he's gone."

The tears spill from my eyes, and for the first time in days, I feel a weight slowly lifting from my chest. "I'm sorry too. I'm just so confused. Lamont sent a letter to me... after all this time, he said he still loved me."

Nichole slowly leans back in her chair, caught off guard. "He sent you a letter? Before he was killed? Lisa, what did it say? If you don't mind telling me."

Slowly, I slip my hand into my bag, retrieve the paper, and hand it to her. I don't watch Nichole's expression as she reads it silently to herself.

"Lisa, I don't understand." She finally says, folding the letter. "Why would he send this to you, and why would he confide in you like this?"

"I don't know."

She waits for me to elaborate on my feelings, but I don't know what to feel; that's why I'm here.

"Lisa," Nichole switches the subject. "How much have you been drinking since you heard the news about Lamont?"

"A lot." I lower my head in shame. Several empty liquor bottles are scattered around my apartment even as we speak. And I know I probably reek of alcohol from every pore. "I have been drunk since Katie told me he was dead."

"Have you done anything else?" Her voice falls flat. "Any relapses?"

"I haven't left my house in days," I snap, folding my arms across my chest. "So, no, I haven't picked up any guys... or done any drugs or self-harming."

"Drinking can be self-destructive too, Lisa."

"Give me a break. I'm grieving. I know Lamont abused me," I say. "I know he hurt those other women. But all I can think about is that he's dead. I will never hear his voice again. And that hurts my heart so much that it feels like I can't breathe. It feels like I'm dead, too."

"I understand that you're upset, Lisa, but you can't forget the things he put you through?"

I nod and shrug my shoulder, my eyes fixating on the floor.

"We've touched on some things that you went through and the toll it took on you as a young adult. But the reality is that you will always have to live with the memories of what happened... and what he did." She speaks. "You were underage. Too young to consent. And although Lamont wants to romanticize what happened between the two of you. It was still sexual abuse and rape."

A part of me knows that. But I still hate that fucking word... rape. I just don't want to admit it or say it out loud. Because if I do, then it will taint everything.

"It doesn't matter now; he's dead."

Nichole's eyes blink several times behind the frames of her glasses. "Doesn't matter? Just because he's dead doesn't mean it doesn't matter. What happened to you matters... What happened to the other women he hurt matters."

I place the letter back in my bag and grab a tissue from the table next to me. Nichole searches for some sign of what I'm thinking. "Lisa, I know you don't think what Lamont did to you affected you, but it did. You've already told me you started doing drugs in college. And began sleeping around just to fill the void he left behind. You tried to kill yourself, sweetie. So, don't sit there and try to dismiss the things Lamont has done just because he's dead. You're still hurting... even now... whether or not you want to admit it to yourself."

"I admit it..." My voice falls flat, fighting the urge to cry some more, but the words still fight to say what I'm feeling. I still have trouble saying the words. "And admit Lamont hurt me. I admit that what we had wasn't love at all... to some people. I admit that —"

I can't say it...

"He raped you," Nichole says. "You can say the word... he assaulted and raped you."

Feeling like I'm going to throw up, squirming in my chair, I nod.

"But you thought it was love?" she adds. "You still want to believe it was love."

I don't answer.

I nod my head — yes. "Can we talk about something else?"

We move on, talking about something else, but I have difficulty keeping up with the conversation. The truth is, for a long time, I thought that what Lamont and I had was love—I fell in love with him. And I thought I was special to him. But it was all lies and dark secrets. The painful memories outweigh the good memories, now that I know better.

"Lisa?" Nichole's voice grabs my attention again. "May I ask, what are you going to do with the money he left you?"

It's something I'd been thinking about for days now.

"I don't know," I say. "I know I don't want it; it doesn't feel right keeping it. It feels like more hush money, like he used to give me before. And I have my own money thanks to this Apple deal; I don't need his."

I pause for a moment, closing my eyes.

"He raped those women." I finally say. "I can't help but think that if I would've said something all those years ago, this would have never happened to them. And for the last few days, I've felt more guilt about that than the fact that he's gone."

Across from me, Nichole sits in silence for a moment. "Wow, Lisa, I think that's the first time you've admitted that what he did to you was abuse. Although I know you're struggling to say the words outright."

"I'm sorry," I say. "I just don't see it as rape. And can't see it that way. But I can admit that sometimes I didn't want to sleep with Lamont. There were times that he hurt me and made me cry. And I felt like a fool

257

for continuing to see him, even after I found out that what he was doing to me was abuse and not love."

"Don't apologize; you were young, and he convinced you that you two were in a relationship." She replies, looking me in my eyes. Then she asks me about the first time I knew it was abuse. And what I felt.

Patiently, she waits for me to stumble and fumble through the details. I tell her about the time a friend, Rachel, told me about her abuse and how it sounded so similar to what was happening to me that I got angry. I talk about how I confronted Lamont about it—how he twisted the truth and convinced me that what we had was nothing like what Rachel had gone through. And how the relationship continued.

I struggle to talk about my feelings as we continue with the session and what being with him did to me. But deep down, Nichole appears to understand everything, even the unspoken words. I talk about being so drunk in college that sometimes I'd wake up in strangers' beds, knowing that I had sex with them, but not knowing the details. Nichole doesn't interrupt; she keeps listening as I confess more in one session than I have in the months we've been working together.

By the end of the hour, Nichole asks me if I felt any better—after getting all of this off my chest, and I do.

"You are stronger than you give yourself credit for," she finally says, hugging me. "few people could've gone through what you went through and been able to handle it."

Immediately, I think about Kira.

At one point towards the end of the session, Nichole says I've been holding on to so much for so long to protect him. And I had so much built up inside me that if I kept it all in, it would destroy what I've worked so hard to build now.

She's right... I've kept his secret for too long.

"The next several days... weeks, and months, you will have to be careful," she adds, "don't shut the people who care about you out. Don't hide from your feelings... and Lisa, leave the Crown and Coke alone for a while. You're drinking for all the wrong reasons, and it will only hurt you in the long run."

Leaving her office, I feel better than I've felt in days... months... years.

I can breathe again.

****

I give myself the weekend to grieve, deciding to return to my life on Monday.

I complete the deal with Apple and give everyone the afternoon off to celebrate. We have a long way to go before going public, but this is a significant first step. Without warning, my phone vibrates on the desk.

Dante: Missing you, it's taking all the strength I have not to leave work and kidnap you; I can't wait to see you tonight.

I'm startled when there is a soft knock on my door. My receptionist pokes his head through the opening of my door, as I thought everyone had left for the day. I text a smiley face and place my phone back on my desk, turning my attention to answering the several dozen emails in my inbox.

"Hey Lisa," he doesn't come all the way in, peeking his head through the partial opening in the door. "There is a woman here to see you. I told her you were in a meeting, but she's insisting that you talk to her."

"Did she give you a name?"

"Natalie Johnson."

Oh God, no... my heart leaps into my throat.

"It's okay," my throat suddenly feels dry. "I'll see her and hold my calls, please."

"Sure thing Ms. Lisa."

I fidget with my blazer and the wrinkles on my blouse, wishing that I'd ironed it this morning. After what seems like forever, a woman knocks twice and then enters. She's gorgeous, with long brown hair freshly done and a supermodel physique. She's dressed to kill, with her expensive Versace clothing and Louis Vuitton bag that screams, "I'm rich."

There is a presence about her that only a person who knows they look good would have. I watch Mrs. Johnson stride in and close the door behind her. Just from the way her eyes intensely stare into mine, I know immediately that she knows who I am, too.

"Miss Rose." She lowers herself into the chair across from me, sizing me up as she does. "I'm guessing you know who I am?"

Of course, I do; you're Lamont's wife.

But I don't say that; instead, I simply lower my eyes from hers and nod, like a child who got caught doing something wrong.

"And I know who you are." she places her purse on her lap. "Or at least I feel like I know you."

Fuck...

I listen attentively, waiting for her to tell me how much she hates me and how I'm so pathetic, but she doesn't.

Natalie tells me how she'd left Monty months ago, and he'd pretty much hid away from everything and everyone before he was killed. And she continues by adding that she's in the city for a few days visiting family after Lamont's funeral, and she just had to find me. A part of me is waiting for the other shoe to drop. Or for Nichole to make a scene, exposing me to everyone in my office and everyone who works for me. I wince at the thought.

"I'm sorry for your loss." I finally say.

"My loss?" She sighs. "It feels more like I should say that to you."

"Why do you say that?" I snap back, instantly regretting my tone.

I watch one of her perfectly sculpted eyebrows raise slightly.

In truth, I know all about Natalie. At first, Monty called several times when they first started dating. I don't know if he was trying to hurt me or make me jealous, but he succeeded in doing both.

In the beginning, I hated her because I wasn't her, and she had Lamont in ways that I could never have him... publicly. But in time, I cared less and less.

I want to believe that she doesn't know anything about Lamont and my recent conversations, but the fact that Natalie even tracked me down makes me think otherwise. What if she exposes me? What if she's here to confront me and ruin what I've worked so hard to build? What if she's recording this and wants to hold it over me later?

Get a grip, Lisa... What would blackmailing me do for her?

I'm sure she doesn't want to attach herself to any of this any more than she has to. I take a deep breath, wanting to believe I can hold my own and approach whatever is coming with a level head.

Another few minutes go by, and the tension in the air is stifling.

Finally, she says, "Can we meet up for drinks? Let's say in about an hour?"

"Sure." I stutter, "There's the Maze Bar around the corner that's the best bar in Manhattan."

"Okay." She abruptly stands. "I'll meet you in an hour."

I say nothing as Natalie leaves, dumbfounded that I was just sitting across from Lamont's wife. I finally exhale the breath I wasn't aware I was holding.

My phone rattles against the glass surface of my desk again, startling me with a jolt.

Dante: Lisa, are you okay?

I exhale, roll my eyes, and tap reply. It's not Dante's fault, but right now, he's distracting me when the last thing I need is a distraction.

I quickly tap out a reply: I was in a meeting. I'll call you when I'm done.

Dante: I'm just checking on you. I don't want you disappearing on me like you have been doing for the last couple of days. I'm going crazy, thinking about you being upset, knowing that there's nothing I can do about it.

Me: I just needed some time. But I'm okay now.

Dante: I'm leaving work soon. I'll be at your place within the next few hours. Or would you rather come to me?

I pause for a moment, thinking about the disaster I left in my apartment. I can't have it cleaned until Wednesday. I shiver at the thought of Dante walking into that hurricane of filth. How can I let him come over and see that? As seconds go by and I check my watch, I text back:

Dante, I'll just come to your place tonight.

My eyes lock on the screen of my phone, watching the time tick away. At a quarter past one, I look at the screen again, gather my things and leave the office. All I can think about is the uncomfortable conversation I'm about to have with the wife of the man I used to be involved with. My mind is riddled with a million questions about what Natalie actually knows. I corral my thoughts away and focus on how I will act and what I will say if she asks me specific questions about the past.

Around the corner, I see Natalie sitting in the Maze bar. Her back faces the window, so she doesn't see me just yet. I think about standing her up and just avoiding this uncomfortable moment altogether, but if she found me at my office. I know she could find me again.

Let's get this over with…

TWENTY-ONE

The Bartender calls, "Natalie!"

The server brings the drink over to the table just as I enter the bar. She lifts her eyes from the screen of her Samsung phone and acknowledges the girl at the bar. The shock on her face almost makes me instantly regret this.

"For a moment there, I didn't think you would come," she says.

"I'm sorry that I'm late." I sit down on the stool across from her. "It was hard getting away from the office."

I'm already thinking of ten million excuses and reasons to cut this little meeting short and leave abruptly, but I don't. Natalie sits and gently sips on the foam of her beer. Her raven black hair hangs over her shoulder as she leans forward. We say nothing at first as we study each other; she reaches for her glass and downs it, just as the server walks up with my whiskey and Coke.

"You didn't even go to the counter to order." Natalie says, "how — "

"I come in here all the time." I smile nervously. "They know my order by heart."

"I can't believe I'm sitting here with you," she says.

I'm not prepared for this. I don't know what to say or even feel about this situation. If you had told me, I'd be sitting at a table with Lamont's wife a week ago. I wouldn't have believed it. I don't know where to start... the adrenaline surges within me, causing my hands to tremble.

"I'm sure you're wondering why I wanted to meet you," Natalie finally says. "I'm questioning that myself at the moment."

"How was the funeral?" I ask, sipping my drink. "I saw pictures on the news."

"It was sad." She sighs. "A lot of crying."

Natalie pauses for a moment, zoning out.

"So, Chloe Roberts has been trying to get an interview with you," she says. "She keeps calling me about you."

"How do you know about that journalist?" I ask, on full high alert.

"I'm sorry that she ambushed you at your office," Natalie adds. "She shouldn't have done that. I told her to be respectful."

"You told her?" I snap, confused. "I told her I had nothing to say to her. Then she told me that something private had been leaked on the internet. I don't even know how she found me."

"I'm sorry, Lisa. Really, I am. I told Chloe about the text messages and emails." Natalie's voice is low, like she feels guilty. "I'm the one who found the phone and discovered the messages. Then I contacted Chloe. She's my cousin."

"Wait? You found the phone and the messages?" I lean forward, trying not to make a scene. "That's how you knew about me? And you gave them to her to do what with?"

Natalie's eyes meet mine.

"I just wanted to be left alone," I say. The tears form in the creases of my eyes.

Fuck… I'm so tired of crying… I think to myself.

"I knew Lamont had loved someone before me."
Natalie continues. "I thought it was your sister...
Katie. Never in a million years did I suspect it was
you."

She finishes her beer, but I don't finish my drink.
I can't shake the feeling that I'm about to throw up.
And I want to leave, but fear grips me. I have to know
what she plans to do with this newfound knowledge
about Lamont and me. And if she knows about the
package he sent.

"So, you know," I say.

"I do," she replies.

The sounds of bottles clanking and soft whispers
in the background distracts me for a moment. The
beer tap spits, and every few minutes, someone walks
up to see if we need anything else. I don't answer,
staring out the window as I process this conversation.

"So, you and he started when you were a—,"
Natalie pauses, with a sad look in her eyes. "That
must've been awful. I can't believe he would do that
to a child."

I lower my gaze, staring at the half-finished glass
of whiskey in front of me. I feel myself slipping away,
distancing myself from the thoughts and memories.

"I'm sorry," she says. "I'm sorry about giving that
information to Chloe."

It's clear to me now Natalie's just as nervous as I
am. I notice her hands are still shaking in her lap, her
eyes looking everywhere but at me. I don't
understand why she's nervous when I'm the one who
should feel ashamed.

"It was in the past. It had nothing to do with you.
So, why did you give what you found to Chloe in the

first place?" I ask. "Were you trying to hurt him... or me?"

Natalie flashes a nervous smile and exhales. "I don't know," she shakes her head. "When I read those messages that the two of you shared, I was angry and disgusted. I'd heard rumors when Lamont and I started dating... rumors that he liked to get carried away with women sometimes. But I never thought that he'd have a relationship with a teenager. I couldn't stomach it. And felt sick to my stomach... I still do when I think about what you must have gone through. I didn't know he was like that."

I shake my head, trying not to think about the details. "No one knew," I speak. "I kept it a secret until it got leaked on that website. Then my world imploded, and suddenly, my family and friends knew everything and started asking so many painful questions."

"I'm sorry. I didn't mean for any of that to happen." She glances at the screen of her phone after placing a credit card on the bill that the server left on the table.

"When the other women started accusing Lamont of doing those horrible things," she adds. "I defended him and believed him when he said they were lying. But then I found that phone... those texts and emails. I saw a different and more twisted side of him. There it was, the truth. It was staring me in the face, and I felt like I had to make him pay for what he did... to you... to those women... and me."

Natalie holds her phone up and taps on the screen.

268

"I only wanted to expose him," she says. "I didn't think about how it would affect anyone else." She sips on her Budlight. "Okay, I'm just going to just ask. When did it start?"

It's not something I'm ready to share with her. I don't want to answer, but she deserves the truth. "I was thirteen," I say. "It's hard to say how it started. I just know it finished when I went off to MIT. Then I didn't hear from him again until he told me he was getting married... to you."

"I thought that knowing would make me feel better, and once I saw you, I would feel differently, but I don't," she says, "I always wondered what Lamont was like before he met me, and now, I wish I could forget it."

I fight with the whiskey twisting in my stomach, smiling uncomfortably as I listen to this woman justify her reasoning for almost ruining my life and digging up things I've tried to forget for so long. I had left Lamont in the past. And now, she's the reason for the chaos that's been wrecking my life for the past few weeks.

"I didn't mean to hurt you," Natalie continues. "I gave the information to Chloe because she said that she wanted to write a story about his victims. Despite that, I was wrong—so, so wrong. I didn't mean to traumatize you all over again."

I ask, "So, did you know your cousin contacted me again, wanting to write a book about my story? Were you in touch with her when she called me about that?" I nod, listening to her apologies.

I already know the answer—Natalie lifts her eyebrow and replies, "I know Chloe is a talented writer, and if she thinks your story could help other victims, then she isn't bullshitting you."

"I told her I would think about it," I say. "But it seems in poor taste now that Lamont is dead."

"You think this is over because he's dead?"

I want to say yes, but I know it isn't true.

"Did you know your husband sent me a letter?" I ask. "He called me a few weeks before he was murdered. I told him I didn't want to talk to him anymore. He tried to reach me again, but I never picked up the phone."

She leans forward; the table rattles. "I know. I know everything. And to tell you the truth, I'm glad Lamont's dead... that means he can't hurt anyone anymore."

I know Natalie's angry with him, but the hate that oozes from her frightens me. It's like all the love she once had for Lamont was dead.

"Yeah, I don't want to think about Lamont anymore after today." She gulps the rest of her beer down. Wiping her lips with the napkin.

"I'm sorry that he did those awful things to you," she adds. "And I feel sorry for the other girls too, but I'm done thinking about him and crying over him."

"I'm sorry." It's all I can get out.

"Can I ask you another question?" Natalie asks.

I nod my head — *yes*.

"Did he ever talk to you about me?" she asks.

My mind is racing and pulling in so many directions that it hurts. I reply, "I remember the day he met you. He called me and told me all about your first date. I don't know if he was trying to make me jealous, but he did."

"He did?"

I blink, staring into my glass. "I knew you were special to him. Because he couldn't stop talking about you...."

Natalie smiles slightly, and it tells me that no matter how much she hates Lamont, a part of her still loves him, too.

"I remember the day he called me and told me he proposed to you. He was so happy... I'd never heard Lamont sound that happy before."

"So, you knew about me?"

"Of course," I say. "And I was happy for him... and you. I knew I could never be with Lamont the way he wanted me to be. It would raise too many questions, and I didn't want to hurt my sister. I could never be to him what you were to him, Natalie. I was his dirty little secret, and you were his world..."

Natalie looks at me with tears in her eyes. "You were so young... when he—"

She tells me how Lamont once confessed that he had a true love before her. He told her the truth about me but neglected to say that I was thirteen when we started a relationship. He called me his first love, said he loved me, but it didn't work out, and he never told Natalie the real reason.

"I spent years trying to move out of your shadow," Natalie confesses, her voice falling flat. "And when I learned the truth and discovered how fucked up, and sick Lamont really was, our entire relationship felt like it was a pile of lies. Once the other accusations came to light, I knew that he'd never stop, and in a way, I became just another one of his victims... and I felt like I needed to do something."

Natalie explains how she eventually stumbled across some old boxes that Lamont was still holding on to. It contained letters, emails, and pictures of me—that she went through; at that moment, she decided that this would be the evidence that could make Lamont pay.

"I just assumed that you would want him to pay for what he did to you, too." She sighs, sliding her phone into her purse.

"I never thought about it," I say. "I'm over it. And I'm trying to move on with my life the way he did."

I stare down at the floor.

"Did he ever force you?" The question came out of nowhere. "I mean, when he got extremely drunk, did he ever have sex with you? Forcefully?"

I shake the painful memories away. "Lamont was a different person when he got drunk. He would do things and not remember anything when he sobered up."

Natalie leans back in the chair. "I understand and can relate." She says. "I could hardly recognize him when he was drunk... he wasn't the man I married. But now, I know I never truly knew him, not like you did."

"I'm sorry."

"So, what exactly are you going to do now?" Natalie shakes as if she's trying to forget some things herself. She exhales and rolls her eyes.

"What do you mean?"

"You know..." Natalie looks around the bar as she orders another beer. "Are you going to come forward? Tell your story?"

"I don't know," I reply. "I don't see the point. Especially now that Lamont's dead."

"It could help others. Lamont's other victims."

"And how does adding my story to theirs help anything at all?"

Natalie tilts her head and takes a gulp of her fresh glass of beer that the server barely sets down. I've had enough of this conversation and only want this to end so that I can meet up with Dante.

"These girls think that they're alone. And the media has been so awful to them. That one poor girl is in the hospital. You were his first… your story could empower them. Or comfort them. Maybe even help them heal."

I think to myself. I don't want that kind of responsibility. Nor did I ask for it.

"But Lamont is dead. These women will never get the justice that they deserve. Trust me, the saying that time heals all wounds is bullshit. The truth won't help anyone. I speak from experience."

Natalie sighs and slams her glass down. For a second or two, all eyes are on us.

"I just want to forget the past," I say. "The memories haunt me every day, but I'm finally trying to move on."

She closes her eyes and inhales. "I can't imagine what you or these other women have gone through. I just remember those nights when Lamont was too drunk to care whether he was hurting me. I remember how helpless I felt in those moments. And it angers me. I think you should call my cousin and just share what you went through. Even if she doesn't publish it, it could help you too."

Natalie shares with me that Chloe was assaulted in college, how she was the only girl who spoke up and exposed a particular frat house for their sexual harassment and abuse of the women on campus. Chloe's article led to several arrests and indictments of the boys on campus. Her courage helped several other women come forward.

It gives me a better understanding of Ms. Roberts and why she's so adamant about telling my story.

"We've all been silent for way too long," Natalie finally says. "there are people who knew that Lamont was like this. And they decided they would rather protect him than get him some help. Money can make almost anything go away, I'm sorry to admit."

I assume she means members of his NFL team, perhaps the coaches and his agent, but no one will admit anything or ask the hard questions.

"Powerful men always have people who can clean up their mess."

"Is that what you think?" I ask.

"No, I know this," she says. "Someone needs to speak for the survivors."

"You think that there might be other women?"

"Yes. I also think that Lamont getting shot wasn't a coincidence." Natalie cups her hands around the beer bottle, pulling it up to her lips. "Lamont normally had an entourage of people around him, but that night, none of his people were with him... not even his bodyguard."

I listen as she continues. "I just don't believe that some random person just ran up and shot him."

She takes a breath, exhaling deeply.

"Look, you can remain anonymous, if you want. My cousin won't betray your trust. Fuck, she quit after her computer got hacked at work, and those messages got leaked. She will protect you. I know she will. She'll do it because she knows how it feels to be alone and scared. Lisa, what you went through... shouldn't be a secret."

I lower my head. "I'm afraid."

"I know it's scary," she adds.

"No, you don't understand," I say. "I'm afraid that if I talk about it... it will destroy this life that I'm trying to build. I may lose everything."

"You were thirteen," Natalie says. "What he did to you... no one should ever go through something like that. There are girls out there right now, confused about what's actually happening to them. They are asking themselves if this is abuse or love? Should I tell someone or not? Am I alone, or will someone understand?"

And with that, the reasons and excuses I had not to do this melts away. I remember being that confused girl. I remember having this big secret that controlled my entire existence. It's scary to think that other girls and women can go through something similar every day. I have often wondered what my life would've been like if I'd never met Lamont at all. Maybe I wouldn't be so fucked up. Perhaps I would be happy.

"Like I said, Natalie," I sigh. "I'm thinking about it, and I will call Chloe soon. Now, I'm sorry, I have to go."

I pay my tab and follow her out of the bar, outside. Dante is parked on the curb, waiting for me, to my relief. I had texted him after my third drink and asked if he could come and get me. Outside, I watch Natalie stumble into a cab before climbing into Dante's BMW i8.

"You want to tell me what that was about?" Dante asks, climbing into the driver's side seat. "I thought you were standing me up again. I thought..." He takes a breath and starts the car.

"Are you okay? Who was that?"

"That was Lamont's wife."

"Oh fuck," he says, "So, you aren't okay."

"I'm fine," I exhale, feeling thankful that things went a lot better than I expected. "Natalie just confessed that she's the one who found my old messages and gave it to that reporter... who is her cousin."

"What the fuck?"

"I know," I continue. "She says that if I tell my story, it could help the other women who accused Lamont. That more people would believe them if I could prove that he'd been doing this long before he was famous."

"I agree you should tell your story, but only if you're ready."

I know Dante wants to know more, but he doesn't press the issue.

"She also wanted to know when was the last time I saw and talked to Lamont before he married her and if I knew about her."

"Did you tell her the truth?"

I sigh, staring out of the window. The buildings sweep past the window in a blur. It's late, and I'm exhausted.

"No," I admit. "The truth would only hurt her more."

TWENTY-TWO

I stare out the window, replaying the conversation I just had. My anxiety is so high that I'm close to having a full-blown panic attack. Dante doesn't say much, guiding the BMW i8 through the streets. The city is tranquil, making the silence between Dante and me even more awkward.

Minutes later, I feel the car pulling into the underground garage of Dante's condo. The fluorescent lights burn my eyes as they whip past the car. The second he pulls the car into a parking space, Dante kills the engine and looks over at me. I know he's been so worried about me the last few days, and I've been actively avoiding him.

"Do you want to talk about it?" He exhales, looking over in my direction.

I unbuckle my seatbelt, sliding across the cool leather seat next to Dante as he scoops me onto his lap and holds me in his massive arms. I fight the tears as I press my lips against his. The kiss is desperate and intense as I try to forget my feelings... the outside world, and all the pain that overwhelms me. He sweeps his tongue over mine, urging me to want him more and more. I moan softly against his lips. His soft tongue explores my mouth. Harnessing every painful thought I have, I focus all of my attention on the heat between us and my desire for him.

"If you keep this up," he breathes. "We won't make it upstairs."

"I don't care."

I rake my fingers through his hair, gripping him hard, pulling him closer to me.

We separate barely as Dante pulls away.

"I love you, but I don't want to have you here in the car," he says, realizing we don't have the privacy that we thought.

"Okay," I murmur, spreading my legs slightly, allowing him to see the color of my Victoria's Secrets lace thong.

"Damn it, Lisa."

Dante's eyes darken. He slides his hand eagerly up my thighs in between my legs and grabs me. I kiss him harder, biting his lip, aware of the ache between my legs and how much I want this man.

"I've missed you these last few days," he says, his grip tightening on my hip. "I was going crazy when I didn't hear from you. I almost came by your apartment, but I wanted to give you space."

"I missed you too." I moan. "Thank you for caring... And the flowers. And the phone calls."

I lick his lips, teasing him, feeling his erection pressing against me.

"Lisa—"

"No more talking," I reply. "Take me upstairs and fuck me."

We barely make it to the elevator. The fire rushes over my skin with anticipation of what's coming. I hadn't seen Dante since before Lamont had died. And for the last few days, I've been alone. Dante kisses me wildly, pressing my back against the back of the elevator. Without warning, he pauses and looks at me.

"Lisa... don't you want to talk?"

"Talk about what?" I catch my breath, feeling the mood souring by the second.

"About everything." Dante stammers. "About Lamont. His death. Natalie. How you are feeling."

My breath rushes out, heat fills my body, both from desire and anger. All I can feel is my flush cheeks. My heart flutters with anticipation, but I want to fuck, not talk. Or feel.

I shrug.

"I'm fine, Dante," I sigh. "I just want to be with you at this moment... is that okay?"

"I want to be with you too, Lisa." Dante rakes his fingers through his hair and walks into the living room. "Damn it, L."

"What?"

Now, I'm annoyed. I can't deal with this now. I don't want to. Right now, I can't take much more from anyone. I'm hanging on by a thread... a thin one.

"Just talk to me."

"I don't want to talk, Dante."

"Then what do you want?"

"I want to feel good," I reply. "I want you to make me feel good."

"You can't fuck away your feelings, Lisa," he finally yells in anger. "I want you to feel you can confide in me and allow me to be here for you. I love you, and I need you... I need you to allow me to help you."

"You are here for me, Dante. You're here with me now."

I come closer, embracing him.

"I'm not pushing you away." I finally say. "This isn't like before. I just need some time to think about everything that's happened. And sort through my feelings. I don't know what I'm feeling. A part of me is relieved that Lamont is finally gone. But I can't deny that the little girl in me is grieving and misses him. I know how fucked up that sounds. But Lamont has dominated my thoughts for too long. So when I'm with you... I just want to be with you."

I pause, grazing my lips over his.

"Sometimes, you are my distraction from everything," I smile. "But in a good way. You feel like home to me. When everything in the world is going to shit, you are my haven... you always have been, Dante. And that scares me sometimes."

Dante's eyes darken, and his gaze grows intense. I'm out of my clothes within a heartbeat, and they fall to the floor. And just like that, he's back in the moment with me, his hands cup my breast, massaging them gently. Within moments, my nipples are hard and sensitive. I moan softly as his lips kiss around the sensitive tips of my nipples. The chaos of the world slips away, becoming white noise in the back of my mind as I get lost in his touch.

"You're my haven too, Lisa."

My fingers fumble with his shirt, tugging the buttons as the adrenaline causes them to tremble. Dante unzips his pants, freeing his erection as his pants fall to his knees. I bite my lip hard as he lifts me and takes me into the bedroom.

Dante hooks my leg over his hip with no time to waste and positions himself between my legs. And slowly eases inside of me as my body eagerly welcomes him. The one thing I love about him is Dante knows when to go slow and when to push me to my limits. Further and further, he eases deep within me, penetrating my soul.

My head sinks into the surface of the pillow, letting out a soft moan as he fills me completely.

"Dante." I breathe.

My body pulses around him as my legs quake and tremble. My fingernails dig deep into the sheets as he pulls me closer to him with each thrust of his hips.

"Fuck, I love you so much, Lisa. I've missed you these last few days. I couldn't do anything else. All I could think about was you." He pins my body to the bed, pushing harder, pushing in deeper as his rhythm speeds up, becoming more relentless in pace.

I gasp for air. "Oh god, Dante... fuck."

Dante cups his hands under my ass without warning, lifting my body slightly. He maneuvers deeper inside, pushing against my core. The pressure of his erection and his powerful strokes pushes me to the edge of all reason. My body tenses with ecstasy, and I unravel under the pressure. I'd been thinking about him for days, too. Although, I don't want to admit it out loud. I crave him like an addict who craves a drug.

"I love you, Lisa."

His words are sincere and drive me wild. I quiver around him again instantly and moan loudly. He's deep, and I love it.

"I love," I reply, barely getting the words out through his punishing thrusts.

The friction of our bodies and the passion between us overwhelms me once again. Urging me to unravel for him again. I close my eyes. The orgasm is so intense that I leave my body in a euphoric way for a moment. My muscles tense, I tighten around him again, spinning out of control.

"Oh god!" My voice quivers.

Under his powerful thrusts, each one feels like a force of nature. I want more of him. I need more of him. I can't get enough. He doesn't stop, even after I've orgasmed for the third time.

"Fuck, Lisa!" I open my eyes, but my vision is blurry.

I surrender all that I am to him at that moment.

"Dante… oh, God. Oh, fuck."

I weaken as the ultimate climax creeps up, taking hold of me. I can't think of anything, as I lose myself.

"God, I love you," he grunts.

He pushes a few more thrusts, and I cum with a scream. As he climaxes too.

"Lisa!" His hoarse voice lets out a dry moan. As he pulls me closer, collapsing next to me on the bed.

My head is spinning, or perhaps it's the room. My legs feel so heavy that I can barely move them. Dante holds me close, laying his head on the pillow next to mine.

"Fuck, baby. I've missed you."

"I can see that."

He laughs. "I can do this all night."

I smile at the thought of it. "You have me now, so let's make the best of it."

He smiles and cradles me in his arms, brushing a soft kiss over the side of my neck.

"Now, you do you want to do? I can make love to you all night. That's my vote." He breathes.

"Dinner," I whisper. "Isn't that what you promised me… dinner? I'm hungry."

"I'm hungry too."

I feel his erection pressing against my body.

"I'm hungry for food, Dante."

He smiles and moves away, slipping out of the covers in all of his magnificent glory. Then he scoops me into his arms and walks into the enormous bathroom.

"Not until we get clean first." He replies.

The water from the shower feels good against my skin. My legs feel weak, but Dante steadies me as he gently washes me with Dove body soap.

"I love you, Dante."

He smiles.

"I love you too."

We step out of the shower together, but at that moment, Dante pauses and looks back at me as I wrap myself in the towel.

"Lisa, I'm curious." Dante exhales. "Why did you lie to Natalie about the last time you saw Dante?"

I hadn't thought about the conversation, not until the question left his lips. Then reality comes rushing back.

"Dante," I sigh, feeling my eyes getting heavy from exhaustion. "Can you do me a favor?"

"Anything."

TWENTY-THREE

It's my Friday, May 20th session with Dr. Nichole Owens, I've been seeing her alone for the last several months that we've been working together, but for the first time... I'm bringing a guest.

At first, I didn't want Dante to come and see me being this vulnerable, but the other night made me aware of how much I wanted Dante — my boyfriend, to be there for me. But neither of us knows where to go beyond that.

My trauma therapy only became beneficial when I truly opened up to the processes. We walk into her office, and Nichole's office is a softly lit room with two armchairs instead of one this time. Nichole is inviting towards Dante as he walks in. His nervousness is visible to both of us. But I appreciate him being there even more than words can express.

"Dante Kingston," she smiles. "Welcome. I've heard so much about you. I'm glad that I can finally put a face to the name."

"Thank you." He smiles nervously. "In truth, I'm shocked that I'm here at all. Lisa is always so private about her thoughts and feelings... even with me."

"I know, but the fact that she's asked you here means that she trusts you," Nichole smirks. "Both of you, please, take a seat."

Today Nichole is wearing a subtle black pants suit with four-inch heels. I listen to them, the click-clack as she walks behind us and takes a seat in her chair across from us.

"Lisa." She shifts her body in the chair. "I must say that it shocked me when you called and asked to bring Dante to your next session. This is genuine progress."

I smile nervously.

"Dante,' she continues. "May I call you Dante?"

He nods.

"Okay," she continues. "I must warn you that this is a judge-free zone. I've worked very hard to make sure that Lisa feels safe here, and I don't want that jeopardized. You may hear things that may upset you, but I'm inviting you to speak freely... but respectfully."

"I understand." He clears his throat. "I just want to be here for her."

I've been nervous all week about what Dante would say or want to talk about in this session. I'm worried about being open and vulnerable. My depression and self-destructive habits are something I constantly struggle with, but I speak very little about the subject to anyone.

Together, Nichole and I have been working on it, but it's been hard in the last few weeks. I hope she can give Dante and me some guidance on how we can have a healthy relationship, because I have no fucking clue.

"Lisa, you asked for Dante to be here," Nichole says, pulling out her pen, "I think we should start there. You two are getting closer. And now you want to talk about the hard stuff, the topics that pulled you apart in the first place... so let's get started."

Here we go...

In most relationships, I'm distant... evasive, and avoid the truth with any partner I'm with; it's been a habit of mine since Lamont. I'd convince myself that I didn't want a genuine connection... but now.

"Okay," I say, "I don't know where to start."

"May I start then?" Dante asks, clasping my hand gently. "I have something that I want to share."

I look up at Dante, not sure if I want to know what he's thinking or what he wants to say. But I nod subtly.

"If I'm being honest," He gives a smile, glancing at me. "I'm scared."

"Scared?" Nichole cocks her head to the side, curious. "Why?"

Dante looks at me. His eyes were full of concern. "When Lisa and I dated in the past, and she told me what happened to her, I didn't know how to react, so I didn't react well. A variety of emotions hit me all at once, but the one that lingered was fear."

Fear? I thought to myself. I wasn't prepared to hear that.

"Why fear Dante?" Nichole asks.

"I didn't know how to be the boyfriend of someone who had been abused. Or raped." He confesses. "Suddenly, I was questioning every thought and move I made from the moment she told me. I questioned how I talked to Lisa. How I touched her. And even being intimate with her. I didn't know how to be there for her. I just wanted to fix it, and because I couldn't... it became incredibly frustrating for me."

He pauses.

"It became too much for me—we ended up pulling away from each other. And I don't want to do that this time around. I'm sad that Lamont is dead. But I'm relieved too."

Dante's honesty cuts me to the core. This is the most sincere thing I think I've ever heard him be. This moment is the first time I realized he didn't break up with me because of what Lamont did or how I felt about it, but because he didn't know how to handle the situation, not wanting to hurt me.

"You didn't want to hurt Lisa?" Nichole asks. "That's understandable and admirable. But you didn't know how to handle your feelings as well as hers."

"Yes, I didn't handle it well either, and ended up hurting her more," Dante says. "People so often turn a blind eye to something like this. It was the first time in my life that someone I knew had been raped... someone I loved."

Nichole nods. "You thought you would've handled it better?"

"Yes." He lowers his gaze. "And now that I got Lisa back, I don't want to make the same mistake again."

"You being here suggest that you won't." Nichole smiles warmly. "You know, people often say that you can tell them anything, but you can never prepare for what comes next."

I'm not thrilled to talk about this or be this vulnerable with anyone, but hearing Dante talk makes me feel I want to let him in more.

"I don't want to mess this up either, Dante," I say. "And want to try... with you. It's just so hard sometimes. It's hard to stay in the moment. To be open and present with you."

"Lisa, I never blamed you for what happened to you," Dante says. "I never saw you any differently, either. The only thing that upset me is how you downplayed it... like it was nothing. Like you were nothing."

"But you did see me differently, Dante, and treated me differently. Even though you didn't intend to."

"I did." He sighs. "I know that now."

I try to raise my eyes to meet his, but it's hard, and I'm embarrassed. Talking about Lamont always makes me feel foolish because I was so in love with him. I thought he could do no wrong. But now I realize I was just one of many of his victims.

"Lisa," Dante shifts his body towards me. "Tell me what happens when you go away?"

I clench my jaw, feeling almost ambushed by the question. "Sometimes, when I'm with you—you go away..."

I feel a sharp pain in my chest.

"It's hard for me," I say. "To stay in the moment. To feel you the way I want to—to enjoy making love to you."

Both Dante and Nichole wait for me to explain; the pain in my chest deepens as the seconds of silence pass. I'm usually can talk about this freely to Nichole, but it's different now with Dante here looking at me and listening to me.

I take a deep breath. "Sometimes, when we are together. I get pulled into... a memory of Lamont and Derek. I can't help it, and I never want to think about them, but I have to consciously work to stay in the moment and feel the moment with you."

It's clear that my answer caught Dante off guard. "You don't enjoy it?" He asks. "You don't enjoy being with me?"

"No," Nichole interjects. "Understand, Dante, that during Lisa's development, she was taught that sex and relationships were one thing, which was what her abusers wanted her to feel. They perverted it and twisted it. When a person experiences trauma, they often leave their body as a defense mechanism. Their mind retreats within themselves to protect them from what is happening to them. And even during consensual sex... it could still happen... even when the person doesn't want to. It's their body reacting like it used to."

"Okay?" Dante says, sounding confused.

Nichole allows me to elaborate.

"I want you, Dante, and want to be with you... I want to feel you." I say. "And sometimes I use sex to feel better, not wanting to deal with the bad feelings I'm feeling. So, when you said that I was using you to feel better the other night, you were right."

I pause.

"Before you, I didn't care about anyone or myself... I was reckless."

"Are we talking about that night I picked you up from your meeting with Natalie Johnson?"

I nod, my eyes fixed on my hands.

"Wait," Nichole says. "Natalie... Lamont's wife?"

I nod again.

"She wants me to share my story and help her cousin write a book about what happened," I say.

"Natalie's the one who leaked the old text messages that Lamont and I shared. He kept the phone, and she found it. I don't see why or how it will help anything to tell my story."

Nichole's eyes flutter in a few rapid blinks. "You didn't have any control over what happened to you before. But you have control now."

I look at Dante and look down again. "I've kept this a secret for so long... it's a part of me."

"And it almost destroyed you, Lisa...." Dante says, "you deserve to be happy. We deserve to be happy. You can't keep pretending that this didn't happen. Or that you're okay because you saw it as a relationship. I think you should think about what Natalie said. You are so much more than this."

Thinking back, I was relieved after the last time I saw Lamont when he and I had our final falling out. When I saw him for the person, he truly was. At the end of my graduation day, he told me he wanted to see me one last time before he married Natalie. That was the worst it had ever been between him and me — where I felt like he'd forced me and was truly not the boy I once knew or loved. The last time Lamont and I were together — wasn't normal.

"Do you want to elaborate, Lisa, about what you are thinking right now?" Nichole asks, "Does Dante know about the last time you saw Lamont?"

The words force the tears I've been struggling to hold back to burst from my eyes. I hide behind my hands, but Dante instinctively holds me close to his chest, comforting me as Nichole looks on and waits.

Eventually, I composed myself enough to speak. "It was the night I graduated from MIT. It was so horrible that I did my best to block it from my mind. And never think or speak about it. And that's why I lied to Natalie about the last time I saw Lamont."

"Tell us what you can," Nichole says. "We're here for you, Lisa."

Still fidgeting with the tissue in my hand, I nod.

"For so long, I was in love with Lamont?" I confess.

Nichole listens intensely. "What he did to you wasn't love. What Dante is doing... being here with you and wanting to learn how to be there for you moving forward — that's love."

"I'm sorry," I say. "I know what you are saying is true, and I appreciate both of you... my way."

"Stop apologizing."

Both of them sit patiently and wait for me to start. But where to start is always the hardest thing for me. I rarely talk about my genuine feelings, about what transpired that night, because the facts are so hard to re-live.

I reluctantly begin...

TWENTY-FOUR

May 27th, 2006

"I can't believe it." I said. "What a perfect day to graduate."

"I can't believe you graduated," Katie laughed, throwing her arms around me. "It was touch and go there for a moment."

The campus was humming with activity. College students, proud parents, and friends had all come out to attend the graduation ceremonies.

The last four years went by in a blur. All around me, students wore their graduation gowns and caps and said their bittersweet goodbyes to friends and professors. I remember being so excited with anticipation of the adventures ahead of me. But through the blur of emotions that whirled within me, there was one lingering thought stabbing in the back of my mind ... Monty. Even though I felt so happy, his shadow still lingered over me like a cloud. I struggled to be in the moment, but I was delighted to have Katie and my dad, Joe, standing by my side.

"I'm very proud of you, Lisa," Joe said. He didn't give compliments too often, so it was a shock to hear those words coming from his lips. "I'm sorry that I can't stay."

"It's okay." I interject, "You came, and that's all that matters."

Our relationship had been strained ever since Derek. Joe couldn't be around me after he learned what happened, and after a few months of him avoiding me, our relationship never recovered.

I told myself over the years that he was just too ashamed that he wasn't there to protect me when I needed him. And it was too painful to think about what Derek had done. After the truth came out, Joe was physically there but emotionally absent for the rest of the time. We spoke little while I lived with him, and I was happy to move away.

Katie was different. Over the years, we became closer; she was my best friend. She listened to my drama and was there when I had my darkest months. Once I even called her drunk out of my mind, upset that I was alone in a guy's house that I'd just met. Katie called a friend and had them pick me up. The next day, she was there by my side. She never judged me. Even when it seemed like I'd lost my way... drinking and partying.

We walked through the MIT campus, and I soaked up the last bit of memories as we made our way to the parking lot. There was a soft breeze that blew through the afternoon scenery.

"Thank you for everything," I said, glancing over at Katie. "I don't know if I would've made it if it weren't for you."

"Don't be ridiculous, Lisa! You would've been just fine. You just had to find your way... just like everyone else in this world." She smiled at me and squeezed my hand. "Plus, now that you're done with college, maybe I will see you more."

I smiled, thinking about how I've missed her enthusiasm and optimism.

"You've been through a lot, Lisa." Katie smiled. "enjoy this moment."

"Oh, I suppose I could be happy for one day."

She sighed softly. "Good, now... are you ready to celebrate?"

I laughed. "Fuck yeah."

We climb into Katie's Range Rover and head into the city. After a fifteen-minute ride through the congested streets, we arrived at the restaurant and pushed through the heavy glass double doors of the local seafood spot.

The hostess showed us to a booth at the other end of the building as we settled down at the table with our menus in hand and ordered two beers and a Salmon dish. The server smiled, disappeared for a few minutes, and delivered two glasses of Guinness and two glasses of water. Katie took one big gulp of the frothy beer. The bitter taste soothed me as I sipped a few gulps of beer down my throat.

Fuck, I needed this. I thought.

I took another sip, wondering what today might have looked like if our mom had been alive.

"I miss mom." I sighed, not wanting to sour the moment.

"I miss her too." Katie's voice was low.

Katie took my hand in hers and looked into my eyes. "She would be very proud of you... of both of us."

I avoided eye contact with Katie for the moment, knowing if I did, I might burst into tears. I didn't want to cry, not now.

"Now, a toast to you. My lovely little sister." Katie smiled and held up her Guinness in the air.

I smiled, raised my glass with hers, and tilted my glass so that the rims barely touched. "Thank you, Katie... I mean it." My glass connected to Katie's, and we gulped down the glass in one swift motion.

"So, are you heading back to Cali?"

"No, there is nothing for me in California."

"Well, come to New York. Stay with me until you figure things out." Katie smiled while ordering another two beers. "Or take a year off as I did."

"I don't know, but I need a break from everything." MIT had been great, but academia and I needed to part ways for a while. I had spent the past year focusing on nothing but overachieving, juggling a thesis, starting a new business, and managing the usual senior burnout moments. I was eager to start the next chapter of my life, far away from campus.

Katie's eyes lit up at the thought of me coming to New York. She'd been seeing a new guy, Paul, and had been eager for me to meet her latest love interest. Paul was an up-and-coming real estate agent that had been showing her places for a client for a few months now. He was the first man she'd dated since Lamont, and she broke up. While she gushed about her new beau, I took a few bites of my salmon and veggies.

Once we finished, Katie agreed to meet up later after clearing out my dorm room. She waved goodbye just as I made my way toward the door, feeling happy about the day. I had just entered the dorm as my phone buzzed in my pocket. Instinctively, I picked it up without looking at the caller ID.

"He sweetheart, I—" I pause the moment I hear Lamont's voice on the other end of the line.

"Congratulations, Lisa." His deep voice vibrated in my ear. My knees weakened a little as I listened. My heart fluttered in my chest as the memory of Lamont flooded my thoughts. A small part of me was humming with desire for him again, even after everything that Lamont had put me through. It was sickening, but I couldn't explain it. I didn't want to see him again, but on the other hand, my body ached to see him again.

"How have you been, Lisa?"

"What do you want, Lamont?" I said, rolling my eyes, pacing back and forth outside of my dorm room. "I've been okay."

"I'm sorry for how I left things the last time we spoke," he murmured desperately. His voice sounded panicked, stressed, and almost afraid. I'd never heard him sound like that before. "Can I see you? Please. I know I promised I would leave you alone when I started seeing Natalie, but now that the wedding is near, I'm freaking the fuck out. A friend is what I need. I need you."

"Lamont." I rolled my eyes at the phone. "I don't know."

"Please, Lisa, I will send a car for you." Lamont pleaded. "I just want to see you for a bit."

"Okay," I relented. "I will see you in twenty minutes."

"I'll send a car."

Twenty-two minutes later, I stepped out onto the street and came face to face with an imposing man standing guard by a black Escalade parked at the curb near the front door.

"Ms. Rose."

He took a step in my direction with a smile. I didn't know why I agreed to see Lamont again. This man had confused me for years. Now that I've been on my own, away from the chaos in California, I'd have a lot of time to think.

"Hi, I'm Jonathan." The driver extended his hand to me and shook my hand gently. He wasn't dressed like a regular driver, more like one of the men in Lamont's entourage. And he stood well over six feet tall and had a muscular frame. He looked like a former football player or another kind of athlete, with dark brown eyes and beautiful dark skin. He was wearing a black T-shirt that strained over his massive muscular arms, and there was a lot of expensive jewelry draped around his neck.

"Hey, Lamont asked me to come to pick you up. And take you to him."

I suppressed every alarm that was going off in my body; it had been so long since I'd seen him. I didn't know what I would say or do when we were face to face.

"Is there any other place that I could take you before you see him, miss Rose?"

"No."

Jonathan smiled and nodded, opening the back door of the SUV for me. I climbed in and quickly texted Katie to let her know I was going out and to text me in an hour. I needed an excuse to leave if I didn't have the willpower to do so independently. As we left the city, I wondered where exactly this man was taking me. At that moment, every horror movie and Unsolved Mystery episode came rushing into the forefront of my thoughts.

"How is he?" I stuttered. "Lamont... I mean."

"He's been stressed," Jonathan said. "You know, with the regular season and planning a wedding."

Oh, yeah... the wedding.

A short thirty minutes later, Jonathan pulled onto Seaport Blvd Penthouse with views of the Harbor and city lights. Unlike his neighbors, though, Lamont spent the extra money to make his condo stand out.

I walked up to the front door alone, swallowing every objection that I had of why I wanted to see him at all. I walked through the lobby towards the elevator. Finally, the elevator doors opened, and before me stood Lamont, staring back at me with a sense of relief that was clearly visible on his face.

"You came." He flashed a sincere smile.

"I wasn't sure that I would," I replied. "And have to finish packing my things from the dorms on campus."

"Yeah." he raked his fingers through his hair. "I heard you graduated. Congratulations."

"Thanks."

I had to admit. Lamont looked good... fantastic. Better than I'd ever seen him look in a long time physically. But the bags under his eyes told me he'd been burning the candle at both ends. He handed me a beer, and we toasted to my accomplishments.

I remember my nerves were frazzled, so I downed my second beer quickly. Then Lamont set down a shot of Crown Royal on the coffee table next to me.

"Lamont, I can't." I said, "I have to get back to campus and finish packing."

My willpower diminished the more I drank, feeling the effects of the alcohol.

The last time I saw Lamont, he told me he was done with me. And for over three years, I was done with him.

"I'm so glad that I'm done with school," my words slurred.

Lamont smiled. "You must have been so busy with studying and college life. Any boyfriends?"

"What about you?" I asked, my voice stumbling. "That is none of your business, Lamont. You told me you were done with me... remember?"

Monty doesn't respond. He's all smiles as he alluded to the real reason he asked me to come to see him tonight.

"I know what you've been up to," he said. "You were probably up here fucking whoever would give you any attention... didn't you?"

There it goes, his jealousy. I thought to myself. Although he's half right.

"Maybe I should go." I gulp my shot. "Can you tell Jonathan to take me back to the dorm, please?"

His eyes looked at me tenderly for a moment.

"You think that I just brought you here to drink?" he asked.

I wipe my mouth. "Then I will call myself a cab or call Katie."

Lamont stared at me, and for the first time that night, fear took hold of me. I saw the anger building up within him. It was clear in his eyes as he clenched his jaw.

"I know you were seeing some guy. At the beginning of your junior year? It didn't last long, I know, but you still were with him. Did you fuck him?

Did he have what was mine? You'd barely even knew him, and you fucked him."

I couldn't believe it. Lamont had been spying on me, even though he didn't want me.

"Fuck you, Lamont," I said, slamming my beer down on the coffee table. "You were the one who told me you were done with me. So, you can't be mad if I move on. You are about to get married in a few days, and you're judging me? To you, I was disposable— you are the one who used me."

"You know it's not like that."

"—you never loved me, Lamont."

"No, that's not true, Lisa. I love you so much that it hurts to think about anyone else ever touching you."

I waited for him to stop, feeling more than ready to leave. This was a mistake, and I was realizing it more and more by the second. I rose to my feet and took a few steps to the door, but Lamont stopped me before I could reach the doorknob.

"Let me leave," I said. "I want to go home, Lamont."

"Baby, you're too drunk; maybe you should stay the night."

"I'm not staying, and I will not fuck you tonight either now; please let me leave."

"You should lie down; you're barely able to stand on your feet." Lamont guided me to the stairs and into the bedroom.

"Lamont, what did you do?"

"Don't touch me." the room was spinning as I plopped on my back, feeling like I was floating. I felt Lamont's hand trying to undress me.

I pushed myself away from him, facing toward the edge of the bed, and that's when I noticed Jonathan was in the room with us.

"Please take me home," I muttered. I tried to move, but my limbs felt too heavy to do anything.

Everything went dark after that...

I awoke briefly to see Lamont getting into bed. My eyes felt too heavy to open, and the images faded in and out like pictures on a projector. I laid there, eyes closed, hearing and feeling everything, but it wasn't just Lamont... it was Jonathan, too.

When I woke again, I was on my back, undressed and completely exposed. Lamont had his head between my legs. His arms were wrapped around my thighs, holding me in place. I tried to move but couldn't. I was frozen, even after I sobered up.

My mind drifted, and I was out of my body, floating above myself in the room. I could feel everything. And even as the tears flowed from my eyes and traveled down my cheeks. Lamont kept going. He wanted to humiliate me, and that's what he did. The images flashed in my mind and seared in the back of my eyelids from that moment on.

When Lamont was done with me, he moved towards the edge of the bed and pushed into me. There was no consent. It felt like I'd blink, and his penis was inside of me.

"Lamont, please don't."

He paused, but only for a moment. "You know you want this. Just shut the fuck up. It's your fault, you know — you drive me so fucking crazy."

I turned my head away as he tried to kiss me. But he just smiled and pushed himself deeper into me, and started moving in and out at a punishing pace.

Jonathan was sitting at the opposite end of the room, staring at us with a dark, menacing gaze. I cringed at the thought of what he was thinking while he watched.

Lamont's rhythm nearly broke me; whatever love I felt for him dissolved with each thrust. This felt dark and wrong... and like something Lamont had planned. I didn't remember it being like this, even when he was drunk at his birthday party. And all I could do was lay there, feeling angry at myself for agreeing to come there in the first place, knowing it was a bad idea.

I shut my eyes and thought about anything. Lectures I recalled for class. My packing list of things I still needed to remove from the dorms.

Twelve Socks...

Ten underwear...

four pairs of shoes.

Six pairs of jeans and ten shirts... four dresses and three blouses...

I needed to turn in my keys and do a walk-through before leaving. I'm meeting Katie at noon tomorrow for lunch...

Lamont moaned against my ear, which brought me back to the moment. He rolled me over on my stomach and pinned me down against the mattress, my face pressed firmly against the fabric of the pillowcase.

He grunted hard and said. "You know that you still love me. I'm deep within you, and you can never forget me."

I hate you. You're hurting me, I thought to myself. But no words came out of my mouth — I couldn't speak. Everything faded in and out of focus. And the alcohol was making me feel sick. Then I understood. He wanted me to feel like I was nothing... and he succeeded. He kept going, faster and harder, until his body stiffened and his essence shot through me. It was okay for him to be with someone else, but not me.

Even then, my thoughts were conflicting... I came there willingly and wanted to see him, so was this rape? Was this love? Or was this just how Lamont showed his love?

When he finished, he said my name over and over. He pulled out, rolling onto his back. Every part of him was slick with sweat, even his forearms, his feet.

"Unbelievable," he said. "This wasn't where I expected my day to end up."

"I'm sorry."

"I mean, it's okay. It's fine." He pushed himself off the bed, put on his pants, and stepped around me. Then went into the bathroom, returned with a spray bottle and rag, got on his hands and knees, and cleaned the floor. I kept my eyes shut tight through the smell of ammonia and pine, my stomach still churned, the bed undulating beneath me.

When he climbed back into bed, he was all over me despite my just having puked and his hands smelling like cleaner. His mouth and hands take me. "You'll be okay," he said. "You're drunk, that's all. Stay here and sleep it off."

In the morning, Jonathan ushered me into the back of the Escalade. Lamont was nowhere to be found; he didn't even bother to say anything or leave a text. The sun was barely up in the sky, and my head was spinning, but neither of them cared.

"Where is he?" I whispered as Jonathan settled in behind the steering wheel. "Where is Lamont?"

"It doesn't matter," Jonathan grunted. "But he left something for you."

Next to me was an envelope with a check and a brief note.

Use the money to start your business or start a life wherever. I know things got out of hand last night. I think we shouldn't contact each other for a while... after all, I'm getting married soon.

The check was for three hundred thousand dollars; at that moment, I'd never felt so cheap before in my life. I didn't come there for the money. I came because Monty said he needed me, and stupidly, I came running. He used me once again to make himself feel better.

"What is this, Jonathan? Hush money?" I snapped. "He's trying to keep me quiet."

"No," Jonathan smiled. "You came over and got too drunk for your own good. Things got out of hand. And that's all."

****

Present Day

The following week passes by in a blur after that session with Nichole. Now that my deal with Apple is finished, things are moving a lot faster. But work is so hectic, I barely have time to think about anything else.

I keep working to mask the pain. I keep moving. Not wanting to stand still, even for a moment. Because when I stop, my heart feels like it wants to burst from my chest. I pretend to care about the projection of new projects and expanding the app's vision.

Everyone's game increased, and I could finally see the light at the end of the tunnel. Dante looks through the blinds of my office, scanning the room for something.

"It's huge... very nice."

He pauses.

"I don't think I've ever been in your office before." He smiles, closing the blinds until it entirely shielded us from everyone outside the office.

Dante walks toward me, pulling me closer to him. I wrap my arms around his neck and held him tightly, not caring if someone were to come in and see us. I love the way he feels in my arms, and I love the way I feel when he hugs me back, tightening his arms around my rib cage. I breathe him in, inhaling the intoxicating scent that is Dante Kingston.

I lose myself in this moment with Dante, allowing the relief of his presence to consume and soothe me. I wrap my leg over his waist, tangling our bodies together as he lifts me up and plants me on my desk.

"Oh my god," I choked. "You just saw me this morning, and you missed me this much," I smirk.

"Shut up, don't make jokes. Everything will be okay." Dante's fingertips sweep a strand of my hair back into place.

"I know it's hard for you sometimes. You were trying to be there for me. I appreciate the effort, but nothing will fix me. My biggest fear is that I will hurt you again, and I don't want to be hurt again. So maybe we can continue to take things slowly."

I pull back as he presses his lips against my forehead. "I love you, Lisa." He whispers softly. "All I am asking you to do is love me… trust me.

Dante skillfully tugs open the buttons of my blouse open and unfastens my bra and moves me, so I'm lying down on the icy surface of my desk. Slowly, he slides up my skirt, leaving me exposed and open to him. The heat radiating from him sets me on fire.

His lips part just enough for me to feel the warmth of his breath. "I want so badly, right here. I want you ready and waiting for me."

He stands, walks over to the door, and locks it. Then pulls his Henley shirt over his head, tossing it away on my couch. He pushes his denim jeans down to the floor, revealing all of his glory underneath the clothes. I take a moment to soak all of him in, admiring every inch of him.

I watch as Dante lowers down to his knees, settling between my thighs. His head slides up and down my clit, his erection presses hard against him as he kisses me from my neck to my lips. I shift my body against the smooth glass surface, feeling the ache between my legs, begging for more of him.

"I want you now, Dante." I breathe, throwing caution to the wind.

"I want you too."

Dante's perfectly chiseled chest stiffens as he positions himself near my opening. He breathes in slowly as he pushes into me with deliberate control. I rake my fingernails over the waves of his curly hair, feeling his muscles hardening under my touch. I ease my hips into him a little more, sliding my hands down to his ass and grinding him harder.

"Oh, fuck." He thrusts forward, planting himself deeper inside me, moving with my increasing speed.

I moan softly, not wanting to make a sound that might alert the others of what we are doing.

Dante looks down into my eyes, thrusting harder and faster. His hands grip my ass cheeks tightly as he steadies my body. "Did you invite me here just to take advantage of me, Ms. Rose?"

I nod. "You said you wanted me now. I couldn't wait either. I thought you said you wanted to make love to me."

"Is that what this is?" Dante grins.

"When you're inside me, I feel your love. I feel your passion for me, and I love you inside me."

He hesitates and then kisses me deeply and passionately, licking and devouring me with his mouth as his thrusts send me to the edge of ecstasy. I quicken and quiver around his cock. Electricity pulses over me as my hips buck and thrash against his hips.

Then Dante lifts me, so I am straddling him on the couch; his cock is still buried deep within me.

"Oh, my god." For a moment, I gasp. I shift my hips and find my center. "I will never get used to that feeling."

"Is that a good thing or a bad thing?" He asks, burying his head in my chest.

I smile. "It's a good thing. I feel good."

Dante sweeps his lips over mine and leans in to kiss me again. I suck him and kiss him passionately. He groans and pushes into my hips further. Our hips crash together, filling me with every thrust. I gasp for air as he makes me unravel for him repeatedly. His cock penetrates my soul with every thrust.

"Oh, God." I clench my arms around his neck, steadying myself as I try to keep up with his pace. "You're right there. You're driving me crazy."

Dante grips my waist and pulls me closer... his strokes are deep, gently he fucks me. "I don't want to lose you again, Lisa. I will be a mess without you."

My heart flutters in my chest as my lungs gasp in the air.

"You aren't alone anymore. I promise. I swear I'm not going anywhere." He hugs me close against his chest.

"I love you, Dante. You're the only one I want to be with."

I lift again, my thighs crashing down against him. He stretches my core with each stroke. He shifts his body and delivers powerful thrusts, working me over his erection, over and over, until my body seizes and stiffens.

"Dante." I plea. "I'm coming."

His skin feels like fire, and Dante clenches his jaw as he pumps into me a few more times. "Come for me, baby."

His words unravel me; my vision blurs as he buries himself inside me. The orgasm that ripples through me is so powerful that my whole body is shaking. My head feels heavy as I collapse on his sculpted chest as he releases a small cry along with his last thrust.

The following morning, a doorbell jolts me awake. Dante loosens his hold around me and slips away, throwing on his clothes from the previous night. We were supposed to go see a movie after we left my office, but after our quickie, all I could think about was getting him home so that we could continue what we started.

"Lisa," Dante pokes his head into the room. "There are two policemen in the living room who wish to speak to you."

My mind is racing. I don't know why the police are here or what they could want from me. I know the investigation of Lamont's murder is ongoing, but that can't be why they are here?

"Lisa, get dressed. The police are downstairs. They want to talk to you."

I sit up quickly as the words finally register in my brain. "Do you know why they are here?"

"No."

"Lisa, this is one of those things that you shouldn't be alone for."

"No, Dante. I will see what it is they want. You can be there, but only if you don't try to control the room in the first five minutes. Please tell me you can respect that."

Dante exhales. "I will behave. I promise. What do you think they're here for? They're going to ask you about Lamont. Do you think they know?"

"I don't know, but whatever it is, I will face it."

My nerves are almost in a complete panic attack before I walk out of the bedroom, with Dante following close behind. I slip into a pair of jeans and throw on a t-shirt. I pray Dante will keep his cool because I don't trust him not to want to jump in to defend me if he feels that I'm being offended. I look a little worse for wear from all the sexual activities the night before, but I still look presentable.

I walk into the living room, and a man and a woman in business suits greet me. The woman is tall and thin, her hair is a sandy blond, and the male is shorter and stockier, like he's had a few too many hamburgers; his hair is thinning on the top. They both appear respectful and friendly, which I am thankful for because my nerves are shot.

The tall woman takes a seat first. "Sorry to track you down here, Ms. Rose. I'm Detective Jane Murray, and this is Detective Eric Wells. We were hoping to speak with you about your involvement with Lamont Johnson."

"Meaning what exactly? What do you mean?" I speak.

Eric Wells reaches into his jacket and pulls out a handful of papers and what looked like call logs. In them, Lamont's number is in constant contact with my number. Then there are photographs from the party that show Lamont pulling me into a corner. My back was against the wall, but I was upset. In another photo, Lamont's mouth was an inch from my lips. And that's when Dante showed up. The memories of that night flood my mind; I look up calmly and wait for the detectives to get to the point.

"These were taken a few nights before Mr. Johnson was murdered. Guests say this party was invitation-only, yet Mr. Johnson showed up. Were you two close?"

I shake my head—no.

"He was my sister's boyfriend; I knew him when I was in high school. After they broke up, I didn't really speak to Lamont. I'd spoken to him a couple times on the phone, but that night was the first time I'd seen him in years."

"He called you almost every night, including the night he was murdered," Wells scoffs.

"I can see that. Lamont called me a lot. I sometimes picked up the phone and sometimes I didn't, but I didn't see him after leaving the party. He called, but I didn't pick up."

"What would he say to you when he called?"

"He often called me drunk, and he never made much sense when he was drunk."

I try to remain calm, but I can't breathe. The pair of detectives glance at each other, exchanging a look in a code that only they understand. Murray pulls out a small black notepad and reads from the scribbles on the paper.

"I guess I'm trying to understand. He was murdered, right? Are you trying to figure out what he said to me or if we were enemies?" The words left my lips before my mind can process them.

Detective Murray fumbles through her notes. "With everything that was going on in his life, we're just trying to figure out why crashing your party was the one thing Mr. Johnson felt like he had to do. Mr. Johnson sent you a certified envelope a few days before his death. We want to know why a man whose life was spiraling down the drain wanted to call and talk to you so much. We're trying to get an account of Mr. Johnson's whereabouts before he went to the strip club that night."

"Oh. I didn't realize that I was being looked into. I have nothing to do with Lamont or what happened that night."

"We understand." Murray shrugs.

"Is there anything else you might be able to tell us? Or why he kept calling you? Like his state of mind the last time you spoke to him."

"I said he needed a friend. I told him I wished I could be that for him, but I couldn't. Honestly, I was really shocked by allegations of these women and how the media has portrayed the victims."

I pause.

"It's no secret that Mr. Johnson had made some enemies, which is why we're talking to anyone who might have known him well. And you seem to know him well enough for Lamont to entrust you with some documents."

I nod. "He sent me something for my eyes only. I'm sorry, but I can't help your investigation." I try to appear concerned and engaged in this interrogation. And don't want to think about this anymore. The Day started out so well, waking up in Dante's arms.

"Can we look at the documents that Mr. Johnson sent you?" The woman detective asks.

"No, those papers were meant for my eyes only, and I will respect Lamont's wishes."

Detective Wells reaches into his pocket and retrieves a business card. "Well, we've taken enough of your time. Here's my card. Thank you for seeing us."

"Thank you, Detectives."

Dante escorts the two detectives to the door, and I sink into the cushions of the seat; my heart flutters so loudly in my chest that I can't hear much of anything else. I'm honestly confused about how they found me; here in Dante's condo. Were they watching me, and if so, for how long? I have done nothing wrong, so I don't think they suspected me of anything. I cut ties with Lamont long ago, and we were careful.

No sooner than they leave, Dante appears.

"Are you okay?"

"Yes. They had photos from the party and wanted to know why Lamont was there. They wanted to know what he sent me in the mail. I explained I didn't really speak to Lamont. And that the papers he sent me were confidential."

"So they think you might've had something to do with Lamont's murder?"

"No, but since he spoke to very few people. They seemed concerned that he kept calling me. Seemed like they were grasping at straws to find a suspect, and so far, they have nothing."

"All right, I won't push the topic any further."

"Dante." I exhale. "Don't pretend that you didn't hear them talk about the certified envelope. I got it a few days after he died."

He pauses for a second. "Okay, do you want to tell me what was in it?" He kisses me and sits next to me on the couch.

"He wrote me a letter." I sigh. "And he gave me a check for a lot of money that I don't know what to do with. I know I don't want to keep it, but I need time to think."

"I understand." Dante pulls me close to his chest. "We don't have to figure everything out right now."

TWENTY-FIVE

May 27th, 2016

It's Friday evening, the moon is slowly rising in the night sky; I scan the Rooftop bar for Katie. I've been avoiding her long enough and can't put it off anymore. Not finding her at first, I choose a seat beside the opposite end of the rooftop. I will not lie. I thought about jumping, but it's only two stories, so I flag down the bartender instead.

"Hello, I'm Sam." the waitress says, with a notepad in her hand. "What can I get you?"

"Crown and Coke, please...." I smile.

As I wait for my drink, the six o'clock news cuts through the noise of the bar. My heart flutters as Lamont's face appears, presumably updates about his murder. They haven't identified a suspect, according to the police. My eyes trace the bottom of the screen to read the caption, "Lamont Johnson's case is still ongoing. So far, they have identified no suspects. And police have no leads. After sexual misconduct and assault, allegations flooded the internet about him."

The news tapered off as I lost focus.

A sick feeling swirls in my gut. I want to move on, forget about Lamont completely. But I'm still a wreck, although I won't admit it to anyone. I'd like his killer to be found, but he had so many enemies towards the end, the suspect list must be extensive. I'm not sure the police will ever get a lead. I am lost in my thoughts as I feel another person standing beside me.

"Have you ordered me a drink yet?"

My body jolts slightly as I turn, seeing Katie standing there with a smug smile on her face. She's clearly just coming from work, wearing a black business suit with a pair of Nine West shoes.

"Oh," I stammer. "No, I didn't. I didn't know how long you were going to be or if you were drinking at all."

Katie raises one of her eyebrows. "Of course, I'm drinking. That's why I suggested this place."

I ask the waitress to return and wait as Katie orders a Single Malt Scotch.

We haven't really talked in the last few weeks; in truth, I've been avoiding Katie like the plague. Things are so complicated right now. There were a few days when I thought that Jason Colewell would find a way to sabotage my Apple deal with Ryan. He can't seem to let that one-night stand go. I was relieved when all the paperwork came back signed and the funds had been transferred, which meant I didn't have to deal with him anymore.

Everything that has been left unsaid between Katie and I, has been weighing on me. I know she has questions about Lamont and about me, but I just can't handle any more drama, especially now that he's gone. An uneasy tension has been lingering between us, and I, for one, just want to move on.

"I wasn't expecting you to show up, honestly," Katie says, trying to cut the tension between us.

"Yeah, I've been lying low ever since — you know."

I shake my head, hiding my expression with a slow sip of my drink. I wonder what is going on in Katie's mind right now and if she's really doing okay.

I shift my body weight uncomfortably on the stool as if I can feel Katie's gaze on me, studying my every move and reaction. Did she want to know how upset I was? To see if I am distraught. If so, I'm not in the mood for the cat-and-mouse game.

Lamont is all I have been talking about for weeks. Even after he is dead, I have to keep talking about him. I'm tired of the comforting and encouraging words; I feel like I have no right to be as happy as I am.

"How is Dante? How are things with you two? Are things getting serious?" I avoid her intense gaze. I'm not used to talking about myself, and when I do, I just feel like a fraud because half of what I'm saying is a lie.

Katie chuckles and sips her Scotch. The waitress just set down.

"Sorry if I am acting weird, Lisa. This thing between us just feels weird... strange, I guess, now that I know the truth... I should be relieved that Lamont is gone, but I'm not."

"I know you are hurting; I'm sorry." God, I feel more guilty now than I've ever felt before.

Katie smiles and blinks for a moment. "I don't know what I feel. Anyway, Lamont is gone; it's over, right? There is some kind of closure for these women."

I return a smile, feeling slightly disarmed. "No, I don't really think it will ever be over for these women. Just because he's gone doesn't mean they have their justice."

"Does anyone know about... you?" Katie's eyes dart around, alert to everyone around us.

I shake my head — no.

"I mean, kind of, but I know who leaked the text messages."

"Really? Who?" she exhales, gulping down more Scotch.

Katie's concern gives me a slight pause. She's more than a little interested in who knows about Lamont and me. Maybe she didn't want to know about the details any more than I wanted to talk about them, but she deserves the truth. I've hidden the truth from her for far too long.

"It was his wife, Natalie Johnson. She came to my office the other day."

Katie picks up on my shift in mood; no matter how carefully I try to hide them from her, she is getting better at reading through my bullshit. It will do me no good to hide what I'm really feeling or pretend that I'm okay.

"What?" Katie inhales sharply.

"I was upset at first; I won't lie," I continue. "To be honest, I wanted to beat that bitch down when she came to my office and admitted it. The reporter is her cousin. Now the reporter wants to write a book with me and talk about my story. Natalie thinks I should, and even though she stabbed me in the back, I kept my composure."

"What the hell, Lisa. Do you think you can trust her?"

"Hell, she could've tried to really hurt me when she found out, but she didn't."

I stare at my whiskey. "I don't know what I'm going to do. I'm grateful that this didn't ruin my business deal, but I'm tired of this ruining my life. I'm tired of carrying all of this with me."

"There's no reason you should have to carry this."

I shrug my shoulders and roll my eyes. "Dante thinks I should work with Chloe and get my story out there. Maybe it will help someone who may be lost right now. Or maybe this is just a bad idea."

"In the end, Lisa, it's your choice. I don't know how you feel about telling your story, but it can't hurt, right? Seriously, you have to stop running from this. You've been protecting everyone... Lamont... Dante... me... it's time to live your life."

I shake my head at the memories creeping in. A wave of nauseous hit me as the memory of Lamont filters to the forethought of my mind. I can't remember being more worn down than I've been in the last several weeks. And somehow, Natalie has been conspiring with Chloe to turn this story into... what? Money? Fame? I don't understand their angles or how I should move forward.

The entire sequence of events has my head spinning in the last few weeks. I just want to feel like I have my life on solid footing and not feel like I'm spiraling.

I quickly gulp down the rest of my whiskey as Katie rubs my shoulder gently in comfort.

"Lisa," she murmurs.

I look up, focusing on her expression and demeanor.

"You aren't alone anymore; you have Dante, and you have me. We will get through whatever happens; next, you no longer have to keep this a secret. If you want to tell your story or not, it's your choice. But if you do this... do it for you. Don't give Lamont the satisfaction of keeping his secrets. You don't have to protect him anymore. Forgive yourself and give yourself time to figure all this out before making your next move. I know how you get; you worry about everyone else before thinking about yourself. But you don't need to do that anymore. We are with you; remember that."

I smile. "Thank you, Katie."

"Lisa."

A man's voice rings out behind me. A familiar scent fills my nostrils as a hand rests on the small of my back. Dante stands close behind me, flashing Katie a warm smile as he greets her. Katie smiles back, and her eyes seem to radiate a sense of happiness. I want to excuse myself from the situation, but I remain steadfast.

"Dante." Katie smiles.

"Katie," he replies. "Did you come here to forget all the stresses of the week?"

"Something like that, Dante, and to catch up with Lisa here. You've been keeping her away from me. I had to catch her while you let her come up for air."

Kill me now... I think to myself. *Can this get any more embarrassing?*

"We should go. We're going to be late for our reservation."

Katie's gaze studies Dante's demeanor. Her jaw tightens as she notices how uncomfortable Dante is. I feel the tension between them. She still believes Dante hurt me the last time we were together... when I was in enough pain to try to end my life. I want to tell her that's not what happened, but I don't think she would even believe me.

"You can't stay and have a drink with us, Dante?"
I put a hand over Dante's and flash a subtle smile,
as if I'm reassuring him that everything is okay.
"Okay, one drink," he smirks quickly.
I nod and signal the waitress, ordering three
shots. And kiss Dante's cheek, eager to diffuse the
tension and my uncomfortableness. I turn back to
Katie and smile.
"So, what are you two up to this weekend?"
"We are heading to the Hamptons to my house on
Mecox Bay at the end of Flying Point Road; it's this
modern home that I just finished. I'm taking Lisa up
there for the week to relax."
Katie nods and turns to me. I smile but tense up
slightly, wishing I could find the right words to make
her feel better. I even thought about inviting her. But
Dante is determined to take me away from the city for
a while, and we can't have a romantic time away with
my sister hanging around.
"When will you be back?"
"Ten days from now." Dante chimes in as we
finish our shots, pay and make our way toward the
exit.
We step out and into the cool night air. Before the
moment gets any more awkward, I give Katie a warm
hug, and we say our goodbyes.
"Hey, are you really doing okay?"
"Yes, Katie. We both have had a fucked-up couple
of weeks here," I reply. "Dante just wants me to get
away for a while."
"And Dante is being good to you," she adds
cheerfully, squeezing me into a gentle hug.
"Better than I deserve, Katie."

Her gaze flashes between us. "Okay. Well, you two get going. I'm sure you can't wait to get out of the city."

I wave shyly while Dante guides me toward the idling black Escalade that's waiting for us on the side of the curb. Moments later, I climb up into the vehicle and smile at the driver Max, the driver/bodyguard Dante hired after Lamont showed up at my party.

I slide onto the soft leather seat next to Dante. Before I say anything, he pulls me onto his lap and presses his lips to mine. The kiss is passionate and intense, as if he hadn't seen me in weeks. He sweeps his thumb over my lips, urging me to suck it. I open my mouth and suck gently, allowing my tongue to dance over his finger. Now, I can finally relax in the arms of the man I love.

****

We leave the city's clutter and chaos and head towards the privacy of a private four-bedroom and five-bathroom house in the Hamptons. The island buzzes with activity as we arrive. We spend the evening visiting shops, trying to stock up on food and provisions that will last us ten days while making a promise to talk about anything but work. Dante laughs and loosens up a bit, which is a relief. I need this, and perhaps he needs this too, because I feel connected to him in the quiet moments we share. We just spend time together most of the night before heading to the house.

I shiver as we step into the cool air that blows in from the sea as I climb out of the Escalade and soak in the view of the 16 x 32' heated Gunite pool and dock. Dante points out the outdoor shower, covered outdoor seating, and dining area next to the pool. And we enter through the ground floor, right off the garage next to the homemade gym and a half-bath. Dante leads me up the staircase straight ahead, which leads to the main floor of the residence. I take a minute to admire the great room, the kitchen, dining, and living area with a wall of glass and sun deck overlooking the water on the Mecox Bay.

There are two guest bedrooms at the top of the stairs that share one bath. I walk into the main bedroom and stare out at Burnett Cove Road and the lovely gardens below. The main bedroom suite is enormous, with his and hers walk-in closets. And dual showers that overlook the Atlantic.

We spend the night ravaging each other; the passion is all-consuming for both of us, which only grows more intense with each second that passes by. All I want is to be with Dante. I want him and need him. And my desire moves me like the ebb and flow of the ocean. Every worry drifts to the background of my mind as I focus on the here and now. And lose all control and reservations that I had before. We'd spent too much time apart with the distractions of the world pulling us apart.

From the day Dante and I started talking a few months ago, he's been so cautious about allowing himself to go all-in with this relationship because I hurt him. And I know he feels the same way about me.

What has grown between us since I let him in has left me with feelings I can no longer ignore.

Between making love all night, the activities in town, and the relaxing feeling of being away from the city, I am exhausted by midnight.

Always acute to my feelings, Dante massages my shoulders, coaxing the warmth from the fireplace to heat my body faster.

"I know it's late, but are you hungry?"

"I could eat."

"Go relax on the deck next to the pool; the firepit should've heated it by now. I'll grab some wine and snacks for us, and I'll join you soon."

I nod, tie the belt of my robe and head out onto the deck with a spectacular view of the dock and the ocean. I sink my sore limbs into one of the Malmo gray wicker/ratan with sunbrella cushions.

Closing my eyes, I let out a long exhale, feeling the warmth of the firepit dance over my skin as the moon rests high in the sky. The sounds of ocean waves crashing against the sandy shore sing me a soft lullaby as I drift to sleep.

Dante joins me, and I jolt awake while he sets a bowl with melons, strawberries, and grapes on the end table. He pours Chateau Lafite Rothschild 2018 into two wine glasses and hands me one.

"Oh, thank you," I smile.

Dante's eyes illuminate warmly as he smiles back at me, wondering what I'm thinking about.

"Are you happy?"

He sits next to me, smirking, before taking a sip of his red wine. "I'm delighted to be here with you,

Lisa. You don't know how much I love being here with you."

My heart smiles and gushes. I tip the glass over my lips, and as the fruity liquid sweeps over my tastebuds, they rejoice. Ten days of peace and quiet with Dante is just what I need. He is my Fortress of Solitude. My home.

"This tastes amazing, Dante. This is a good choice, and it was a good idea to get away for a while."

"Yeah, I built this house over seven months ago. I wanted you to be the first person who I brought here."

I laugh. "Are you serious? I can't be the first girl you've brought up here."

His eyes beam as he stares at me and smirks with a severe nature. The humor in my words fell flat as I thought about what he was saying. I inhale, suddenly feeling overwhelmed by the sudden realization.

"Yes, I made this, hoping it would be our home someday." Dante takes another sip of wine. I wanted to surprise you with it on our honeymoon... but...."

"I dumped you and hurt you," I say, feeling embarrassed.

"Yeah." He nods, taking a full gulp of wine. "But you are here with me now, and that's all I can ask for."

I sigh, take a long sip, and quickly swallow.

Oh my God.

I straighten, "I'm so sorry, Dante." I stare at the condensation on the glass, frozen and cursing myself for hurting him the way I did. Dante smiles, kneeling down in front of my chair, rubbing his hand along my bare thighs up my robe.

"Don't do this, Lisa." He grins. "Don't spoil this night for us by thinking about the past. We are here now; that's all that matters to me."

I inhale sharply as I watch Dante reach for a ring box out of his pocket and places it on the glass table.

"This is how serious I am about us. This isn't the ring I offered you before; I thought I'd upgrade it. I know you love me when I haven't made it so easy for you to... But Lisa, I'm willing to ask again... putting everything on the line one more time, as long as there's a chance that you might say yes."

I swallow hard, feeling my throat drying up almost instantly. Tears swell in my eyes as I meet Dante's gaze.

"Are you crazy... brave... or stupid?" I whisper.

"A bit of all the above, but this is where I am; I want to spend my life with you, as your husband. I want to call this our home and know that when I walk inside, you'll be here. And want to lie next to you every night, making love to you and waking up with you next to me."

I shake my head, tears falling freely down my cheeks. I want to say more words, but nothing meaningful comes to mind.

Dante brushes away the stream of tears on my cheeks and hands me a tissue. He lifts the lid of the ring box, retrieves the ring, and holds it between his forefinger and thumb. He reaches for my hand, still kneeling on one knee, looking up at me.

"Lisa, will you marry me?"

I stare into his eyes, now brightened by the moonlight. I feel a sense of déjà vu; the last time we were here, I made the worse choice of my life. His words still echoed in my mind and mirrored what he said tonight.

"Are you sure you want to do this again?"

Dante smirks; he's never looked more terrified in his whole life. "Yes, Lisa, I've been sure for a very long time."

"I'm so scared right now."

His eyes widen. "I'm terrified right now, too. But I don't want another day to go by without you knowing how I really feel about you. You're the one I want to be with. And even if you can't give me an answer now, I—."

"Yes."

"Yes?"

I nod my head—*yes*.

I listen to my heart, expecting the heartbeat to be racing, but my heart is calm. I never thought he'd ask me again. To be Dante's wife, to trust someone exclusively, irrevocably. This is what I wanted but never thought I deserved. Deep down, I know he loves me. And as much as the thought of losing him terrifies me, I want a chance at forever with Dante. He's home. He's my heart. I loved this man more than I've ever loved anything or anyone.

"Yes," I repeat softly.

Dante smiles. "Yes?"

I smile and say it louder. "Yes, Dante, I will marry you!"

"Whoa!"

"Yes—I want to marry you. I love you." I laugh softly.

Dante smiles from ear to ear as he slips the 3ct Radiant Sidestone Engagement Ring in Platinum that's both striking and sophisticated. The ring is crafted in platinum with six perfectly matched emerald-cut diamond prong-set alongside the center diamond, which immediately catches the eye. It draws my eyes to the emerald cut diamonds are the perfect accent for the band.

"I love you, L. I know he hurt, but I'm going to spend my life showing you only happiness."

I hold his face in my hands as he smiles, and a tear pools in his eyes. "You said yes." He exhales. "You said yes."

TWENTY-SIX

Ten days goes by to quickly...

As soon as I get back into the city on Monday the 6th, I'm determine to call Katie and make amends once and for all; things have been strained between us ever since she found out about Lamont. For days, I've rehearsed what I might say to her, and now that Dante has proposed, I just want to share some good news with my older sister.

Now that Lamont is dead, I know she's feeling various emotions. I decide to go to her office out of desperation, knowing that I just don't have the strength to call her.

For a few hours, I stand outside the large glass windowpane, staring at my older sister, hard at work, closing deals for spoiled actors and musicians. My body freezes, not wanting to go in.

I stand there for a few more minutes until I lose my nerve completely.

I'm nearly half a block away when I hear my name ringing out over the city noise. Katie stands at the end of the block just before the intersection. I notice she's cut her hair in a pixie style since I left for the Hamptons. She's wearing a black classic single-breasted suit blazer and dress pants with high heels. As I stand there, unable to move, my heart pounds in my chest so hard that I feel like I'm going the pass out. We stare at each other until she crosses the street to greet me.

"Were you really just going to stop by without coming in to say anything to me?" she asks, out of breath from her quick sprint. "I've been calling you for nearly two weeks now. How was your trip?"

I'm not prepared, I thought I would be, but seeing her here in front of me, I still can't find the right words. I want to apologize, but I'm sorry never feels like enough. And want to tell her I didn't mean to hurt her. I want to say that I'm not okay, but I'm trying to improve. But none of those things come out.

"You looked busy," I reply sheepishly. "And I didn't want to disturb you. I just wanted to say that I'm okay."

"Are you?" Katie asks. "Because you haven't been by my office since you worked for me when you first moved to the city."

"I didn't know what to say to you," I say under my breath.

"I know. And I understand. But I don't want you to push me away, Lisa. I don't know how I feel about Lamont or his death... BUT one thing I know is that I love you, and I don't blame you for what happened. I never did. And I just want you to be okay... to be happy."

"A lot has been going on with me... since. You know. And I just needed some time to deal. I never wanted this to... what I did with him... to touch you, Katie."

Katie comes closer to me and throws her arms around me, hugging me so tightly I can barely breathe.

"It wasn't you... it was never your fault," Katie huffs. "You were just a child. Come, let's get some coffee."

"Aren't you busy, Kat?" I ask.

"I can make time for my little sister."

We go to 777 Coffee. It's only a quick ride from Katie's office, but it's her favorite place. Kate pays for my Rum Latte and orders cappuccino and an egg and cheese empanadas. Standing in line, we say nothing, imagining the several hundred ways this conversation will go.

"Thank you for my latte," I say, playing with the engagement ring on my finger, seeing if she will notice.

"It's my pleasure," Katie says. "You rarely let me do anything for you anymore — "

It's true; as sad as that sounds, she's right.

Brenda, the barista, expertly works the coffee machine, grinding the beans and steaming the milk into a foam.

We sit near the end of the shop, near the wall, for privacy.

"Lisa, are really you okay?" Katie asks. "I've been so worried about you ever since the news broke about... well, you know. I went to the funeral. It was harder than I thought to see him laying there."

It hurts her to say his name, even though he's dead.

I smile nervously and gently blow the steam away from my latte.

"I'm sorry," she says. "That's a dumb thing to ask."

She's nervous too. It's visibly clear to me now. Her hands are trembling, even though it's warm outside.

"I'm fine, Katie," I say. "I've just thrown myself into my work and my relationship with Dante."

Katie smiles, understanding precisely what I mean. "I know what you mean," she says. "This is going to be my best month yet... I've made over twenty million in deals."

I flash a smile. "That's great, Kat; congratulation."

"What about you?" She lifts her empanada, tears it in half, and hands me a piece. "What's been going on?"

"Well, I just got back from my vacation with Dante." I grin. "I've been going through a lot of therapy and soul searching. I've been approached to have my story told in a book...."

I pause.

"Dante proposed to me..., and I said yes."

Katie holds her hand up to her mouth, processing the avalanche of new information that I'm throwing at her.

"Oh wow," she says, blinking rapidly, "It seems I've missed quite a bit in the last few weeks. I'm glad that you are sticking with therapy, and Dante proposed? Congratulations.... Wow!"

She sets the coffee on the surface of the table and exhales. "I was engaged once; I remember how excited I felt at the moment."

The statement catches me off guard; I know Lamont proposed to her once, but she never talks about what happened and why they broke up.

"I know, Katie," I say. "And I'm sorry."

Her words bring me off the high I've been on with Dante.

"It doesn't matter now." Katie shrugs.

"No, Katie." I snap. "It's a big deal, and we can't go on avoiding this. Avoiding him. We need to talk about this... without the anger, shame, and regret."

"Well, Lamont proposed while you were away at MIT," she says, "the August before your sophomore year. I was over the moon at first. I thought I was going to get everything I wanted... the real-life from rags to riches story."

I try to keep the muscles in my face as relaxed as possible as I think back to that year. I remember Lamont saw me at school. We had a fight because he accused me of sleeping with my study partner, Tyson Collins, which was true, but none of his business, either.

"Obviously, I didn't know about you," Katie continues. "But something felt rushed and wrong about the whole thing. Lamont wanted me to give up everything for him. My career and dreams. And he seemed more distant than ever after he asked me to marry him. Most days, instead of feeling closer, I felt abandoned... and alone."

I nod subtly, listening to her every word as I try to push the images of Lamont out of my mind before a panic attack grips me. I know the memories hurt her as much as they hurt me, and shortly after the proposal, they broke up... but it's time to ask.

I push the words out, "So, why did the engagement end?"

Somehow, I know it had something to do with me, but what happened?

Katie shakes her head before replying, "He was home for the week and got really drunk. We were making love, and it turned into... something horrible... aggressive... something dark."

She pauses.

"He got so abusive and didn't seem to care that he was hurting me. Was it ever like that with you?" she asks. "Did he?"

"Sometimes towards the end," I reply. "Lamont would get aggressive... violent."

Katie leans back into the seat and exhales hard as tears accumulate in her eyes. "I never saw that side of him until that night. Afterward, we had a huge argument, and...."

"And what, Kat?"

"He said your name."

She waits for some kind of expression or reaction from me once I hear the statement—but there's nothing I can say.

"Oh, Kat, I'm so sorry." I sip my latte and play with the foam. "I never wanted to hurt you," I add. "I tried so many times to stop him, but...."

My head floods with memories of the pain that I've caused her. This is just as much my fault as it is Lamont's fault. I loved him. I didn't want to let him go. He was my everything. In desperation, he once said he'd hurt himself and Katie if I left him. He did that every time. Our entire relationship was nothing but pain and guilt and gaslighting. I see that now more than anything.

"But what?" Katie asks.

"He made me feel like the entire relationship was my fault... my idea like I seduced him, and it was me who was hurting you. Every time I threatened to break things off, Lamont threatened to kill himself, or worse."

"Can I ask you another question?" Katie asks.

I barely have a moment to register the question as my brain processes everything. I've beat myself up for so long because I questioned how and why I seduced him. It's been a lingering question that I can never forgive myself for believing.

"How many times?" she reluctantly asks, playing with her coffee cup.

Still lost in my flashback, I answer, "It started when I was thirteen. Every time you were asleep. Or asked him to watch me because you had to work. If Lamont could sneak a moment alone with me, he would."

"When did he stop... when did it end, Lisa?"

I blink rapidly; every minute of this conversation feels like I'm piercing my sister's heart with a hot poker. "He called me the night before he married Natalie... drunk. But nothing happened... I mean, we didn't... even though he wanted to. Before that, he had been too aggressive, violent with me on my graduation night — that's when it was over for me."

Katie lowers her head, her eyes glaring intensely at her cappuccino.

"That's the person you ran off to see that night."

"He called me after the restaurant and begged to see me." My voice is above a whisper.

It's refreshing.

Katie knows the truth, nevertheless, my nerves are shot from anxiety at the thought of what she's thinking. A part of me wishes she would yell... tell me she hates me and that I've ruined her life. Tell me I'm the worse sister in the world. And say to me I'm a piece of shit. But she doesn't; instead, Katie is understanding and loving, which only makes me feel worse.

"So it was after that argument that you knew about us?" I ask.

"No… not exactly," Katie says. "But I had my suspicions. Of course, Lamont tried to explain it away, stating that he was drunk and meant nothing by it. But after that argument, something just didn't feel right. And as much as I wanted to be with him, I couldn't stay with him while having these lingering questions. And after what happened with Derek, I didn't want to discuss the topic with you again. You had changed so much after what happened. There were times I thought I would find you dead. When no one believed what happened and you retreated into yourself. I just couldn't ask for the truth this time."

This is the longest conversation Katie, and I have had in months, and neither one of us wanted it to end. Katie finishes her drink, even though it's clear that she doesn't want to. And I finish my latte, even though it's cold.

"So, I once asked Lamont, and I believed him at first when he said that nothing ever happened between the two of you. It's embarrassing to admit now because, looking back, it was right in my face. You'd become so distant and withdrawn, even before Derek. Of course, something was going on. I was just… too blind to see it." Katie lowers her head again, looking down, averting her eyes from mine. "I didn't want to see it."

Katie goes on, telling me how she's been looking into his victims more. How she spoke to a therapist about me and "grooming." We talk until the coffee shop closes, the sun has gone down, and the streetlights illuminate the asphalt.

"I'm happy for you, Lisa," Katie admits, standing next to me on the curb. "And I'm proud of you."

"For what?"

"For trying to be better. Even if you decided not to tell your story. You are the bravest person I know. I don't know too many people who have gone through what you went through. Despite that, you are here, fighting for your happiness. I know it's difficult."

The tears leave streaks on my foundation as they roll down my cheeks. Her words mean more to me than Katie will ever know. And even though she has no reason to forgive me, she has. And I'm grateful.

TWENTY-SEVEN

June 2006

After graduating from MIT, I moved in with Katie for a few months. And applied to every odd job that I could think of. And finally, Katie took pity on me and allowed me to work as her personal assistant for six months. It's a job that made me realize I could never work for someone else. I wanted to be my own boss, and I started working on my own business. The problem was I had talent/ drive/ and a vision, but no money or investors to back me. That was, until Monty called me out of the blue.

"I'll be fine," I told him. "I don't have any experience with running a business, but I'm willing to put in the work."

When I lay in bed, I did a ton of research on owning a tech business. I found an efficient apartment, using some of the money Monty had put in my account that I hadn't touched since high school. Determination was the only thing that drove me at the time, that and Monty's money. I had an idea of how to make life a little easier, but it was just an idea at the moment.

Monty called sporadically and wanted to come by to see me, but I always told him no... even though I wanted to see him. One night he called and said he was coming down anyway and would find me. I refused to see him, but I couldn't stop him either.

When he arrived in the city, my phone blew up constantly from the moment he landed. After a while, I answered it so he wouldn't bother me anymore.

"Please, baby, I'm getting married in a few days. Don't you want to see me?"

"Monty, it's late."

Under my covers, I was wearing my favorite Victoria's Secrets shorts, a tank-top T-shirt, and nothing else. I had no intention of going out that night or seeing Lamont a few days before he married someone else. I'd spent the entire day looking at office spaces to rent, and I was exhausted... too exhausted for this conversation.

He said he only wanted to see me, and I fell for that. He said he made a reservation at a seafood restaurant downtown, so I didn't have to worry about him trying anything.

"Ten minutes?" he pleaded. "Just give me ten minutes."

"Monty," I replied. "I can't... not after last time."

"That's why I'm here... to apologize."

My jaw clenched. I knew I would give in the moment I answered the phone.

"I'll give you five minutes," I said impatiently, knowing that wasn't a victory. "And don't you dare think you're coming into my place."

"We'll see," he replied. "You know you miss me."

It was true, but I would not admit it... not to him.

I shook my head and quickly hung up.

I knew I'd regret it, but I was always a fool for him. Monty still had a way of disarming me. I could be furiously mad at him one minute and begging for his touch the next. He was the only man who made me feel that way. And it's so fucking frustrating.

The moment Lamont pulled into the parking garage, he called me. "I'm here."

"I'll be down soon," I replied.

"You sure you don't want me to come up?" He smirked on the phone.

"No… I'll come down to you." I stayed strong.

"I'm in the black Bentley Continental GT."

"Okay."

As soon as I got in the luxurious car, he frowned, took a drink of Scotch, and stared at me. I tried to still appear angry with him, but Lamont knew I was full of shit, that I had no plan beyond entering the car.

"You should've let me come up," Monty said. I sensed his anger and frustration with my stubbornness. He smelled like liquor, and I immediately noticed the residue of white powder that I assumed was cocaine. It was the off-season, and he looked terrible.

"Why are you here, Lamont?" I rolled my eyes, annoyed with myself. "We haven't spoken in months."

After a moment of awkward silence, Lamont spoke. "I've been thinking about you a lot lately. I miss you. I wanted to see you before I — I just wanted to see you."

His words cut me straight through my heart, and all of my stubbornness melted away. All I could think about was how in a few days, he'd be married, and we would be over forever, and suddenly, that fact upset me more than anything Monty did.

"Am I supposed to say something?" I asked, crossing my arms over my chest. "I won't... this is your choice."

At first, he shot me a glare and finished his glass of Scotch.

"You and I could never be together... you know that," his words slurred. It was the first time he's really looked at me and told the truth.

"Lamont, I know that." I folded my arms across my chest. "So, why are you here?"

"I just wanted to see you one last time as a free man, without a wife."

"Have you been seeing anyone?" he asked, leaning back against the soft beige leather seats. "I just want to know."

"No," I lied. I hadn't been in a serious relationship, but I had been sleeping around... a lot. But I would not tell him that.

"Oh," he said, "I know I'm getting married, but the problem is. I love you still, and no matter how much time passes, I'll always love that thirteen-year-old girl and what we were."

"I'm not that girl anymore," I sighed. "I haven't been for a very long time."

"I know." His voice was low.

That was when I realized this was where we would always end up. I had done my best to try and let him go, but Monty being here with me on that night was him asking permission to be with Natalie.

With my hand on the door handle, I was ready to leave. I didn't want to play this game with him. I was too old for games. And too old for him.

I went months without contact with him while I was attending MIT, and I managed just fine.

"I have to go." I sigh. "You're five minutes are up."

"Come on," Monty placed his hand on me. "You can't tell me you don't think of me."

Even though I didn't want to, I thought of him every second of the day. I did everything I could to not think about Lamont. I went on many dates, had sex with faceless men, and had a love/hate relationship with sex. But nothing filled the void that Monty had left.

"You've got serious issues, Monty," I finally said. "And I don't want to be one of them anymore."

I thought about the other night...

I was on a first date with someone I met on Plenty of Fish. I had lobster and steamed veggies. We were halfway through our drinks when my date asked, "Can we just skip the cat-and-mouse game and just go have sex?" I nearly choked on my Crown, shocked by his boldness.

"Sure," I replied.

Afterward, we walked toward the back of the restaurant; the man said, "Is here okay?"

"It's the back office?" I asked.

"Yes."

It was apparent that he targeted me from the moment we started chatting. We didn't have a genuine connection, and he wasn't anything special, but he wanted me, and I was horny. He took me right there on the desk. And I left my body like I usually did. He did whatever he wanted to me, and I let him.

TWENTY-EIGHT

"Don't go, Lisa," Monty said, leaning over to close the Bentley's door.

"Take your shirt off and lie back." He added.

"No," I exhaled, "I told you that nothing was going to happen between us ever again. You can't just keep fucking up, Monty, then apologize."

I paused and looked into his eyes.

"Money doesn't fix everything."

He grinned, not listening to a word I said. And tugged at my shirt. "Come on, take your shirt off, Lisa."

He pulled his cock from his pants and looked at me with a needing gaze.

"I'm not in the mood, Monty."

"Lisa, you know me. This is who I am. You know that."

His breath was warm, but the stench of liquor was the only thing I could smell. I held my breath from the aroma and reached for the door handle again.

His fingers unbuttoned my shirt, and I heard his pants unzip and slide down.

"Lie back and don't make me repeat myself again." He demanded.

I released the breath I'd been holding, suddenly feeling like I was that thirteen-year-old again. The one who was eager to please him. Arguing with him would only make things worst, but I didn't want this, and I knew it.

I was frozen. Monty had an intimidating stature, and he'd get more violent when he was drunk or high, and I didn't want to anger him. If I'd known he was drunk when he called, I wouldn't have picked up the phone.

I was scared... for various reasons, but mostly I was kicking myself for falling for Monty's bullshit again.

"Lay back." He said more forcibly. "Please."

I obeyed and lay down against the back of the leather cushion, resting my palms on the back of the seat, and didn't argue. Monty unbuttoned my jeans and tugged them down to my hips. I wanted to protest, but the words would not form. Our last several times together were painful and violent; I didn't want this time to be like that. I didn't want to remember my last time with Monty to be hurtful or violent... so I yielded.

I watched Monty as he kissed a trail along my neck to my bra. The more I relaxed, the better it would be.

"I love you," he murmured. "I never stopped loving you. Your body... Lisa drives me crazy."

He looked up at me.

"Tell me you want me." He added.

I didn't answer, but he didn't care.

"I wish I could be with you," He continued to kiss my body. "I don't love her as much as I love you... you know that, right?"

He unfastened my bra with one swift motion, allowing my breast to spill out. The air felt chilly on my bare skin. What was he going to do to me? I shivered at the thought as he sucked and licked my nipples, and my body reacted to the sensation.

"Your body is so beautiful."

I quiver from the heat of his touch. "Monty I—" My throat felt dry, and I couldn't speak.

I opened my mouth, but Monty kissed me before I could even object. I arched into his kiss, submitting to the lust between us.

He pressed a kiss to my throat, licking my hot flesh. Then Monty traveled back down to my breasts; his hand was gently massaging. His tongue danced circles over my hard nipples. Once he was ready, he slid a hand into my underwear and rubbed my sex.

"I want to fuck you one last time. Please, let me say goodbye properly. I don't want the last time to be the last memory you have of me."

His hands electrified my skin, sending waves of sensations rippling through my body.

Why can't I feel this way with any other guy? I thought. Why is it only him who can drive me wild?

I moaned softly at his touch, my hands gripping the leather tightly. My body ached to burst for him.

Monty stripped the clothes from me and pushed them on the car floor before positioning his body over mine.

"Monty." My voice was hoarse. I wasn't sure if I could do this. My mind was racing in several directions at once.

"It's okay, baby. I will be gentle," he murmured. "Just like our first time."

Clearly, he remembered our first time a lot differently than I remembered it.

He pulled his shirt off. There we were, naked in the Bentley, in a parking garage. I felt like this was my low. I went from feeling like his girlfriend to feeling like his whore.

"Do you feel how hard you make me?" He said. "Only you can do this to me."

I remember this was the first time I didn't believe a word Monty was saying....

"I've been hard all day thinking about spending this time with you. I needed to see you. And needed to feel you again."

My hips circled into the motion of his fingers as he massaged and fingered me, sliding through my wet lips and inside of my sex.

I closed my eyes and retreated into myself. But without warning, Monty tugged on my nipple hard with one hand.

"Don't close your eyes." He said. "I want you to look at me. I want you to see me make you cum."

I panicked when I looked in the rearview mirror and saw someone walking past the car. I could only think about what would happen if we got caught by anyone or they made this public.

"Monty..."

He continued to ignore me, spreading my legs around him, positioning them on his shoulders. He slowly pushed inside, easing his cock deep inside me and driving out any doubt left in me. I moaned, feeling the heat in my limbs and the electricity build in my body. Then Monty took my mouth as he aggressively fucked me and possessed my body.

Minute by minute, Monty crashed into me, finding a relentless rhythm that was almost more than I could bear.

He breathed hard against my ear, moaning and grunting with each thrust.

"Lisa, oh God...." His lips trembled.

"That's it, baby. Give it to me. Tell me it's mine and will always be mine."

My name left his lips in a soft moan. An explosion erupted from behind my eyes as I convulsed and seized under him.

"Fuck, Lisa... Fuck!"

Once I regained my senses and the feeling back into my limbs. I slowly slipped back into my jeans and shirt, thoroughly disgusted with myself.

"Man," Monty sighed, glistening in sweat and gasping for air. "That was one for the books."

"No..." I snapped, pushing the car handle, "*THAT* was the last time you will ever touch me... Goodbye, Lamont...forever."

I slammed the door before he could respond and raced upstairs before I regretted this. That was the last time I saw Lamont. I didn't hear from him again until these accusations surfaced.

TWENTY-NINE

Tuesday, June 7th
Present Day...

In Nichole's office, I ask, "Do you think less of me, doctor?"

It's not how we usually start a session, but the thought has been weighing on my mind for days now. I've been fighting the urge to drink, and my baser animalistic needs are being met by Dante, but there is still so much weighing on me... I feel smothered. For once in my life, everything seems to be going well. It almost gives me hope, and having hope can be dangerous, especially when it's taken away.

"I could never think less of you after what you've gone through. The secrets you were forced to keep and the things you've been forced to endure. The only thing I wish is that you would've told me sooner so that we could work through it together. And find an easier way to move forward a lot smoother than we did," Nichole smiles, cleaning her glasses. "You went through a major self-destructive spiral after you and Dante broke up several months ago. The drinking... the cutting... the one nightstand with random strangers... you did anything to fill the void so that you couldn't think about your pain."

"Yes," I sigh. "I know... that much; I can admit it to myself now."

Shifting in her chair, perching herself on the armrest, Dr. Nichole stares at me, studying me like she always does, and waits for me to tell her what's really bothering me. I focus on everything but her gaze, my watch, the window, the condensation on my glass of water. I tip my head up to finally look at her. And then I say it, "Katie told me why she and Lamont broke up."

"Oh, when did you learn this?"

"Recently."

I straighten my posture, but only for a moment. "She told me they got into an argument, and during the heat of the moment, he mistakenly called out my name while addressing her. I've known this whole time that somehow I was the reason they'd broken up. But Katie never told me."

"So, were you the cause of the argument?" Nichole asks, "Or —"

"No," I shook my head. "Katie said that Lamont had come over one night drunk and got aggressive and very violent with her, and it scared her."

"Was he ever like that when he was with you?"

"Only when he was drunk." My voice is barely above a whisper as I answer. "When he was drunk... things would get bad... it was the only time that I ever felt like what I wanted didn't matter. Like I was being —"

I hesitate to say because admitting it makes me feel it... like a victim, his victim.

"Raped?"

All those years ago, he told me he loved me. It never felt like a lie or a line to keep me under his control. I loved him too. It never felt wrong at the time, but now all I feel like is a naïve fool to believe the fairytale of the prince falling in love with a nobody.

Nichole doesn't flinch and remains expressionless; she only shifts ever so slightly in her seat.

"I know what these girls have gone through," I say. "I know all too well. He made them feel special, too, like they were the only people in the world who understood him and he could be himself with. Then he touched them, long before they knew if they were consenting or not; or what they were consenting to. For so long, I wanted and wished he would have picked me... stayed with me. And that thought makes me feel—so—disgusted with myself sometimes. Still... I miss him. Ever since his murder, the guilt has only increased."

Nichole's eyelashes blink a few times, processing all the things I've just confessed.

"I could have ended things," I say. "or told Katie. Maybe if I had said something back then, there would be a lot fewer victims right now. But I didn't want to at the time because I thought I brought out that darker part of him."

"Lisa, do you hear yourself? You were thirteen. A baby. You didn't know what you wanted at that time; none of us did. You saw him as a friend and had a crush on him. BUT that will never excuse what he did to you or what he did to these women. You couldn't have foreseen any of this, and none of it is your fault."

"But I was the first, and he didn't start hurting these other women until I cut him out of my life completely. A part of me knew that what we were doing was wrong. He told me he couldn't be around me without wanting to touch me or be with me... in that way."

"Lisa, stop."

"Lamont made his choices. He probably would have found another naïve girl if it hadn't been you. Men like him often can't stop themselves."

"I know, but—" I say.

"No," she interjects. "Stop carrying this darkness like you were the problem. You are a great and wonderful person. Just because HE put this darkness in you, you don't have to have the shadow of his actions follow you forever."

"I'm afraid I might not have a choice in that," I say, lowering my head again. "I still feel him in me. I will always feel him inside of me. Every relationship... every intimate moment... every man I fuck. I feel Lamont."

I pause.

"I feel like he took something from me. I can never get back."

"He did take something from you, Lisa," Nichole replies. "He took your innocence... your childhood... your trust in men, and your trust in your own judgment."

Without warning, I feel like I can't breathe, holding my head in my hands, and Nichole comes over... hugs me, and tells me to breathe. I miss Lamont's, and I hate that I do.

"I'm so fucking tired of feeling this way," I whisper. "I'm tired of hearing his voice in every whisper. Or feeling him in the middle of the night. I'm happy with Dante. He makes me happier than I've ever felt, so why can't I let Lamont go?"

Nichole's crouching down, leaning on the arm or the chair, and patting my shoulders.

"It's okay to be tired." She sighs. "You have been carrying a heavyweight for so long. You have to let it go. Just let go."

My breathing steadies as Nichole steadies me; her hands massage my back in a circle motion.

Softly, she says, "If you can let go of the guilt and forgive yourself—"

"No, I can't." I sink my head further into my hands, shielding my tears. "I let it go."

"You have too," she says. "Just allow yourself to feel. Stop holding the pain in. Just stay in the moment with me and know that you are safe."

I exhale and hang my head. "I'm sorry."

"That's fine," she says. "You don't have to be sorry about anything."

"I just feel..." I cry freely, soaking my sleeve. My face scrunches up from the pain of the memories. "I just thought it was a love story. I thought I was special. I really just wanted to be special to someone."

"We all do at that age," Nichole says.

"Because if it isn't genuine love or something special, then what else could he call it?"

Her eyes stare at me with such empathy.

"I gave him my childhood," I say. "I loved him."

Nichole continues to cradle my hand in hers. "No, he took your childhood. It's okay for you to be sad or mad. But you have to feel it to let it go."

I cry until the end of our session, it's overdue and I feel better the moment I leave her office. I know what I need to do now. I know how I'm going to help these girls, if I can and I'm seriously considering taking Chloe Robert up on her offer to work with her.

Finally, I feel like I have a purpose...

THIRTY

July 20th, 2016
Present Day...

Warm sun rays dance into the bedroom from the window, stirring me awake; no bad dreams tonight. No guilt or shame. Just peace. I wake up with the man I love lying next to me, and I wonder whether I am dreaming. I don't want to disturb him as I watch him sleeping peacefully. Not wanting to wake him, I don't move an inch. Dante's warm body is sprawled out over the ruffled sheets.

The comforter is at the foot of the bed. We scattered our clothes along the floor, leaving a trail from the door to the bed. The black cotton sheets barely cover the bed, and the entire bedroom looks messy. It looks like a tornado went through the room, and we're left in the carnage. Slowly Dante stirs, moaning as he lifts his head to look at me and smiles. I place my head on his bare chest, feeling his warmth radiate from him.

"There you are," he stretches. "My beautiful fiancé."

Fiancé? That still sounds so strange to me.

"How did you sleep?" he mumbles, caressing my hair. "I didn't hurt you last night, did I?"

I smile, look up at him, and shake my head as I melt into his embrace. I reach up, outlining his face with my fingertips. Trailing my hand down his arms, down the tops of his chest, and down underneath the sheets. He catches me there and smiles.

"I'd think that you would have had enough last night. If you go any further, we might not make it out of bed."

"I don't mind that too much."

Dante smiles again, kissing my wandering fingers.

We had such a fantastic night, the best night. We didn't just fuck, but made love. And for the first time, I felt normal; he makes me feel that way. My body aches, but I still want more of him. All of him, all the time. But today is the big day, and I'm avoiding the reality of the situation. The past can no longer hurt us, and I'm willing to leave it where it is, and we can be happy and stronger.

Throughout all of this, something has changed between us; Dante never left my side. He knows all of me, and yet he's still here. I let him in, and I didn't scare him away with my darkness. Through all the drama, our connection has only grown stronger.

Now we trust each other. I can allow myself to be vulnerable with someone for the first time in my entire life, sometimes that scares me. But the question of "What if he sees all of me and doesn't like what he sees?" has been answered. It feels so foreign to me. I pushed him away and hurt him, yet he came back into my life, just as I needed him the most. And I feel free.

The way Dante touched me made love to me last night; I felt the love and warmth. I felt fulfilled in ways that I'd only seen in movies. It felt like the perfect way to end things if we lived in a movie. The camera would pan out, and the end credits would roll.

But do I really deserve a happy ending? The thought lingers in my mind.

As we lay there in bed together, he cradles me tightly in his arms, with the promise of never letting me go. I can lay there all day, but the rest of the world beckons.

"Are you okay?" He kisses the back of my shoulder, tracing his fingertips along my arm. "Last night was so intense."

"Last night was perfect, Dante."

I catch his hand, suck his fingertips, and guide him down between my thighs. He hesitates before touching my sex.

"Lisa, I—"

"It's okay." I push my hips against his hand. "For the first time, I am okay. I realize that you're all I need. You always were, but now I'm not afraid anymore."

"You're not?" He smiles, making sure.

"I'm sure that I love you."

Slowly, he slides his fingers inside of me, gently stroking in and out, awakening the most intimate parts of my body. I place my hand on him, pressing his fingers deeper, reassuring him I'm okay as I let out a soft moan. His rhythm picks up, and more moans escape my lips; my body has a mind of its own. The pressure and tension ripples from my head to my toes, forcing my muscles to constrict.

Dante shifts his body, leaning down to kiss my lips. Then my neck. Then my breast. His breath ignites my sensitive skin as he sucks and plays with my nipples.

"Dante," I breathe. My hand reaches for his erection.

"You drive me crazy," he presses his cock against me. "I can't get enough of you."

"I know… me either."

I stroke him gently, teasing him. My urges take over me completely; as much as I try to play coy, all I want is for him to ravage me.

Dante grips my hand tightly as I continue stroking him, controlling me as I pleasure him. His dominance entices me and sometimes frightens me, but I believe him when he says he'll never hurt me.

"If you keep doing that, I will have to do something about it."

"I want you too, Dante. So do something about it."

"I'm going to fuck you so hard that you'll feel me all day," he murmurs, shifting himself, positioning his body on top of mine. "Are you ready for me, baby?"

I lay back, bracing myself for the pleasures that are coming. He eases inside me slowly and deep. His thrust is deliberate and controlled as he rolls his hips inward and deeper. I moan softly with every thrust.

"I love you, Lisa."

"I love you too, Dante."

His pace gradually hastens, sinking in and out of me, holding my body in place as he pumps harder and faster. I cry out, gripping a fist full of sheets in both hands as electricity of pleasure shoots through me. And it drives me wild as he fills me completely.

"Fuck me."

"Oh, I plan to," he grunts with a sharp exhale. "I could fuck you all day."

Dante's body crashes into mine as I pull him closer to me, bracing myself for more. Without warning, he pauses, then flips me on my stomach... face down against the pillows.

I can hardly take it, feeling my entire body explode."Fuck, Dante." I cry out when he reinserts himself. His pace picks up again as I scramble to hang on to anything tangible. His hand slaps my ass hard, and I unravel instantly as the climax consumes me entirely, ripping through every cell in my body. I lose all sense of reason and control, just as Dante reaches the edge. He sinks deep inside, grunts, and his body stills. Dante slips out of me and rolls onto his side, pulling me closer to him, my head resting against his chest.

Everything goes quiet; the room stills as my vision refocuses. Dante hugs me tightly in his arms as we lay there, catching our breaths. He's right. I could do that all day. I could lay there with him all day.

"We have to get up and get ready." I finally say, rolling over to look at him. "It's going to be a long and challenging day,"

"I know," he sighs. "I just wanted to start the day on a positive note. I don't know how it will end after your meeting." He sweeps a stray strand of hair from my face, kissing my forehead.

As much as I don't want him to, Dante loosens his grip, releasing me and allowing me to get up from the bed. My knees feel like jelly as I brace myself to stand. I need a shower. He does too.

"I'm going for a shower," I smile, lacing my fingers between his. "Care to join me?"

"Definitely," he smiles. "Although I might just make you wet all over again."

I grin. "Promises... promises."

"You know me, Lisa. I always keep my promises."

"I'm counting on it."

He gets up, scooping me in his arms, and carries me into the bathroom.

Our shower is long, and even though my body is sore and tired, we make love again with the warm water cascading overhead. Finally satisfied, we finish our shower and step out.

Dante gets ready before me, and when I rejoin him in the living room, I hear him speaking to someone over the phone.

"Okay, Katie, I will let her know."

"Oh, are you conspiring with my sister about something?" I ask. "My birthday isn't for a while."

I pause, reading his expression.

"Is everything okay?"

Dante looks at me, but I can't tell what's going on in his head.

"Dante?"

He blinks, "The first victim, Kira, is out of the hospital. Katie wanted to look into it, and she thought you might want to know."

"I'm glad she's okay now." I lower my head.

He rubs his head and exhales. "I just hope she gets the help that she needs. Lord only knows what coming forward has done to her life... it had to be something bad for her to want to kill herself."

I lift my eyebrow, switching the coffee machine on. "Yeah, I have been thinking about that."

He looks up at me. "Think about what?"

"I've been thinking about how I can help these girls. And feel somewhat responsible for what they are going through right now. I know it's not my fault, but I feel for them."

"So, what are you thinking about doing? I don't think they're going to get much justice, even though Lamont is dead. And I've heard that accusing him has cost one woman her job. Even with Lamont dead, they aren't getting much of a break."

My chest falls into my stomach as I sigh. "I'm thinking about giving the victims some of the money that Lamont left for me. I don't want it, nor do I need it... it feels like dirty money... hush money, and I know I can put it to better use."

My thoughts drift on all the positive things I can do with the millions that Lamont left.

"That sounds like a good idea, Lisa." Dante smiles. "I think it would be good for them as well as being good for you, too."

He pauses, sipping the fresh coffee I'd just made.

"You need to do this," he exhales.

"You think so?" Tears line the borders of my eyes. "I've been thinking about it for a while."

"You need to heal and continue to move forward. I'm here for you. I always will be. I know it won't be easy, but I'm not going anywhere. You're stronger than you give yourself credit for, and the first step is owning what happened to you. Then you can help others. Just take it one day at a time... and I will be here with you."

I close my eyes. "I don't want to think about it right now. But I will work on giving these women some peace...."

My tears fall, but I don't hide from Dante. I let him in. I let him touch me... hold me... and comfort me.

He hushes me... his baritone voice soothes me as he pulls me close into his embrace. I melt against him and let the tears fall.

I'm so nervous about today, agreeing to meet Chloe Roberts and hear her offer out. Over the last couple of weeks, she and I have spoken several times over the phone. And finally, I feel comfortable enough to meet her face to face.

"I know you are nervous about today. You're afraid of being vulnerable, but everything will be okay. You're strong. And you never left your past break you... that's what I admire the most about you." He holds me a little tighter and kisses my forehead. "You can do this. I know you can. I will be here with a bottle of wine when you get home."

****

In the afternoon, I meet Chloe Roberts at her place. It's a small condo on the East side of Manhattan. My mind is racing the entire elevator ride up to her place, listing every reason in the world that I should turn back. But I'm undeterred. Swinging the door open on my second knock, Chloe greets me and leads me deeper into her place, inviting me to sit and get comfortable in her chair. I admire the warm décor of her living room, which is filled with flower paintings suspended on the walls. She smiles at me and gestures for me to sit on the soft cushion chair across from the sofa... the only thing between us is a glass coffee table.

She's nervous too...

There are several articles scattered on the coffee table about Lamont and information about the other victims, as well as several handwritten notes. My nerves are in a frenzy, my heart flutters in my chest. I fidget with my clothes as she readies herself, finally grabbing her tape recorder. I want to turn back. The fear mounts with every second, but I stay strong, thinking about what Dr. Owens and Dante said to me. Silently, I wait for her to be ready.

"Do you want something to drink?" She says nervously. "I can get you some water or a Coke."

I'd like a drink... I think to myself.

"No," I force a smile. "I'm okay."

"Oh, okay," Chloe exhales, shifting her body against the couch. "I really appreciate you for doing this. I know this is hard. I'm just about ready."

My stomach drops.

I'm slowly coming to terms with everything that Lamont did to me... his death, and everything that's happened in the last several weeks. Every thought... every memory will always trigger me and threaten my happiness.

A part of me will always be stuck in the past, but I can't stay there anymore. And the thought of that is the only thing keeping me here right now. This is another healthy way for me to own up to everything and work through it on my own terms. But I don't know Chloe. She wants to convince me she cares, but only time will tell if that is true. Still, she's a stranger to me, so I will remain cautious.

Finally set up, Chloe looks up at me and smiles. "I'm sorry about Mr. Johnson. I wanted him to pay for what he did to those women. Not die."

My mind slips into the memory of Lamont sitting in my room at night, caressing me and touching me. Just as I'm about to get lost in the flashback, I breathe sharply, shake my head, and refocus.

"Thank you," I reply, fiddling with my clothes. "It's sad for everyone involved. Mr. Johnson brought something unique to the game of football."

"That's not what I meant, but you're right."

"I know, Chloe," I smile. "But no matter what he did, he was special to someone. And he had people who loved him very much."

She checks the batteries of her digital tape recorder on the table between us one last time. And then positions her pen above a piece of paper to write her own separate notes.

"I know you're nervous, but I promise you, I won't write or publish anything that you don't personally pre-approve. To reassure you, I mean what I say, here it is in writing… an agreement between you and me. If we get to the end of this, I will scrap it, and you don't like it. I'm not here to exploit you in any way. All you need to do is sit here and tell your story, any details that you feel comfortable talking about. Stop as much as you need to. And I'll play it back to you when we're done."

"You don't need to play it back to me." I blurt out. "I only want to talk about this once. If that's okay."

"Yes," she smiles. "Sorry, of course. I understand."

Chloe presses the red RECORD button on the device. "This is my first sitting with Lisa Rose. Are you ready?"

I closed my eyes, exhaling hard. Instinctively, I fidget with my clothes one last time. Then open my eyes and look down at my engagement ring.

"He didn't ruin you... And he can't hurt you anymore...." Dante's words echo in my brain.

"Oh my God, that's an exquisite engagement ring," Chloe says, picking up on my nervous demeanor.

"Thank you." The corners of my mouth pull into a slight grin. "I know it sounds crazy, but I've been a mess for so long, living, barely surviving, drinking away the pain with no end in sight. I was functional but so fucked up inside and afraid to allow myself to feel anything. But one good thing that has come out of all this is that I finally feel like I'm in control. And that Lamont's hold on me is loosening. I'd put what Lamont did to me in the back of my mind, but I'd never dealt with it. Now, I am, and I finally feel some hope for the future."

Chloe smirks, nodding her head... Then clears her throat and postures.

"Let's begin. Shall we?"